Maelcom

Daimon Desire

MAELCOM

Daimon Desire

KATE BIGEL

InWorld Studios Publishing

Maelcom Daimon Desire
Copyright © 2017, Kate Bigel
Print Edition
Cover Art by InWorld Studios
Published by InWorld Studios Released December 2017

Print ISBN: 978-0-9985558-2-9

ALSO BY KATE BIGEL

Sorcha in Snowflakes

Naberius Daimon Soldier

To all the soldiers who have served.
Thank you.

ACKNOWLEDGEMENTS

To my husband who supports me in every way and leaves me alone to write.

Thanks to my writing groups and the feedback, they provide. Thanks to LC for all your feedback. Thanks to my sister. Thanks to Romance Writers of America and the Los Angeles Chapter (LARWA).

Big thanks to two amazing editors, Julia Ganis (juliaedits.com) as copy editor and Kimberly Cannon as proofing editor.

Thanks to Raine for being a sounding board and looking at drafts.

Thanks to the virtual community of writers on Twitter. You keep me laughing.

Thanks to my readers who find me, follow me on social media and reach out to tell me how much they love my stories. You are the best!

Thanks to all the soldiers who have served and are serving their country.

CHAPTER 1

Maelcom

MAELCOM MADE HIS WAY DOWN the crowded street trying to avoid bumping into any of the people. Too much random energy made him restless and distracted. Most Daimons enjoyed the cities, the people, and the endless energy. But he was conducting an investigation and needed to locate the author of an intelligence report that mentioned the existence of Daimons. He was here to evaluate the risk that this person posed. Secrecy was key to the protection of the Daimon Realm.

The streets of Stockholm were full of people enjoying the warm evenings of late summer. Stone facades were washed with the orange light of sunset. Another couple stopped to kiss but Maelcom zigzagged around them.

Giggling and laughing, a group of women strolled three abreast with arms entwined. Stuck behind them, he slowed his pace while he stared at their long, glossy hair, tight clothes, short skirts, and legs—he could see lots of pale, slender legs.

The man who sold him low-level intel regarding European intelligence efforts had requested a meeting. Maelcom had many such informants and used different ones for different areas of expertise to ensure his information-gathering efforts remained under the radar. He had built a list of potential information sources from when he worked for various intelligence groups, and there was a level of trust extended to him because he was considered an insider.

A man and woman headed right for him while they stared into each other's eyes. He turned to dodge them and go around the man, but his hand brushed the woman's forearm. "Excuse me," he muttered, but he couldn't resist a tiny sip of energy because he was tired. It was sweet and pure. An energy of love.

He would never feel that. Never stayed long enough with women. They either wanted relationships or more money, and sometimes if he flashed too much money around, they wanted a relationship. He liked women comfortable with their sexuality and having a good time so he could always part ways in an amiable manner. But he'd been alone for a while and the lack of sex made him moody.

When he had business in Stockholm, Maelcom always stayed in the Sodermalm area, one of the larger islands that made up the city, because he preferred the hotels located there. Small, discreet luxury hotels. A blend of students, artists, tradesmen and working professionals made the area interesting and vibrant.

Personally, he preferred Denmark over Sweden—people were calmer and quieter there. He'd served in the Special Forces in Denmark for several years and it was where he'd acclimated to life in the Earth Realm, a safe sort of transition to life here. But really, he missed California, all that space and the ability to hide in his big SUV with black windows while he drove everywhere he needed to go. Most of all, he loved surfing the ocean there, escaping from the buzz of the busy world into the quiet of the water.

He straightened his tailored suit coat and ran his hand down the front of his black designer shirt. His goal was to blend in with the crowd. There were many tall men in the city and he blended despite the fact he didn't look typically Swedish.

All Daimons had mixed Earth and Daimon heritage— some said pure Daimons had never existed, and the proof was that they could shift between two forms, one human and the other a horned, fierce beast. His darker skin combined with the blue eyes made people assume he was the child of some immigrant who married a Scandinavian, which was more accurate than they could appreciate. His ancestors were ancient Mongols who married Daimons back when Daimons lived in the Earth Realm.

He had agreed to meet his informant at a popular bar.

He had picked the bar from a guidebook the hotel left in his room which listed "Top Five Most Expensive Bars in Stockholm." It was impersonal and busy.

First, he walked past the bar to see the crowd and to view any possible exit routes. He turned back when he came to the end of the block to ensure he wasn't followed. Old habits.

The bar was all glass and dark wood, like a room from a Daimon palace in the mountains. The hostess, a curvy redhead, smiled up as if she recognized him. "Your friend is at the back table. He told me to look out for a big guy." She smiled wide.

He scowled down at her which he regretted immediately as she took a step back. A friend jokingly said his scowl made him look like he ate babies. He did not intend to frighten her but he disliked being noticed, and his size was something he could not control.

"Sorry, thank you," he said, softening his tone so her shoulders relaxed and she happily gestured to the table. He walked to the back of the bar where his contact sat with a drink in front of him. "Nils. Good to see you," Maelcom said.

Nils was a chubby man with a modest job and a demanding wife, which was why he sold information. The type of intelligence he sold was specific and never mission critical. Always low-level stuff. "Maelcom." He grinned like he was imagining the money he would be paid at the end of the meeting.

Tucking his chin-length dark hair behind his ears, Maelcom tried to appear relaxed, but his brain buzzed with a strange tension. It might be the crowded city, the hunt, or his general struggle with his life after fighting in the Daimon Wars.

Nils narrowed his eyes at Maelcom. "Every woman in this place stared at you walking in, despite that surly expression on your face."

"I look appropriate for the city," Maelcom said confidently. He had put effort into his conservative businessman look but women always stared at him. They liked his body, they liked his money, they loved his hair. He could shave his head to look meaner but he liked his hair long—he liked the phantom tickle when his hair swung over the place his horns emerged when he shifted forms. It reminded him of his other self, but he never transformed with women here in the Earth Realm.

"You look appropriate but you're too unique-looking to blend in," Nils said.

Nils annoyed him with his inadvertently accurate assessment. Maelcom spoke softly, letting a hint of annoyance creep into his voice. "I simply need the name of the person who submitted the report."

Nils rolled his eyes at Maelcom. "Calm down. Price is the usual."

"No problem," Maelcom said, and he took out his phone to make the transfer via a third party e-payment system. "Done."

A folded piece of paper was laid on the table. "Name and current address." Nils gestured to the waitress for the bill. "You're paying. I got here early and ate dinner so the amount is correct. Call me anytime."

"Of course, perhaps we can have dinner again as I need to know what the budget expenditure for Swedish Intelligence for the next two years. No details—just the percentage breakdowns." Maelcom took a sip of his single malt whisky. Straight up, no ice.

Maelcom was Daimon Lead in the Earth Realm on intelligence issues. His commander needed him to establish current European intelligence priorities while he was taking care of business. Finding out what they spent money on was the easiest way to figure out what they considered important.

Nils grinned and slapped his hands together. "Easy. I'll message you on GamerChat when I am done. Compensation is the usual rate." Nils slid out of the booth and stood.

They communicated via the GamerChat app. Everyone talked about crazy things to do with their multiplayer gaming campaigns so their discussions blended with the general conversation if they kept it all phrased in terms of planning a campaign.

Maelcom stood and thumped Nils on his shoulder with the casual bluster of a businessman finishing a meeting. "I'll see you soon. Good evening."

Nils left and Maelcom took out his phone. He punched in the address that Nils had given him and found information on who leased the apartment.

His commander, Naberius Vasteras, wanted to find the author of the report on the existence of Daimons so they could evaluate the risk. Maelcom wanted to just locate the man and kill him. The report had been full of half-truths and pure fabrications, as the author assumed Daimons were some biotech-enhanced soldier experiment, but still, risk was risk, and the only way to be sure would be to eliminate it. But Naberius's mate, Jessalyn, was an ex-US intelligence analyst and she was working to ensure it was disregarded as a crackpot report. Naberius and Jessalyn worried that a mysterious death of an intelligence agent could provoke unwanted attention.

The whole debacle had started with a human soldier skipping out from a challenging training exercise at the Greenland training facility. This lazy soldier had been hiding in an off-limits area and had seen some Daimons shift into their Daimon form and then later, told a low-level intelligence analyst who had written up the sighting in a report. Maelcom was proceeding cautiously: first find the intelligence analyst, then he would move on to dealing with the young soldier.

Maelcom paid the bill and left a generous tip.

THE NAME OF THE INTELLIGENCE ANALYST was Anders Frisson, a pale, plain-looking man with thick glasses or, at least that's what his government ID picture showed.

The apartment was under his roommate's name, Agnes Gustafson. She could be a girlfriend or just a roommate, but he would investigate her to ensure she wasn't involved. He made his way to the street where Anders lived and leaned against a large stone doorway, pretending to check his phone while he did some casual surveillance.

He searched for Agnes Gustafson on social websites and found lots of photos online, her in an art gallery talking to artists and her with groups of people at social events. Thin, with long, wavy blonde hair. In the social photographs, she was called Nessa, which was a diminutive of Agnes. She glowed in the pictures, looking at the camera with a big smile, always laughing. In a short flowery dress, she could pass for an illustration of a fairy from a child's storybook.

Suddenly, he remembered a book he'd had as a child with pictures of Små folk. It was those pictures he was thinking of. A people that used to live in the Daimon Realm and the Earth Realm. They were thought to have all been exterminated in the Great Killings a thousand years ago.

The door slammed and two people walked out—the same people whose pictures he had just been looking at. They were talking intently about something but he couldn't get the meaning exactly. Daimon hearing was sharp but not extraordinary. He sniffed their scents. One was acrid and sweaty. The other sweet like summer, like flowers.

He watched while the woman waved her hands around, talking rapidly and at length until Anders put his hands up in a conciliatory gesture, agreeing to whatever she had proposed in her long diatribe. They stopped talking, and Nessa played with her phone. Finally, a third person came running down the street shouting apologies. Nessa screamed "Olaf" and threw her arms around the man. Together, they walked south toward an area that had several taverns and bars, and Maelcom followed.

The woman, Nessa, wore a stretchy dress in blue that almost looked painted on and was completely open in the back. Her bare skin was exposed from her shoulders to just above the dip and swell of her round bottom. Shoulder blades like sharp wings. He could count the knobs on her spine all the way down to her lower back.

He shifted his eyes to the man under investigation, Anders Frisson. A twitchy man with a sharp face and insistent gestures, ordinary, pale brown hair. Nothing noteworthy except the way he jabbed his finger in the air when talking.

The goal was information-gathering and, then, containment of the situation. Maelcom was glad that just killing the man was not the automatic solution even if it was his default option. Maelcom wanted to find, no, he needed to find other ways to solve problems. He was done with being a killer.

Maelcom followed the group of friends down several streets until they came to a neighborhood bar with signs declaring homemade beer and craft cocktails. It reminded him of Gusion's bar back in the Bay Area. This place was a comfortable neighborhood bar with art on the walls and loud music.

The men went in, but the woman, Nessa, turned to look across the dark street. She was searching for something. He sank back farther into the shadows. Her enormous brown eyes sparkled in the street lights. Her blonde hair was a wild halo—so much hair on such a thin person.

The door opened and the light shone around her. A voice called out, "Nessa. Come on…" The person's voice got lost in a mumble but she laughed and went inside.

He frowned. She had looked in his direction like she could see him clearly hiding in the dark of the doorway.

CHAPTER 2

Nessa

SHE WAS LATE. The main group of her friends had already arrived and each new addition was greeted with big hellos and enthusiastic chatter. She kissed everybody's cheeks, hugged, joked with everyone and sat down at a long wooden table.

The plain wooden chair dug into the vertebrae of her back. Maybe she was too bony to wear the tight backless dress. She needed flowing clothes to hide her thinness and emphasize her modest curves. Someone had given her friend Olaf the dress as payment instead of cash and he'd come dancing into her apartment, saying "Versace" over and over again till she put it on. She straightened up so her spine didn't hit the back of the chair.

Olaf said she was fat compared to the models with whom he worked in the fashion industry. His performance art career did not pay the rent, particularly now that he had veered into avant-garde cabaret theater with drag queens singing in fabulous outfits. She adored him and attended all his shows.

Tonight was a semi-regular gathering of friends who had known each other since university. She loved hanging out with this varied group of friends, mostly artists of all sorts working in visual art, fashion, theater and cinema. No one was datable because they were either married, gay or simply knew too much about each other to make it viable. It made the whole get-together very relaxing. She probably should have saved the dress for another night but it was new so she'd worn it.

In truth, she had sort of given up on dating—just no luck with men. Her last boyfriend had moved to Thailand without even telling her. They hadn't been madly in love but it still hurt. He left a letter saying he had to do it this way or she would have talked him into staying even though she didn't love him. It was discouraging to realize that he was correct, and she hardly missed him at all.

Many of her friends were involved in relationships, moving in with lovers, some even getting married. She felt like the odd man out. She wanted love, to have her hand held, to have kisses every day, a friend, a lover. It was good she had her art or she would have been lost; making art was like a relationship, just not physical.

All the men she met treated her like a little cute girl. Once, a man had actually patted her on the head like a dog or a child. She wanted something different, but she couldn't quite put her finger on what it was.

She had developed a technique to evaluate men, besides their moronic impress-the-girl chatter. She kissed them as soon as possible on a date, ideally within the first hour. It was enough intimacy to see if they connected—kissing, like sex, was wordless communication. It was certainly a lot less risky than sleeping with people she didn't know that well. Having them fail the kiss test when she was half-naked was awkward. That had happened once and she promised herself not to let it happen again.

So a kiss as soon as possible seemed like a brilliant idea, but it was possible the idea put unfair pressure on her dates and made her seem—well, odd. The last guy she had kissed in the foyer of her apartment building before going out had asked her if she was drunk. So embarrassing. Maybe guys she passed over were just having a bad day. Maybe kissing wasn't important in a long-term relationship. But that was inconceivable and it upset her just thinking about it.

Olaf had snickered when she explained her approach and he'd argued that fucking was the best way to get to know someone. For her, sex confused the issue. It was difficult to be discriminating about a relationship when it felt so good. So, she ran around kissing men. Some of them were delighted with her kisses. Some were not.

She eyed the crowd—she knew too much about their

love lives, so they were off-limits. So unfair. She should ask the marrieds to bring one new person a month to their meetings to help out the single friends.

Everyone told her to use dating apps, but those terrified her as everyone also told her, sometimes even in the same conversation, horrible stories of people they'd met through those same apps. Her one date with a guy she'd met online was so epically horrific that the events of their date became her go-to funny story at parties to make people laugh. People tended to laugh hard at that story.

The front door opened too fast, banging the doorstop and making her look up quickly at the entrance. A man walked in, and she blinked her eyes repeatedly to make sure she wasn't seeing things.

Tall, strong wall of—*no*, not just handsome, something more. His face was like a hero from a comic book, hard slashing lines. An interesting, strong face. A stubble of a beard coming in. Intense blue eyes. Maybe he was a Russian hockey player or maybe a mobster. Probably just a businessman. His long, wavy dark hair was so luxurious that she wanted to run her fingers through it. His black suit jacket hugged his broad shoulders, beautifully cut and tailored to his massive body.

"Olaf, look, look. Yum. Yum," she said. "I want to order one of those models. Wrap him up for me."

Olaf sighed. "Yummy and straight. Why do you pretend to talk like a bad girl when you're not? That man would pat you on the head and you know how that makes you crazy.

You always are attracted to big, tall men, which has proven disastrous. Wait—I take that back because I should be supportive. We'll find you a big, huge man if that's what you want." He blew a kiss in her direction.

"It has not been disastrous," she complained even though it had been. She went back to staring at the man. Olaf talked to her about some plans he was making but it was hard to concentrate.

Olaf poked her. "So what do you think?"

She raised her eyebrows while she tried to think about what he had been saying. "You might take off to Paris because otherwise what are you doing with your life?"

He laughed. "I never said the thing about what I'm doing with my life."

She smirked. "I added that."

Her friend Natalie leaned over. "A living god at ten o'clock."

"Already tracking him. You're slow," Olaf said.

Nessa pretended to be shocked. "Natalie! You're married!"

"Married, not dead." Natalie leaned against her husband's shoulder while he earnestly discussed politics with a friend.

Olaf leaned forward and tapped her on the arm. "Nessa, go talk to him. If you don't, Tatianna will when she gets here. I'll buy the next round of drinks if you go say hello and ask him his name."

Natalie nodded. "Tatianna would like him. She fancies

them big and muscular, but she is out of town. Anyway, she adores you. She would throw him your way, considering that terrible date you had. She would cheer you on."

Tatianna was their most beautiful friend and a talented commercial photographer. A sweetheart to her friends but she admitted freely and frankly to have a very strong sexual drive. Her heritage was part-Swedish and something else because Tatianna was vague on her family. Nessa adored her because she was so brave and unapologetic. Why couldn't she be tall with big breasts and baby-fine straight hair and fearlessly go through men like a reaper in a field of wheat?

Nessa pushed her curly hair over her shoulder with a sigh. She could use a strong drink for some liquid courage to take Olaf up on his dare. "So, Olaf, you're going to buy a round for the whole table if I go talk to him. Right?"

Olaf nodded. "Just don't talk *too* much. You will scare him away."

Nessa stuck her tongue out at him and turned to the table. "I'll do it for the greater good of the group. You all owe me one for the drinks Olaf will buy you." She pointed at them while they all raised their glasses to her.

Natalie smirked. "The hardships our Nessa endures," she said.

Hesitating, Nessa pretended to check her phone while peeking at the man from the corner of her eyes. His eyes were on her, and she knew it—his glance was warm and she could feel it. But when she looked at him directly, he turned away.

Olaf made meowing noises because she was stalling. She scowled and gritted her teeth. Olaf was right—she pretended to be all bad-girl but really she didn't like to be intimate with almost-strangers. Apparently she had trust issues still, or so her therapist said.

Leaning up against the bar, the man had ordered a beer and surveyed the room casually. His gaze passed over her and then returned to take a long look at her. The color of his eyes washed over her, a pale ocean-blue.

Feeling bold, she grinned and winked at him. There was a hard line between his eyes as if he was concentrating. So long as he kept looking at her, she didn't care. When their gaze connected briefly, his mouth flattened as if he was displeased. He pushed his hair behind his ears and turned away.

What was so wrong with a wink? Men were so messed up nowadays. You made the first move, they freaked. You didn't, and you went home alone. She was determined to liven up her life. It needed to be more than just painting and working at the gallery. She got up and wandered over to where the blue-eyed hunk of sexy leaned against the bar.

"Hello, I'm Nessa. I'm here with my friends over there. You live in the neighborhood?" She worried she sounded dorky and uncool so she gave him her biggest smile. He was a lot bigger up close and she was in boots that had two-inch heels. Her lips were at the top of his chest. *Hmm.* A broad and muscular chest.

Stop. Be cool, Nessa.

He answered in a beautiful deep voice. "No, I'm just visiting Stockholm."

His voice was a rich rumble which she could feel in her chest. It was surprisingly warm, with a quiet sincerity to the tone. "What's your name?" she asked.

"Maelcom Skov-Baern."

He held her gaze with a directness that she liked. He answered her promptly like a soldier would to a commanding officer. But he was not grinning or flirting.

Time to be bold. She stuck her chin out and flipped her hair over her shoulder. Maybe she'd invite him to her table. It would liven up the evening. "You're Scandinavian but you're Danish? I can hear it in your Swedish. You want to come over and have a drink with me and my friends? It's okay—we won't tease you for being Danish. Can I call you Mal?" She reached out and tugged his arm with a flirty smile to get him to move toward their table.

He froze and tilted his head to eye her with a peculiar intensity. "My name is Maelcom, not Mal. Your name is Nessa. Is it short for something?"

She received a little electric zing through her hand. *Strange.* "Agnes. Nessa is short for Agnes, *Maelcom.* I get it, no nicknames. Hey, you gave me a shock by the way. Static electricity. I guess I'm electric. Sorry, I am chattering a lot. Would you like to sit with me and my friends?"

"I don't know." He rubbed his neck without meeting her eyes.

"Please, I've drinks riding on this," she blurted out.

Great. Now she sounded like she was begging a guy to hang out with her, but she didn't want to look hopeless in front of her friends.

He narrowed those blue eyes at her. "Yes," he whispered.

She could barely hear it but she watched his lips shape the word. *Beautiful voice* was her only thought. "Come on, then." She jerked her head and he followed her to the table. "Hey, people. Pay attention. This is Maelcom. He's visiting from Denmark and he collects art. Make him feel welcome and he might buy a painting."

Her friends smiled and waved. Someone shouted out, "Hooray, Maelcom."

She turned to him and whispered, "I know you don't collect art. That's cool but they're all artists who're trying desperately to sell their art so I like to give them hope. You might like a painting as a memento from Stockholm."

"But I do like art. And I collect art. I didn't understand how you knew," he said with a surprised tone.

It was easy to spot a potential art buyer after working in a gallery. You looked for money. His coat was tailored perfectly for him and she knew that a jacket like that ran thousands of euros. Expensive clothes meant money, and people with money bought art. Simple formula.

"I work at a contemporary art gallery so I'm used to trying to get people to buy art. It was just a wild guess. But if you do collect art, these people are all very talented artists and their work is very inexpensive."

"I buy paintings and drawings of nature. I like landscapes."

Really, she loved customers who had specific preferences. "All right, try talking to Elena down at the other end of the table. Long black hair. She does watercolors—huge and amazing landscapes, sort of modern realism. Who have you bought? Anyone I might know?"

"Paintings by Sorcha Rosenbloom and some drawings by Tse-Ting Lo."

"I have heard of Sorcha Rosenbloom. She's American, right? I saw her work at the Venice Biennale last year."

"Yes."

"Cool." She peered up at him. "You know your eyes are amazing." She had gone up on her toes to peer at them. She was very close to him and could feel the puff of his hot breath on her face.

"So are yours," he muttered.

"Mine are just boring brown eyes—yours are unique," she said while still staring at him.

"I should sit down," he said abruptly.

He took a chair next to Anders and introduced himself to the people sitting around the table. That was disappointing. Why did he sit next to her crazy roommate? The one person who annoyed her. She'd only invited him to be nice to him since she'd asked him to move out of the apartment.

And now Anders would talk endlessly about his obsessions, inevitably blabbering on about aliens from space, conspiracy theories and how the government created monsters in secrets labs. She once tried to convince him that he should write a sci-fi novel about some wild events he assured her were on-going, super top secret and hush-hush. He told her he didn't appreciate her not believing him and stomped away angry.

Anders used to work in the government as some kind of researcher but he'd quit his job recently. Nessa speculated he had been fired because he seemed depressed and kept leaving the house all dressed up as if he had job interviews.

She had rented out her spare bedroom because she needed extra cash, and a roommate was the easiest way to get some money. That had been the biggest mistake of the year.

Right before they'd left the apartment, Anders tried to tell her about some genetically-modified humans he thought might be aliens, but she just cut him off. Told him she didn't believe in that stuff so he better back off on the alien conspiracy stories. On the spur of the moment, she decided to inform him that a cousin was coming to live with her and that she needed to consider family first, so he needed to vacate the room. He appeared unhappy, but he agreed to move out before her beloved and imaginary cousin arrived.

She tried to edge nearer to Maelcom. He glanced sideways at her just as she noisily scooted her chair closer. She gave him a little wave and fluttered her eyelashes. Anders was babbling about government conspiracies. Maelcom turned back to Anders. *Shit.*

Olaf pulled at her arm to get her attention. "Your

roommate is the black hole of boring. He just sucked your big hunk of Genghis Khan into crazy talk and now he won't release him."

"*I know.* But he's not my roommate for long. I gave him his notice tonight. The official story is my cousin is coming to live with me because I didn't want to hurt his feelings. So if he asks, back me up. Her name is Nina. Second cousin." She whispered it to Olaf so only he could hear but she swore she saw Maelcom's head jerk as if he could hear her whispers.

"Thank god for Nina, your nonexistent cousin. I was starting to dread coming over to your place because the last time Anders talked about government conspiracies for an hour. A whole goddamned hour. I felt bad because he seemed so lonely, so I listened," Olaf said.

"Poor Olaf. Imagine what I put up with living with him." She turned to the people near her. "How about I get some chips for the table?" Several people nodded and gave her the thumbs-up.

Anders and Maelcom were still deep in conversation. Clearly, smiling and flirting had not worked. She loved when people smiled at her, and it made sense that it would be reciprocated.

"Nessa, please order a plate of chips. I'm starving," Anders whined.

He didn't offer to pay, of course. "I'm sharing with Olaf and his two friends. I don't think there'll be enough. Maybe you two can get your own?" Nessa narrowed her eyes at him but he'd already turned away.

Maelcom gave her a puzzled glance and Anders ignored her. She twirled away and stomped unhappily to the bar, muttering to herself. It was inconceivable that her annoying roommate had monopolized the handsome guy and then expected her to buy him food.

The bar had gotten crowded. Carefully, she squeezed through the people to the bar and into a little space next to a broad-shouldered man.

He turned to face her and smiled. "You can push up beside me anytime," he said with a grin.

It was a cheesy line and he delivered it with a little bit of embarrassment. The guy looked like a farm boy—young, all healthy and ruddy and slightly chubby.

She smiled back. "Sorry, I'm trying to order some chips from the bartender."

"I know, it's very busy. When he comes back, I will make sure he attends to you. Leave it to me. Can I buy you a drink? An apology for being just a country boy, but you are the prettiest girl here. My name is Thorsen. Call me Thor." He winked at her.

She sent a prayer of thanks to the universe for sending her a nice-looking man. He kept eyeballing her dress, which she found uncomfortable, but hey, beggars couldn't be choosers and she'd worn the dress to attract attention. She tugged the hem lower. "I'm Nessa. You live in the neighborhood? This is my favorite bar." Forget men who wouldn't pay attention to her. She would chat this guy up just to prove to herself that she wasn't a complete loser.

CHAPTER 3

Maelcom

MAELCOM THOUGHT THAT INTERACTING in a relaxed situation with the subject of his investigation would give him a better understanding of the risk. Information freely given was more valuable than information provided under duress. It was a delicate situation. They didn't want to overact if Anders was a minor annoyance as that could draw unwarranted attention.

Unfortunately for Maelcom, Anders droned on and on about non-relevant topics in response to Maelcom's brief questions. He'd prefer listening to Nessa talk—her voice had a little rasp to it. She talked fast and blurred her words together but it was melodious compared to Anders's drone.

But still, he needed to listen to Anders's weird and

wacky ideas with feigned interest. The safety of the Daimon Realm was at stake. Anders was on a longwinded diatribe about pyramids, Vikings, Africa, race issues and more.

Surprisingly, he was accurate about a couple of facts, but mostly not. Aliens from space—ridiculous.

The race issues in the Earth Realm confused Maelcom, but he had learned a great deal in his time here. Some treated him oddly no doubt because of his skin color. They would wrinkle their foreheads and ask where he was from. Denmark, he would say. He tried to understand it in the same light as the conflicts between the three different Daimon groups, but he couldn't quite grasp the human obsession with skin color. Perhaps it was all the same thing—hatred of the other, the inability to see them as the same. The Daimon wars were driven by rulers attempting to maintain control over different Daimon groups, and the differences were obsessed over. But thankfully those Daimons died and more progressive and visionary leaders took control. The wars ended and the focus was turned to unity and peace. Maelcom still had problems with Ice Daimons—he had spent so long hating them.

Maelcom tracked Nessa out of the corner of his eye. Was she some sort of player or a flirt? Fickle and man-hungry? No, he knew these kinds of women and she was different from the sexually adventurous women he had partnered. She was earnest, even naïve. When she'd walked up to him at the bar, all sweet and nervous, it had stunned him. That smile, which she doled like it wasn't powerful or enchanting. Now that beautiful smile was being given to some stupid blond man at the bar.

"Maelcom, are you listening to me?" Anders complained in a high-pitched voice. "I have to tell you about biologically altered humans called Daimons."

Maelcom jerked his head and casually widened his eyes like he was surprised. "You mean devils?" he said, deliberately misunderstanding him. "That's ridiculous. You're joking, aren't you? Demons don't really exist. I mean, that's insane." He chuckled but it came out rusty and choked.

"No, no, not a demon—this is a Daimon. There is a type of soldier called by this name. It sounds benign but it isn't. I tried to get my superiors alerted to this possibility but they ignored me. I uploaded the report to our US counterparts and they ignored it. Then I received an official reprimand, which is bullshit, and they put me on a leave of absence without pay. I think they want me to quit." He pouted like a child at this perceived injustice.

"Aaah, they probably don't realize how observant and intelligent you are. Government people are not very smart," Maelcom said. Anders had all the details wrong and it made Maelcom feel more confident that the rumors would die on their own. "Did someone tell you about this? Who? Are they trustworthy?" Maelcom asked, pushing for more details.

"I was at a lecture on military experiments by an investigative reporter, and this young soldier sits next to me. So we start talking and he tells me he has seen the result of some of these experiments. After the talk, we went to get a coffee. I told him I believed him and that I worked for Swedish Intelligence. He was glad that someone believed him. So, he tells me about how on a training mission he saw these men transform somehow into beast-like soldiers. Their skin color appeared metallic, and they were inhumanly fast, like someone had sped up the film. He said they fought with swords, their hands were huge and they roared like beasts when they fought. Something was weird about their heads, but they wore large fur caps."

"Maybe he had been drinking?"

"No, completely sober and serious. He was telling the truth. He wasn't overly specific—he described it like you would if you saw something unbelievable," Anders said.

Maelcom was surprised at the sharpness of the observation. "Where did this happen? Here in Sweden he saw these demons?"

"Daimons, not demons. This all took place at a training facility in Greenland and there were strict regulations about where the soldiers could be, but he had wandered into one of these restricted areas which were marked with biohazard signs. He told a senior officer and was severely reprimanded for being in the restricted area and put on leave. Right? I think they were some bio-experiment to produce a super soldier but they didn't want him knowing about these experiments. I wrote a report based on his testimony and developed a theory that someone is doing this research illegally, probably funded by the Russians. The Russians love that kind of thing. There's something fishy with the owner of the training facility—the guy who is listed is a ghost, like he just popped into existence eight years ago and now has top-level NATO military clearance. My boss won't listen to me. They say all top intelligence guys have no record like this Naberius guy. But really that's not true anymore in this day and age. Plus, why would a training center have biohazard signs. You see?" He tapped his forehead. "I've figured it out."

A small, unpleasant headache grew in Maelcom's brain because of Anders's incessant drone. Maelcom himself had put up those signs to keep people away from those areas so Daimons would have places to train and spar in their Daimon form. Who knew a soldier trying to skive off a training mission would hide in a secure off-limits zone?

"I'm listening. I think it's very interesting," Maelcom said, lying with pretend solemnity while he kept track of Nessa. She might be important. Good investigators didn't overlook little details. He could just see a flash of long, curly hair at the back of the bar and the head of the blond man she had been talking to. She was mostly hidden by people but he caught her scent amongst the crowd, a light flower smell drifting under perfumes and colognes.

"I think it's the details on how they fought that are interesting. They used old Viking swords." Anders sat back with a triumphant look on his face as if that finalized it.

Fuck. He briefly considered kidnapping Anders to simplify his life. It would be easy to knock him out and then Naberius could decide what to do with him. But Naberius wouldn't want that as it would draw attention and Maelcom envisioned much screaming from Anders. "Very interesting. I think you are onto something. Anders, what's your phone number? I know someone who'll want to meet you. A government person." A necessary lie, and Anders quickly told him his phone number.

While Anders babbled, Maelcom kept tracking Nessa in the corner of his eye. It was stupid, but perhaps she knew something about Daimons. A far-fetched idea but he assumed it must be the reason for his interest.

People kept walking in front of him blocking his line of sight. He shifted his chair over slightly to have a better view while Anders babbled on.

Nessa was walking to the rear of the room toward an exit door when he saw her stumble oddly. He lost her behind a group of people looking for a table and for several seconds they blocked his line of sight. The people parted and he saw the blond man grab her arm and sneer at her in an unpleasant way. Her eyes were glassy and the man dragged her out the back door while she punched his arm repeatedly with her clenched fist. No one else seemed to notice.

"I'll be right back," Maelcom said breaking into a run, pushing people out of his way. He didn't care if Anders heard him, he had to make sure she was okay. He slammed the rear exit door open then sniffed the air. A male scent with cheap cologne to the left.

Turning to his left and slightly around the corner, he

saw Nessa sprawled on the hood of a car and a man loosening his belt. Shit, he wanted to kill him with his bare hands.

All of a sudden, she jerked her leg up, kneeing the guy hard in the balls. A high-pitched scream and he staggered back into Maelcom's waiting hands. Closing his fingers hard around the neck of the disgusting man, he squeezed with a steady pressure, just enough to put him to sleep. He glanced at Nessa briefly but it appeared she had passed out.

Regrettably, he had decided to stop killing people. Well, if at all possible. He could make an exception but it was more important to help Nessa, so he flung the unconscious man to the ground. He hated rapists and abusers but he'd make sure the police put this animal in prison.

Completely by accident, he stepped on the man's fingers, pushing down with his boot till he heard a crunch. *Oops.* Picking up the man's wallet, he snapped a photo of the identification card and replaced everything, just in case someone dropped the ball. He dialed the police—the direct number of a high-level officer he knew from his Special Forces days.

A quick visual check of Nessa had him worried. Her eyelids were half open and she appeared barely able to move her body. It was amazing that she'd kneed the guy in the balls. He could see her breathing, semi-conscious, but clearly she had been drugged. He took her pulse, her skin warm and soft under his rough hands. He frowned at the erratic tempo and the weak level of energy in her body.

Leaning in, he whispered in her ear. "It's Maelcom. I'm here to help. Blink if you hear me." She blinked several times and a tear rolled down her face. "No, no, don't worry. I'm going to just fix your dress. I have called the police. We'll take care of you." He cooed softly, like taking care of a hurt animal, while delicately and discreetly arranging her skimpy dress so it covered her.

Her purse was on the ground and he picked it up, putting it over his shoulder. He brushed her hair gently from her face, her eyes closed. She looked like a sleeping angel.

"You will be fine but you need a doctor. I don't know how strong a drug he gave you."

Her energy tasted erratic and sick. Considering his options rapidly, he calculated the fastest way for her to receive medical attention would be to bring her to his hotel where he could have a doctor waiting. He could simultaneously direct efforts against this guy, take care of Nessa and deal with the Anders problem. Efficiency.

He dialed his phone. "This is Maelcom Skov-Baern. I want a suite prepared now with the hotel doctor and nurse to be there prepared to care for a woman who has ingested rohypnol or some similar drug. I'll be there in minutes. The police will be arriving to assist." The concierge responded with a simple affirmative and Maelcom hung up.

The man on the ground groaned and moved. Maelcom could feel a disruption in his own appearance, like a ripple of energy pushing out from his core through his human form—the beginning of a shift. He wanted to transform into his Daimon form and shake his horns at the man before killing him. He growled. *No. Not a killer.* He was in control. The disruption faded. Instead, he turned and kicked the unconscious man in the ribs. Broken ribs were a bitch in jail.

He scooped Nessa up in his arms. His right hand splayed against the bony wing of her bare shoulder and he took a sip of her energy—he could taste the drug she had been given. He gave her some energy back even though she couldn't use it. She was so light in his arms. Delicate and soft.

She nuzzled against his chest, said something incomprehensible and gave a low moan. Her hair tickled his chin and he kissed her head for some unknown reason. Because she was hurt, that's what it was. Like a lamb on his family's farm.

Sirens came blaring down the street and he strode down the alley toward the main street as the police pulled up. The senior officer came to attention as he informed him that the man on the ground was the attacker. "I'm taking Nessa to my hotel where a doctor is waiting. Meet me there," he commanded. The officer saluted and turned to direct his men.

Her energy was fluctuating. Dodging people on the sidewalk, protecting her with his shoulders and arms, Maelcom raced to the hotel with her in his arms.

CHAPTER 4

Nessa

HER BODY ACHED and her lips were dry. She tried to swallow but it hurt. She could hear voices but it took a lot of effort to open her eyes. They were gummy-stuck closed. As she rubbed them the room came slowly into focus.

An older man's voice said her name. "Nessa? I'm Dr. Sorensen, the hotel doctor. You were drugged and hurt but you're safe now."

She turned her face to the sound of his voice. A man in a white coat came into focus, a chubby face with glasses. *A doctor?*

He patted her hand. "Can you talk?"

"Yes. Where am I? What happened?"

The doctor turned and waved at a woman beside him

with dark hair. "Nessa, you're at the Hotel Alta on Summersgatan. I'm Officer Lucia Larsen. I'm here as your advocate, to help you. You don't have to talk or say anything unless you wish. You were drugged and assaulted. We have the man in custody and charges have been filed against him."

Nessa sat up in the bed and a wave of nausea swelled up inside her. "What? I was having a drink at the bar and—Oh, I'm going be sick." The doctor placed a bowl in front of her face and she puked up a lot of liquid. The policewoman handed her a towel and she wiped her mouth. "Thanks." She collapsed back on the pillow, feeling dizzy.

The doctor shook his head. "Move slowly until the drug has fully left your system. Physically, you're fine. We gave you some fluids to help flush the drug from your body. You might feel some dizziness and exhaustion for the next day. You had some trouble breathing before. Can you take a deep breath for me?"

A cold metal stethoscope was placed on her chest while she inhaled and exhaled.

"Your breathing is normal and clear," said the doctor.

Nessa pulled the blankets up around her and nodded. "I feel hungover and very tired. I remember everything but it was hard to move my limbs, like I was frozen. I felt sick, like I was going to puke, and this guy dragged me outside. I wanted to go to the bathroom but he dragged me outside and tried to attack me. I could feel adrenaline rush through me and I kneed him in the balls. Then I couldn't move anymore. Was I raped?" She rasped out the question. The terror of the situation was creeping up on her and made her feel breathless.

The policewoman shook her head. "No. I believe you immobilized him and then someone came and knocked the attacker out."

Nessa swallowed, trying to generate spit in her achingly dry throat. "His name was Thorsen," she croaked. "He said to call him Thor. Fucking hell. I thought he was harmless and silly. A nice country boy calling himself Thor." It was horrible to remember being so helpless and her eyes stung with tears. She was a stupid, stupid girl.

The policewoman squeezed her hand to comfort her. She smelled like Nivea cream and coffee. "Yes, that's the man they arrested. He is a predator. We have been trying to catch him for months. You're banged up and bruised from when he dragged you and threw you onto a car."

"Ouch, no wonder I ache. Why am I at a hotel?"

"It's two blocks from the bar you were at. Maelcom Skov-Baern found you and brought you here," the police-woman said.

"You don't have a lot of body fat to metabolize the drug and we worried that you would flatline from an arrhythmia. This hotel has me as their private doctor on call for the clients," the doctor explained.

"When I arrived, the doctor was here with a nurse. They had examined you and had already given you fluids to flush the drugs you were given, which is standard protocol. My

Captain said you were a VIP," said the policewoman.

Nessa wrinkled her nose, confused. "Me? A VIP? Really? I'm an artist. I work at a gallery part-time. My dad is a well-known artist, he is kind of famous. But I mean—Maelcom could have brought me home or to the hospital." She thought about him, all serious in black, and she remembered his whisper that he would help her.

The doctor stepped forward. "The man who knocked out your attacker was Maelcom, ex-Danish Special Forces soldier, a Jægerkorpset. The head of police knows him. He told the police he didn't know where you lived and he wanted to get you medical treatment quickly. He was worried about your respiration and heartbeat. When you arrived that was my concern but we had you on oxygen inside of five minutes of your arrival, and an IV of saline fluids, and you stabilized. We can arrange for you to be transported to a hospital now if you want."

Nessa shivered. She felt exhausted and sick. No way was she standing up and going to a busy hospital and talking to new doctors and nurses. "No, I'll stay. I'm better now anyway. I don't want to go anywhere. I just need to sleep."

The room was dark and calm with walls painted green, the color of new leaves in the springtime, and some decent paintings of flowers hung on the walls. It seemed hushed in the room like it had soundproofed windows and thick walls.

The doctor nodded. "That's a good idea. With sleep and fluids, you'll be back at one hundred percent by tomorrow."

"What about my friends?"

The policewoman said, "They were told you were receiving medical care and could not have visitors, but a Mr. Olaf Pedersen will not stop calling. So call him back soon."

Olaf would not stop until she talked to him. Her mouth tasted horrible and her bladder was full. "Later."

"Do you want to call your father?"

"My father is in New York for an opening. Don't call him, this is a big show for him at a major museum. Umm, I need to use the toilet."

The doctor said, "That's because of the IV. You have a lot of liquid in you. Can you stand?"

"Yeah, thanks." Nessa stood and the whole room spun for a second. She took a deep breath and things steadied.

The policewoman helped her to the bathroom and back. Nessa texted Olaf because she was too tired to talk, and promised to call soon. He texted emoji hearts back to her.

After draining a glass of ginger ale, she crawled underneath the silky sheets and snuggled into the soft pillows.

The policewoman said her goodbyes and left her phone number on the nightstand. She told Nessa to call if she felt worse, although Maelcom would apparently be checking in on her.

Nessa couldn't summon enough energy to talk so she flapped her hand as thanks and fell into a deep, dreamless sleep.

Later, Nessa opened her eyes feeling as if she had slept for hours. She stood up and put on the thick hotel robe that was lying at the foot of the bed. Standing beside the huge bed, she ran her fingertips over the sheets which were thick and soft. This was a luxury hotel. She wiggled her toes in the plush, cream-colored carpet.

Someone knocked at the door. A deep voice rumbled out, "Nessa, it's Maelcom, we met at the bar. May I come in?"

It was the voice of that soldier, the rugged businessman with the crazy blue eyes who helped her. She remembered that. "Yes. Yes. Come in."

The door opened. Maelcom stepped in and left the door partially open behind him. "I'm just checking if you are okay or if you need anything."

"You know I remember you helping me. It's a bit foggy but I remember you picking me up. Thank you. You stopped my attacker and called the police." She cleared her throat because her voice was scratchy.

"You stopped him, you kicked him. I just finished the job you started. You are strong to fight back like you did."

"Then it was a team effort because I think you saved me from being badly hurt."

He nodded and held out a plastic shopping bag. His eyes skidded across her face then looked away. "Here are some clothes. I'll return in an hour to escort you home." He shifted his weight from foot to foot and sniffed the air with a frown.

Automatically, she mimicked him and sniffed. A stale odor wafted up. Ugh, it was her and she needed a shower.

"Wow, I need to shower. Yes, come back later. I'll be

ready." She looked away, embarrassed because she hated smelling like old sweat.

He bowed and left without saying a thing, which was a little strange. His body language was deferential and concerned. But no eye contact. Maybe he was feeling embarrassed for her.

Nessa made her way slowly to the bathroom. A dull pain in her head pulsed, making her fuzzy and slow. She remembered the entire night at the bar like some weird, lucid dream. Everything was clear but strange, as if it happened to someone else. But it didn't. It happened to her.

Her face in the mirror appeared as pale as the white nightgown she wore. She vaguely remembered the nurse helping her put it on. Opening a bag on the floor, she saw her dress which smelled like vomit. She quickly rolled up the bag and kicked it toward the trash.

After she pulled the nightgown off, she saw fingertip-shaped bruises on her arms and around her wrists where someone had held her too tight.

"Fucking hell. That asshole hurt me," she muttered. She hoped Thorsen would be in jail for a long time. No one else would be hurt by him.

There was a huge showerhead and jets from the side which massaged her with hot water. It soothed her. Then she scrubbed every inch of her body with a washcloth and lots of soap.

If Maelcom hadn't shown up, Thor would have recovered from the kick in the balls and really hurt her. She wasn't crazy about soldiers. She was a pacifist—but she had plenty of friends who'd joined the military. They really didn't fight wars though. Some did UN tours in the Middle East or did rescue work, and they trained constantly.

Her heart raced at the thought of the close call she'd had. *Like almost being hit by a bus—you step back for some inexplicable reason and it whooshes by your face and your heart explodes because you were so close to death.*

Maelcom had been watching her carefully in the bar. All the people she passed on the way out had assumed she was drunk when Thorsen dragged her outside while she tried to punch him. Someone had even laughed at them, thinking they were joking around. Somehow Maelcom, from across the bar, had known something was wrong. Lucky for her.

CHAPTER 5

Maelcom

THINGS HAD GONE OFF THE RAILS with his investigation and it annoyed Maelcom. He liked when his efforts progressed cleanly and without a lot of publicity. Somehow last night he had abandoned his mission and run through the streets of Stockholm with a drugged woman in his arms and checked her into one of Stockholm's most exclusive hotels.

Could this be a manifestation of his depression come back to haunt him? Usually he had his space-outs or reveries where he would sink into an unreachable state, but impulsive behavior was a new thing. Dragging his hand through his hair, he realized he had even dropped kisses on the head of an unconscious woman. Totally out of control. He took a deep breath to clear his mind.

Perhaps he could gain control if he shifted into his Daimon form, but he preferred to be outside in the woods, under the stars, or in the mountains, not in a hotel room. The solitude of nature calmed him, which was why he liked surfing. The quiet floating out beyond the breakers. Once, he went at night and surfed in his Daimon form, horns and all, but it was too damn cold so he never did it again.

He stared out the window at the cloudy sky and half-translucent reflection of his face. Leaning his forehead against the cool glass, he decided he was fine. His energy was good.

He picked up the phone and called his commander. "Naberius, I've had a slight delay in dealing with Anders. I had to help someone in danger, a woman was attacked. She was the roommate of Anders Frisson, and her name is on the lease for the apartment where Anders is currently residing. I do not believe she is involved but I need to confirm absolutely he is a lone agent. He has some fellow conspiracy friends but they all have their own obsessions, and I don't think he has managed to convince any of them that 'whales' are real. I was going to kidnap him but he would scream a lot. I hate screamers."

"Whales" was a stand-in word for Daimon. Saying the word "Daimons" out loud was avoided in public or in any communications. They changed euphemisms regularly and had been using whales recently as a placeholder. The year before it was dolphins. Maelcom was partial to sea animals. Gusion kept pitching Marvel hero names because he was a fan, but Naberius ignored him.

Naberius's sigh floated in over the phone. "Do not joke. No kidnapping."

He wasn't joking. Why couldn't people tell when he was joking and when he was serious? "You will be glad to know I rejected the simplest solution which was to kill him."

"Those were the options you came up with? Killing and kidnapping?" Naberius said casually.

"Ah yes, but he is definitely a screamer. So don't worry. I will continue gathering intel and I have some other ideas to essentially co-opt him. Something tempting which he will be eager to sign up for and will allow us to contain him." He spun the heavy red-gold ring on his finger. All the men in Naberius's personal guard wore one. "I think it's the safest option."

Naberius was silent for a second. "Fine, spin your intricate webs, Maelcom, and try not kill or kidnap people. You're my friend—I don't want you spacing out."

Naberius was a thoughtful leader, and Maelcom had called him General in the Daimon Wars but here in the Earth Realm, they didn't use titles. "Earlier this year I was worrying about you, but you were fine. That last incident of mine was a freak occurrence." He'd had one of his space-outs on finding the dead body of a young man who had looked like his brother. He snapped out of it, no worries. He was getting better.

"You're like Gusion. Stubborn," Naberius said.

Maelcom heard the concern in his friend's voice. Shit,

he should not have mentioned kidnapping and killing as a possibility. "I'm far less stubborn than Gusion, just not as charming with the ladies."

He heard a woman's voice in the background talking to Naberius. Jessalyn, his wife and mate.

"Hold on. Yes, Jessalyn just told me that report is considered dead on the radar of any US intelligence agency. People have it filed under Looney Tunes crazy. Her words. Anders is the last loose end, so let's just ensure he is a lone agent and lock him down with whatever tricky web you have devised," Naberius said.

"Give my regards to Lady Jessalyn."

"Shhh. No titles. She gets all angry about the titles, says it's against the burgeoning democratic ideals and the elected government in our realm. Don't bring it up. I dislike arguing politics with Jessalyn," Naberius said in a hushed tone.

Love had changed the legendary general. Made him happier and more cautious. Their exile on earth had been a ruse to remove Naberius from the pressures and pain of his life after the wars. Naberius had been commander of the Jotun Daimon armies and was eldest son of the most powerful families in the Realm. Exile had worked for him and the Daimons who had accompanied him.

"You just hate our politics. Listen, Gusion texted me an update. He believes that there are some remaining associates of Rayme around." The rebel leader, Rayme, had attempted to destroy the peace by kidnapping Jessalyn and attempting to lure Naberius to his death.

"Yes, some support personnel. We will track them down. Listen, something is off with Gusion. He doesn't joke around as much. He didn't even get excited when I told him I was going with him and the men to Comix Con dressed as a Viking warrior."

"Is he listening to Metal, Rock or Country?"

"Metal, as usual. He listens to country?" Naberius sounded bewildered.

Gusion was fearsome as a Daimon soldier, but here on earth he was a happy-go-lucky human obsessed with cosplay, music and his bar. "Call me when he listens to country music. But metal? Shit, he's fine. But get Bobby to talk to him. Bobby won't let up until Gusion tells him what's happening."

"True that. Okay, Gusion believes those support people are in Scandinavia. Perhaps left there to secure an alternate escape route or to hold down a base of operations."

"I've been here, but I haven't been focused on scenting for anyone."

Maelcom heard Naberius's sigh over the phone. "The intel came from individuals who saw the light in the old country and gave us the number of people who came through, but no one had names. We are short at least two from our count. They may have simply gone AWOL and underground, but we need to find them."

"I'll look but I need to finish dealing with Anders before giving it my full attention. Unless you want Gusion to come over and hunt them."

"I would prefer him not to be in the field for now."

"No problem. Talk later."

"Later. And stop helping all the pretty women in trouble."

"How did you know she is pretty?" Maelcom asked a nanosecond before he realized he had fallen into a trap.

Naberius laughed at him, muttered a goodbye and hung up.

Maelcom frowned at the phone. Was it time to stop by Nessa's room and ask how she was doing? Perhaps she needed closer monitoring, just to make sure she was recovering. He felt responsible for her.

A detective who worked for Maelcom was watching Anders. He had been seen returning to the apartment then leaving. Maelcom's hired hand had lost him in the crowds of the train station, which was why Maelcom didn't like to outsource important work.

He would escort Nessa home soon and use the opportunity to look around for clues as to where Anders went and perhaps gather other information. He had Anders's phone number and ran a trace. He could find him easily but some background information would be useful.

Maelcom found himself at Nessa's door, and knocked. He remembered holding her, small and nestled in his arms, such sweet energy. Her voice called out, "One minute."

Daimons took energy from each other governed by custom and tradition. Like a handshake or hug. They needed high levels of energy to maintain their human forms, but it was easy in the Earth Realm nowadays. People hugged, kissed and shook hands; women touched him when they flirted and men thumped his shoulder. His fellow Daimons gave him plenty of energy but he did like the wild sparkle of energy from people here in the Earth Realm.

"Take your time. It's me, Maelcom," he said to the closed door. He leaned his ear against the door. Movement and shuffling.

He had sipped some of Nessa's energy to evaluate her health, but he had also impulsively kissed her head. Was that a violation in her drugged state? He had been terrified that she would die. A stupid fear, but she was so thin and her breathing so erratic that when he tasted the bitter poison in her energy, he had given in to fear and pressed that kiss to her head with a prayer to the gods. And he was an unbeliever.

Carrying her in his arms reminded him of lambs on his family farm in the Daimon Realm when, as a young boy, he worked as a shepherd for the family herds. The mother ewe would trot at his side as he carried her new offspring. He hated farming but he loved animals and the peaceful stillness of country life.

Nessa opened the door, all pink and showered, with wet hair. "Maelcom. Come in." Nessa's soft husky voice licked at his brain.

He looked at his feet, feeling awkward and enormous. She was willowy, pale and earnest. Looks were often deceiving. Frail but she was steely strong on the inside. He had tasted her energy, and he knew inside there was a steely strength like a willow tree.

"The medication is still wearing off. The doctor said you might have balance issues."

"I'm fine. A slight headache. I ordered some breakfast. The food helped give me energy. I'll head home soon."

"I will escort you home when you are ready." He stood near the door with his hands behind his back.

Observant brown eyes turned in his direction and he held her glance. "Why?" she asked bluntly.

He tilted his head, surprised at the question. "The doctor said you might be dizzy for a while. I'm worried about you," he confessed. He didn't mean to be so honest, but something about those big, liquid-brown eyes made him tell the exact truth to her.

Nessa gave him a crooked smile. "Oh, you are sweet but I'm feeling better. You know, the policewoman said you were a soldier, Special Forces or something. You rescued me. I guess you are trained in observation because you saw me being dragged out. No one else noticed. And then you knocked the guy out which is cool even though I'm a pacifist, but sort of a pragmatic pacifist—you know, we need some soldiers to fight truly evil people. I have friends who serve in the Swedish army. They do a lot of rescue stuff and—" She put her hand over her mouth. "I tend to talk a lot. Sorry."

He blinked his eyes at the torrent of words. "It's fine.

You should know I'm no longer a soldier. I'm retired and I am in private investigations and intelligence work. But in the Special Forces, I excelled at rescuing people in dangerous situations." He bowed slightly to her.

Nessa stared at him. "Like Superman," she said softly. She stood awkwardly in a too-large sweatshirt, fiddling with the sleeves, and sweatpants so baggy that she had to hold up the pants with one hand.

"No." He had seen the movie. "Definitely not. More like the Incredible Hulk."

"Hah! Good one. I like the Hulk, too." She snorted a laugh while trying to push up the sleeves on an enormous shirt but they kept unrolling.

The hotel had provided clothes on his request that were the wrong size and it annoyed him.

She plucked at the shirt. "I don't think I thanked you for the clothes and everything."

Maelcom shifted his feet restlessly. He should have gotten to her sooner. And he was using her to gain access to Anders's place of residence. "You don't have to keep thanking me."

She made a funny face and put her hands on her hips. "You know, I can thank you as many times as I want and you're just going to have to put up with it." She stuck out her chin and stared at him with a stubborn curl to her lip.

He liked to see her feisty with eyes bright and alert. She was recovered if she had the energy to scold him. He was happy being scolded. Strange.

"And I'll pay you back for the hotel. Can you tell me how much the room was?"

Maelcom scratched his jaw. This was a luxury hotel and he knew that Nessa worked at a gallery and as an artist— both jobs paid modestly. How could he get her to accept it as a gift? An idea popped into his head. "You're an artist. I'll take one of your paintings or drawings in payment."

Nessa stared at him. Her chocolate brown eyes blinked a couple of time before she answered.

"A trade? Well, you might need to take two—this place is very expensive and I ordered a big breakfast," she said.

Her hair was damp and just starting to dry into long ringlets hanging down her back. The scrubbed face and rosy cheeks made her appear younger than he knew her to be. Her driver's license said she was twenty-six years old. His Daimon age was almost a hundred years, but as Gusion always said, it was like dog years compared to humans.

"Two drawings, then," he said with a definite nod. "When should we leave for your apartment?"

"Soon?" Nessa hesitated. "I only have these clothes. The dress I was wearing is covered in vomit but I literally don't think I can walk in these pants. They're too big."

Maelcom stared unhappily at the pants which were rolled several times but seemed to unroll every time she moved. "I apologize. I'll go and get something else for you."

"Hey, wait a minute. You know, last night? I was going to flirt with you at the bar but you started talking to Anders." She pushed the wet hair back from her face. "I went to order food from the bartender and since you didn't want to talk to me, I flirted with Thorsen. I'm not blaming you. It's his fault. I'm just thinking." Her expression was sad and she bit her lip.

He spun his ring while thinking about how he had wanted to talk to her, or at least listen to her talk and not the annoying Anders. His energy levels pulsed in anger at Anders and Thorsen but he said firmly, "You should flirt as much as you want and not be hurt because of it. I wished I had talked to you instead of Anders but I'm not interested in flirting."

"Are you married or do you have a girlfriend or a boyfriend?" she asked with polite intent.

Maelcom shook his head solemnly. "No. Not married, no girlfriend, no boyfriend. I'm on an assignment and I don't flirt while working." It was a lie. He had been with women on assignment. Maybe not flirting, more like having company for the evening. There was something about her that made him lie about his habits. He didn't want to flirt with her because he was drawn to her, interested in her.

A flicker of disappointment showed on her face but she shrugged. "I didn't mean to put you on the spot. Just curious because you talked a lot to Anders and we didn't get a chance to talk."

"No. Anders talked a lot."

"I know, exactly—he's very irritating when he starts to go on and on about his theories. All ridiculous things. I wonder if he is mentally stable. Anyway, once you start talking with him, it's a slippery slope, and before you know it, hours have gone by."

He stared at her. "I would have flirted with you but I was working."

"Oh, it's okay. Don't worry about it," she said but her shoulders tensed.

"You *are* interesting and beautiful," he said firmly. "Very unlike Anders. I wanted to talk to you. I should have talked to you." He never considered that she would take his lack of interest personally.

She laughed. "Very unlike Anders? You are funny. You don't have to compliment me. I understand. You needed to focus on your whatever you're doing."

He tilted his head while he examined her. "Yes, I do."

She waved her hand like the whole thing was nothing. "Anyway, you saved me and I like you. You are like my own personal hero. I think we're going to be good friends so I need to give you fair warning that I talk a lot. I can't help it. When we get to know each other more, you will see that I can be exhausting. After a couple of hours, most people ask to me to stop talking so much." She held up her hands in a stop-right-there gesture.

His eyes moved to her raised hands, his stomach clenching at the bruises on her wrists. Someone growled.

She ignored him and stared at him with her eyes half closed. "Hey, can I draw you instead for our deal about the drawings? Or I will draw you and give you one of my other drawings—any one you want. That would be a valuable payment. I have a terrible time finding interesting male models. It's very important to draw interesting-looking people." She licked her lips and raised her eyebrows in question. "I like to draw people who aren't Swedish and you qualify. Plus, all your muscles. They are great to draw." She made a little whirling gesture with her index finger then placed her finger on her lips with a *smack* sound.

Lips. Maelcom cast his eyes down as he pondered the idea of being looked at so carefully by her. It made him feel hot.

She stepped closer and put her hand on his arm. "It's okay if you don't want to."

He sipped her energy, a little taste, almost not trusting the honesty of her request. But her energy was clean. Her pale hand with those terrible bruises rested on his forearm and again he experienced a tremor of anger in his energy which threatened to disrupt his form. He tapped it down, controlling it easily.

"You can draw me if you want." The words flew out of his mouth before he could think. Some strange impulsiveness had overtaken him.

"Really? Your face is amazing, too. Your eyes, cheekbones, forehead, all strong lines, great to draw."

He didn't know what to say so he tried for distraction. "Do I have to stand in a pose?"

She wrinkled her nose. "Ha. No. You can just stand or sit for me, whatever is comfortable for you. I want to draw you. Not some artistic or cheesy pose, just natural."

He looked down as he thought. Her feet were bare and her toes scrunched into the carpet.

"They forgot to buy you socks," he muttered nonsensically.

"It's not cold. I grew up not wearing socks."

"Why didn't you have socks growing up?" he demanded.

She looked surprised at his abrupt tone. "Umm, I didn't have socks because my mother was a crazy religious woman who believed socks were an unnatural coddling of children. She was a freak. Now I have many socks at home. I'll put some on when we get there."

"You can wear a pair of mine."

She smirked at his boots. "You're funny. I could probably wear your socks as a dress. I'll be fine."

He frowned. His feet were a size fourteen but he didn't think she could wear his sock as a dress. Warm and dry feet were the most important thing in the command of soldiers.

She shook her head at him. "Don't worry, Maelcom. I'll be all right." Her confident voice had a sweet bounce to it, the up and down like a song of assurance, a song of comfort.

Why did she want to comfort him? He was a warrior known for his ruthless, bloody victories. Even his human form reflected this truth. But no, she had ready smiles and cheerfulness for him. Even bruised and hurt by evil, she stood straight with her shoulders thrown back and smiling at the world, happy and strong.

"Let me dry my hair. I'll be ready in thirty minutes?"

She bent over and rolled the pants up to her knees. Like a child in an adult's clothes. "It's ridiculous, right? I think these are men's pants. Is there some tape around here? Maybe I could tape them up. We used to call it poor-man's tailoring when I was in university."

"No," he said forcefully. She looked confused but not scared by his command voice. He rubbed his face. "I'm sorry. I'll be back with clothes that fit in twenty minutes." He ducked out of the room before she could argue with him. Those were ridiculous clothes. She couldn't even walk without her pants falling off.

In the lobby, he located the concierge. "The clothes you bought were far too large. Where's the closest store for women's clothes?" After effusive apologies by hotel, he was directed to a store two buildings away on the same block.

A young woman in a long, gray T-shirt dress with a long, colorful scarf welcomed him. "How can I help?"

He narrowed his eyes and thanked his luck. She was the same height as Nessa. "My wife needs clothes. I want the red jacket in the window. And the dress you are wearing in your size and the scarf." He handed her his credit card. It was important for Nessa to stay warm.

CHAPTER 6

Nessa

MAELCOM ESCORTED HER DOWNSTAIRS, staying close to her like he was her bodyguard, like she was a VIP. He hovered over and around her, not letting anyone near, all in black and very serious. It was cool. If she was a celebrity, she would totally have men like him as her bodyguards. Big, powerful, serious men with soft, deep voices keeping the paparazzi at bay.

He was like the yin to her yang. Tall, male, mahogany dark hair, shy and muscled. She was pale blonde hair, with no muscles, talking all the time and wearing bright colors. Opposites.

She flipped her hair over her shoulder, stuck her nose in the air and strutted through the luxurious hotel lobby as people stared at them. This was what it must feel like to be a rock star—all eyes were turned to her. *La-di-da.* The life of the rich and famous.

It was funny—she had never really noticed Maelcom's hotel because there was only a tiny, discreet sign near the door denoting it as a hotel, and the doorman wore a dark suit that made him look like a businessman waiting outside a building. It was only inside that she saw it was an exclusive establishment, all hushed leather and cream carpets. It was a place for wealthy tourists who wanted a low-key luxury experience with all the trimmings.

After she dried her hair, he had returned with new clothes and insisted she wear them because they would fit her better. The red jacket was cut in moto style but was made of fuzzy soft fleece with a lightning bolt on the back— an ironic jacket. She told him to let her borrow a sweatshirt of his which he claimed he didn't own. She suggested he could go get clothes from her apartment and he frowned so unhappily that she gave up and wore the clothes he bought her.

The dress was a simple long T-shirt dress in a beautiful soft cotton, and cut in a clever way so that it clung to her body, giving the impression of curves, and the jacket was cozy.

On the street, the sun was out and the sky clear, but there was a chill in the shadows. She stood for a second on the sidewalk and lifted her face to the sun. The warmth was pleasant. "The sun is out today."

"Are you feeling sick?" He held her shoulder with his huge, warm hand like she was going to fall or something.

"Don't fuss over me, I'm totally recovered. I always heal fast. Yes, I'm a little hungover but I'm weirdly happy because I helped catch a sick freak who has been messing with the women of Stockholm. You should be proud because you were a big part of it turning out the way it did. If you hadn't caught him and made sure the police hauled him away, I'd have been more upset. But I feel victorious, like we did something important."

"When you fight what you know is evil, justice has been served," he said in a soft voice.

She closed her eyes and breathed in deeply. The wind held a hint of the sea. The briny smell of water was present in the breezes off the water as the city of Stockholm is spread over a multitude of islands. "Justice has been served. We took a criminal off the streets and the women of Stockholm are safer now."

She put out her fist. He hesitated a second and then presented his fist. They bumped softly, his huge hand against her regular-sized one.

"Let me get a taxi," he said.

"No, no, lazybones Maelcom. It's only a couple of blocks. I need the fresh air."

He opened his mouth to argue but she gave him a serious look. He stopped, examined his boots carefully and then nodded. *Phew.* She didn't want to argue—not because she was scared of him but because she wanted to spend more time with him on their walk.

They proceeded at a relaxed pace. Sodermalm was one of the larger islands and it had a laid back feel. It was not so busy as downtown and had more interesting shops. Her apartment was only a couple of blocks away. A vibrant neighborhood, half fancy and half hipster, with cool stores and galleries.

"I'll hold your arm. The doctor said you might experience dizziness for around twenty-four hours. You need to take it slow and chill."

He spoke funny sometimes, reminding her of an older Swedish country grandparent. Very proper and even old-fashioned. But occasionally he would use an American phrase like "chill" and the blend was odd. She couldn't decide if it was because he spoke several languages or if it was his tendency for terseness which made everything sound slightly off.

"Maelcom, I'm fairly sure I puked up all the drug." She wrinkled her nose at the memory. "I'll take it slow. Being outside in the fresh air is helping clear my head."

He frowned and nodded. *A little tightly wound and definitely not chill*, she thought to herself.

"Come on, I want to stop at this bakery. It's down this street and I'm still hungry." She tucked her hand in the crook of his arm. It was nice because his body threw off a lot of heat. "You're so warm. The breeze is off the ocean today." She moved herself closer to him.

As they walked, she chatted about the neighborhood

and about what each store had that was special or unique to cover up her sudden attack of nerves. She knew she was failing at trying not to overwhelm him with her chatter. Her brain said *stop* but her mouth kept talking.

Oh look, her favorite stationery store, and there an amazing flower shop, and finally a wonderful gallery of ceramics. She pointed these out to him and he listened carefully to her. She waved to her friend in the gallery who smiled and waved back.

"She owns the gallery and she's a renowned expert on contemporary ceramics. I go to all their shows. I love clay but I'm not gifted that way. My thing is paper, drawing or painting, watercolor mostly—this way I don't compete with my dad who is the oil painting master of Sweden. Do you know him? Eric Gustafson. It's tricky when your father is your country's most famous painter and you decide to become an artist, too. The king gave him a medal, you know, at a special ceremony. I could show my work under a different name, but the art world is small and they all know me anyway so why bother. Sometimes it helps get me noticed but I'm trying to do my own thing, you know? Be my own artist. I'm working on writing and illustrating my own fantastical stories. Like arty graphic novel stuff." She stopped to take a breath.

"What stories?" he said in a confused manner.

That was cool—he listened. She pointed to her head. "The ones up there. I mean, I make up stories and I draw them. My art is all about imagined stories or poems that are in my brain, so I started actually writing them. I might publish the drawings and the stories together. Like a picture book for grown-ups. Or a poetic graphical novel."

"I would read your stories," he said in his deep voice. She wanted to put her ear to his chest and see if he rumbled when he talked. She wouldn't, of course, but she imagined it would feel lovely.

"Okay, I'll show you some. Do you read any sci-fi or fantasy?"

"No. But I read poetry."

She stopped walking. "You're not kidding, are you?"

"No."

"I write my stories in verse. Oh, this is so good. I'll show you them and you tell me what you think. Just be gentle." She hunched her shoulders. "I'm sensitive to harsh feedback."

He stared at her but not really at her, sort of right past her. Because, she realized, he didn't like looking into her eyes. It was like he stared at her forehead or her ear. When he did look into her eyes, she felt it inside like a fire deep in her chest.

"Come on." She grabbed his arm and steered him into a store with large close-up photographs of bread hanging in the window. "My friend Tatianna did those photos. Oh, you should meet her. She's very beautiful and an amazing photographer. So talented. She's like my best friend combined with the older sister I never had. Everyone flirts with Tatianna." The moment she said it, she became a little angry with Maelcom, which was ridiculously unfair considering Tatianna wasn't even there and he wasn't flirting with her. Irrational. It was probably a side effect of the drugs.

He scratched his jaw. "I don't think I would."

She ignored him. Like, who could resist Tatianna? She opened the door and walked in. "Does this place smell amazing? Close your eyes and breathe it in. Come on."

He obeyed her and closed his eyes and breathed in. "It smells like a farm kitchen."

She punched his arm. "Yes, yes. Exactly. You have a good nose to guess that."

"Nessa, hello." Her friend Christophe appeared behind the counter, grinning. He leaned forward and kissed both her cheeks.

"Hello, Christophe, how are you? I brought a friend. We're dying for some oat farm bread and two of the little sweet cakes."

Christophe became her friend when she moved into the neighborhood. He was married to a fellow artist, Gretta, and they often saw each other at openings and museums. "My little Nessa. Yes, yes. Here is the bread. The sweet cakes are my gift. You need to eat more or you'll blow away in the winter wind."

She giggled. "I love sweet cakes. Thank you, Christophe. Is Gretta around?"

"No, she's in her studio under strict orders no one can interrupt her," Christophe said.

Maelcom stood there glaring at Christophe as if he was trying to make up his mind about something. Why was he being so stern? She shoved her elbow at him. "Don't mind my friend. His grandmother died and he's very sad, not grumpy."

It was stupid to lie but she didn't want Christophe's feelings hurt. She lied to cover up Maelcom's weird reaction, but she also knew the reaction Christophe would have at news like that. It was just a little lie because Maelcom was being so weird with her friend and it would serve him right to get a Christophe hug.

Christophe placed his hands on his heart. "How sad. How terrible," he muttered and he came out from behind the counter. "I'm so sorry," he said, throwing his arms around Maelcom for a big hug and a squeeze. Nessa coughed and tried not to laugh.

Maelcom patted Christophe on the shoulder and stepped back out of his embrace. He had this silent and stern vibe but when he talked, he was gentle. That was the real Maelcom, the one in his voice, the one who mumbled a soft, "Thank you. Thank you," to Christophe.

Nessa grinned, happy that Maelcom was nice to her effusive friend.

"A grandmother is a special relationship. Am I right?" Christophe said earnestly.

"She was very old and lived a long life but thank you for reminding me of her. She loved to bake," Maelcom said.

Christophe smiled, happy that he was able to comfort

someone. He was a very spiritual baker, and making people happy with baked items and hugs were his thing.

"Have a good day." She stuffed money in his hand because she knew Christophe would try to give her the bread and cakes for free. "I pay. But you give some bread today to someone who can't."

Christophe sighed. "*Ja. Ja.* Good day." And he hugged and kissed both her cheeks again.

Maelcom nodded at Christophe and held the door open for her.

"I feel like a celebrity with my tall, strong bodyguard because *I* always bring security when buying cake." She sashayed past him.

"You should. You're not very strong," he observed seriously.

"I think I'm fairly average for a woman my age but since I'm skinny, people assume I'm weak." She sighed and flexed her arm. "But feel that. I lift weights."

He delicately squeezed her muscle. "Hum," he muttered, not appearing impressed.

"Whatever. I have very good arm strength for someone like me. It's just comparative weirdness because everyone here in Sweden is so tall and I'm not." Opening the bakery bag, she ripped off a piece of the still warm bread to eat. "Why is fresh bread so amazing?" she said before taking a big bite.

Maelcom stared at her mouth while she chewed the bread and then looked at the sidewalk with studied care.

"My grandmother was very old when she died but she would have laughed at me being hugged by a baker."

He spoke plainly and with the first tiny bit of humor she had ever seen him display. It was sweet. Of course he loved his grandmother—everyone loved their mormor.

"I'm glad your grandmother laughed a lot. It must not be genetic," she teased.

He nodded. "Yes, you're correct." He remained silent, waiting for her to talk again.

As she ripped another hunk of the bread, she noticed the bruises on her wrist. She pulled the jacket sleeve down. It was weird how she could go from laughing fun to feeling scared. Those bruises reminded her of how close she had come to really being hurt. The memory made a surge of adrenaline course through her body, made her lips prickle and sweat break out on her forehead.

"Nessa." Maelcom took her hand and stroked it, his fingers hot on her cold hand. "You're safe."

His touch grounded her and she squeezed his hand back. "I know. It can take a while for bad memories to fade. I know. Thank you for walking me home."

"I've learned a lot about the area. I know the best bakery and the best galleries in Stockholm now." He said this seriously but it made her smile because that was him being nice, even a little funny. He kept her hand in the crook of his elbow, walking slower to match her stride.

After another block, they arrived at her apartment. It was an old building from the nineteen twenties, and all the apartments were very spacious. A cousin had bought it as an investment and let her take a large apartment on a high floor for half of what it was worth. She had the part-time gallery job for expenses and time to paint, but life in Stockholm was expensive, so she took a roommate.

She unlocked the front door and waved him in. "We have to walk up to the top floor, sixth floor, no elevator. That's what you get in an old building. It's good exercise. I run up, sometimes two steps at a time."

"You shouldn't run," he said seriously as if she was going to start leaping up the stairs the moment she saw them. Funny man. She should, just to freak him out because he didn't believe she was completely recovered.

Hers was the most spacious apartment at the top of the building, but the hardest to rent without an elevator. The apartment had two bedrooms, a separate dining room and living room. The dining room, her studio, was a perfect space for drawing and painting, with old-fashioned sliding doors that separated it from the living room.

"Come on. I don't think Anders is home. Yay. I'll make coffee and we have the sweet cakes." She fished out her keys and jangled them. *Drawing him would be amazing.* She wondered if she could schedule him for the next week.

CHAPTER 7

Maelcom

HE HAD PICKED OUT CLOTHES that would be comfortable for Nessa but the dress was not as baggy as it had been on the salesgirl. It clung to her body in a sexy manner even though she was slender. And the V-neck in front was too low, providing him distracting glimpses from his height. He was disgusted with himself as she had just been hurt by that animal at the bar so he kept his eyes up, not quite looking her in the eyes but staring at her face.

"Sit. Gotta put some leggings on. My legs are cold. But I love this jacket. It's so cozy and funny with the lightning bolt. I can't believe you want me to keep this. I kept all the tags—you can just return it."

"It is a gift. You like it so you should keep it," he said

stubbornly.

"Make yourself at home." She disappeared into her bedroom and he was left alone in her living room. He eyed her tiny two-seat couch draped in colorful blankets and chose to remain standing in order to examine everything in the room while he waited.

Electric blue running shoes beside the door in Nessa's size. Bookshelves stuffed full of books. There were paintings and prints on all the walls.

The drawings were Nessa's—he knew it even before he saw the initials AG. Agnes Gustafson. A big one above the couch was drawn with colored pencils and depicted two people running in a forest with birds swooping around them. Her drawing was like her energy—quick, light and fast. There was a warm light in the scene. She had infused it with her own energy. Interesting. The painting near the front door must be her father's. He recognized a different style to the paint strokes—it was a picture of Nessa, younger, jumping in the air. It was a picture that glowed with the love of a parent.

He peeked into the adjoining room, tidy and organized with a work table with neat piles of drawing paper, and shelves with paint tubes and jars. On the wall there was a drawing of a woman flying with feathered wings over a mountainous landscape, more like a bird than an angel. It looked like a dream or a story. He would have to ask her.

On the other side of the apartment, there was a door that was slightly open. He strode over and looked inside. It appeared to be Anders's room. Maelcom sniffed. It smelled like Anders and looked like him too—pale, sparsely furnished, with a cross on the wall and several posters of the Norse gods. An old laptop sat on the desk and several closed moving boxes were stacked next to it.

He slipped into the room and stopped to listen for Nessa. Now, was his opportunity to take a quick look for clues. He heard a faucet and her talking loudly on the phone declaring "Oh, Olaf" as the start of every sentence and then retelling the events of the night. She must be in the bathroom, from the echo, and her voice sounded happy. Who had phone conversations with friends in a bathroom? Nessa, apparently. She was effusive and laughing, her little melody of talk. His stomach twisted as he considered what might have happened if he hadn't been there at the bar. He was damn glad he'd broken the man's hand.

Peering in the open draws, he saw nothing. No clothes. No shoes. It looked like Anders was already gone.

He opened the laptop on the desk and quickly clicked the spacebar. Why had Anders left this? There was an option to enter as a guest, which was helpful for him trying to hack in and bad for the security of Anders's computer. Sitting down in the chair, his fingers flew across the keyboard as he set up a hack of the hard drive. He opened the browser, typed in the path to the team's server, which would execute a command to run a program to break into the hidden folders under Anders's user account. It was going well—he was almost done. He peered at the screen intently as the information copied to a secure location.

He took out his phone to text his status to Naberius but he sniffed the air, and he looked up to see Nessa standing in the doorway. "Hello, Nessa."

She stood, head cocked to the side with her arms crossed. "What's going on, Maelcom? You're snooping on Anders's computer. I don't like the way my brain is trying to link all this up, and the results are not good. Tell me what is happening and why. Right now." She tapped the toes of one of her black ballet slippers. No wonder he hadn't heard her. The odd thing was she didn't look mad, but as if she was annoyed at not being informed.

He opened his mouth to lie, to tell her he was just using the computer to check something on the internet. She tilted her head and raised an eyebrow. This woman was perceptive and she would know the difference, he just knew it. Plus, he was a notoriously bad liar. He'd never had to lie until he came to the Earth Realm and here he needed to lie a lot. New life, new problems. He would tell her the truth. A partial truth.

"Last night, at the bar, I was there following your roommate. I work for European Intelligence and Anders violated intelligence protocols, stole and leaked secured material. I was sent to gather more information so my superiors can decide if Anders is a continued securtiy risk."

She narrowed her eyes. "Which European intelligence agency?"

Of course, she pinpointed his one lie. "I can't tell you

because you don't have clearance. My subgroup reports into NATO Intelligence. I have identification, but do you know what Danish Intelligence IDs look like?" He pulled out an ID which he needed for the contract work he did for the Danish Special Forces and showed it to her.

She peered at it like it might bite her and flapped her hand at it. "Oh, I don't know what to look for. It seems very authentic. Terrible picture though, Maelcom. You look unhappy." She looked concerned which was ridiculous.

He had been unhappy at the time of the picture, he remembered. "Will you allow me to break into his computer?" he asked.

She snapped her fingers. "Absolutely. Right? You're on a mission. Or an investigation. I don't even think you need my permission. The police already told me you are ex-Special Forces and probably you work for Intelligence because you have all the connections. At least, I think you do. Let me say, I have always found Anders very strange. Not like people who usually go to work in government, who are very straight and boring. I mean, he was boring but also crazy. Right? I can't believe he stole government secrets. I bet he did it because he is all conspiracy theory about certain things and he stole some information that proves his theories. Am I right? I bet I am. But will people be hurt or killed by his actions? I mean, we cannot let that happen. He's not a political terrorist?" She gasped in horror at the idea.

Maelcom scratched his jaw. "He's not dangerous, he's

not a terrorist, but I'm simply ensuring that he doesn't intend to leak any more critical information which could compromise national and European security. I can't judge his mental state."

"What kind of information did he leak?"

"I can't tell you because you don't have clearance."

She waggled her finger at him. "Now I understand why you talked to him so much at the bar. Listen, Anders is freaking nuts. My friend, Tatianna, thinks he has mental issues, but I just think he's naïve and slightly crazy. Anything strange in the world, he thinks it's a plot or aliens and the government is out to get him or his friends, plus he's very religious. He thinks Olaf is mentally troubled because Olaf is gay. Can you imagine? I'm a very accepting person socially and politically, but Anders is too much. If he is doing illegal stuff, I hope you stop it, and I will help you. But if Anders is up to something, it's probably just fantastical conspiracy theories. Nevertheless, I feel like a crime-fighting superhero, potentially facing my second baddie in two days." She stopped and took a deep breath and bit her lips. "I'm so happy that you were following Anders. It was lucky for me. And now I can help you."

He tried to make sense of her torrent of words and decided to answer simply. "Yes, you're helping by letting me look at his computer," he said.

She wiggled her eyebrows. "You find anything incriminating? Did you figure out his password?"

"No. I'm waiting for a program to decrypt and copy his

hard drive." Again, he was honest. It was too hard to lie to her, like he would be lying to a friend or a fellow soldier. Thinking about her as a friend made him uncomfortable. A friend with a lithe body and soft skin smelling of petals. No, those were not friend thoughts.

She rubbed her hands together. "Oooh, spy stuff. But don't bother, I know his password. See, helping already."

"How do you know his password?"

"He told me." She rose up on her toes and rocked back on her heels.

"You lie." Odd, he'd known immediately that she lied.

She deflated. "How could you tell?"

"You rocked back and forth on the balls of your feet. Usually you stand firm and straight at me while talking, except for your hands."

"You watch me carefully with those pretty eyes of yours," she said. "I can tell when you lie, too. See, we are meant to be friends."

Woman often complimented his eyes but no one had ever called him pretty. He—Maelcom, the Smashing Fist of Death in Daimon Armies—had pretty eyes? It was disconcerting. "I got my eyes from my mother. My family background is what you know as Mongolian and Danish people, but generations long past."

The "mostly Daimon" part he couldn't tell her about. His ancestors were the last to flee the Earth Realm during the great genocides of the Daimons. His human form reflected the ancient mix of humans who had children with

Daimons since the beginning of recorded history.

"That's kind of cool that you tracked that information down. I'm very boring. Did you do one of those genetic tests? I did one that you mail in," she said. "I'm eighty percent Scandinavian, eighteen percent Celtic and two percent North African. I don't think they are super accurate tests. It could be that I'm related to a slave brought back from a raid. You know the Vikings took many Celtic slaves in attacks on Scotland and Ireland. They were violent people back then. But they might have got a slave from North Africa. Who knows?" She spread her hands at the mystery of her past.

Figured she had Celtic blood, she looked like a wood sprite, like a Små folk. "So, you said you know Anders's password?"

"*Asgard1*. Capital A. Yes, I watched him type it once while we were watching TV together in the living room. He had his laptop on his knees and he thought I had fallen asleep on the couch. Such a cliché, right?"

Maelcom typed in *Asgaard1*. It worked. He copied the files to a remote server and pushed the chair back to wait. "I wonder why he didn't take his computer if he left."

"Wait. You think he is *gone* gone?" She peeked in the empty drawers of the chest. "Wow, you are right. He cleared out. He didn't take the computer because the battery is dead. It needs to be plugged in all the time or it won't turn on. It's very old. He has a tablet with a portable keyboard that he uses now for everything."

Nessa sat down cross-legged on the bed and looked around the room. She still wore the T-shirt dress and the sky blue scarf he bought her, but she had put on bright red leggings. She looked soft and cozy.

"It's so grim and plain in here," she said, wrinkling her nose at the room. "My next roommate will be someone way more positive. I need a yoga teacher in here, someone peaceful and centered, and then I would get free yoga instruction. If Anders ends up being a criminal, you will note in your report or whatever that his roommate cooperated with the authorities. You know that Anders belongs to a right-wing church group? They hate everyone. Hey, you could recommend me for a commendation or a medal. I'd like a medal," she said with her eyes sparkling.

He was getting used to her voluminous bursts of thoughts. It was like a wave of noise but it didn't give him a headache. The instrument of her voice was husky and melodic with a touch of laughter in it. "I don't think they give medals for that." Maelcom stared at his hands. He was nervous looking at her all the time but his eyes kept going back to her face anyway. Usually he didn't care to stare into the eyes of people unless they were friends or fellow soldiers.

"I'm joking, Maelcom. When I was in school, I used to get lots of medals. Different color ribbons, shiny, elaborate medals. My dad kept them in a special chest. He called it Nessa's treasure box that he made himself with little paintings of birds carrying medals, it's wonderful, I still have it at his house." She waved her hands in the air as if imaginary medals were there.

He had many medals that he had left behind in the Daimon Realm. They were like she described, shiny and impressive. She could have his medals. They meant nothing to him. The thought of his medals for service in the war made him feel cold and frozen. A darkness folded around him and there was a hum in his chest like a single note.

And then he awoke. A soft touch and a smell of flowers.

"Maelcom, hello. You spaced out. You must be tired," she said softly. She patted his forearm, a delicate hand full of sparkly energy. Her energy had fizz to it.

The moment she touched him, he snapped back. Her energy grounded him to the here and now. Even with his Daimon soldiers who had strong energy, it took him a while to break out of his quiet reveries. He was still damaged from the wars.

"Just thinking. I focus on problems very single-mindedly," he muttered and patted her hand in a thank-you while giving some energy back, as was polite among Daimons.

She made a little noise and let go of his arm. "Static electricity. It's you. It always happens with you." She laughed.

It was true, he seemed a little out of control with her energy. "You know where Anders went?" he asked, wanting to change the topic.

"Yes. Are you going to pose for me or do you have to rush off on a super-secret mission?"

"I need to find Anders first. It's very important. But I swear I'll let you draw me. Where did he go?"

"Naked? I can draw you naked?" she said eagerly with her pale blonde eyebrows high on her forehead.

Maelcom thought about it. "No," he said firmly. He didn't want to be stared at by this Celtic fairy girl. Just thinking about it made his cock twitch. *Nope. Pants stay on.*

She pouted. "How about no shirt? It's interesting to draw muscles, and you look like you have a lot of muscles. I want to do a huge, enormous drawing." She spread her arms wide to indicate a proposed size of paper, or so he imagined.

Maelcom scratched his head. "How long will it take?" He imagined himself standing with no shirt and only his pants on while she danced around as she drew him. He shifted uncomfortably.

"I'll do some studies, take some photos. It would take around four hours. Is that cool?"

He nodded. In a car, he could engage in a mild flirtation with her despite the unease in his chest and the worry in his belly. Something about her. The talk of photographs sent his mind to cameras then pornography then naked women and then—naked Nessa. *Shit.* He spun the gold ring on his finger nervously.

She kept chattering on. "So, we can stop on the way to the music festival and see if Anders is at his friend's farm. If not, we can push on and see if he is at the concert. I could use a ride. The train is *so* slow and if we drive we can stop at all the beautiful places. I know a place to swim on the way.

It's really a beautiful drive."

What was she talking about now? Swimming? Music festival? He shook away his dirty thoughts. "Anders is at a music festival?"

"He will be. We both have tickets to the EDM festival. Don't you dance? Anders likes EDM but whatever, that's how we met. I don't get the religious person interest in EDM but hey I can't judge. I like strange things and people probably wonder about me. I love medieval religious paintings, you know those? The altarpieces. All those dimpled baby Jesuses."

He didn't know how to respond because he didn't understand what she was talking about so he just stuck with the one fact he understood from her conversation. "There is a concert featuring EDM, which is…?"

"Electronic dance music. Are you messing with me?"

He shook his head. "No. So you and Anders have tickets to the concert?"

"Festival. It's a two-day music festival in the country. They hold it every year north of Gothenburg. It's mad fun."

He stopped and replayed the conversation in his head. "Where is Anders?" he said patiently.

It had been a tough twenty-four hours for her. Perhaps that was why she sounded scattered, although perhaps that was simply how she was always. She reminded him of when Bobby smoked weed and babbled on in detail about waves.

"I didn't tell you about his friend's farm? Anders was planning on going to see some friend, a soldier, before the concert. He told me the other night. I thought he was going to move out after. Anyway, they are in on some conspiracy alien thing but I don't know any details. I try not to listen too closely. He is like—what did Olaf call him? A black hole of boring. Is that cruel sounding? Maybe I'm being mean. I don't mean to be, but really. Am I right?"

"Huh," Maelcom grunted. He had arranged with a friend to give Anders a low-level job in a private think tank. The company was run by someone he knew from the Danish Special Forces. Anders would be watched and given zero security clearance. There would be no talking to other government offices because it was a private firm. But Maelcom needed to find him as the more Anders ran around talking, the bigger the risk. "Anders is going to the farm and then this music festival? And how can I get a ticket?"

She pursed her lips in thought. "I know a guy who scalps tickets. You pay double the price but he delivers."

"It's fine, I can get tickets. What's the name of the festival?"

"Electric Power Flowerdance. Flowerdance is one word. Power it up." She gave a little shimmy with her shoulders and clenched her fist.

He blinked. "What?"

"That's their tag line—'Power it up.'"

She was funny but he didn't crack a smile. He texted the concierge that he needed a ticket to Electric Flowerdance. Maelcom's phone dinged back, ticket purchased. The ticket would be backup in case he missed finding Anders at the farm.

"We were going to go together but he decided to leave early to go to this guy's place after I told him he had to move out."

"You have the address of this place?"

"I have the name of the family and the farm. I told you, Anders never shuts up. The father was a famous hockey player, so the name stuck in my head. And he was bragging that he was going to meet the son of the greatest Swedish hockey legend. Told me all about some farmhouse they have in the country but they live in Spain half the year. I can show you where he is. I have to say, Maelcom, I'm glad to catch a ride with you."

"Did I say that? I might go alone and meet you at the festival."

She pouted and then blinked her eyes. "Please? Is it because I'm a pacifist or is it because I talk too much? I have friends who serve in the Swedish army and I support them. I don't impose my beliefs on others. I won't talk too much, I promise. We could go as a couple so it won't look as suspicious as if you, a big, huge guy in expensive black clothes, were all alone. You could probably claim to be a music producer or an industry guy. You could be undercover with me on your arm, just another hapless boyfriend dragged by his girlfriend to an EDM festival. Come on, Maelcom, let me come with you."

He would take her with him but some perverse little

devil inside him liked to see her beg. He would like to see her naked, begging him to fuck her. *Shit.* Not a good line of thought. He grunted and stared at the computer.

"Please. I'll be good." She stared intently at him and Maelcom nearly groaned out loud. She needed to stop the dirty talk.

He turned away to pick up his phone, attempting to appear cool and unaffected. "Yes. Yes. You can come with me. If we find Anders at the farm then I might have to return to the city with him. Okay?"

"Really? I could take the train the rest of the way. It's no problem. Or if he is not there we can go look for him together at the festival. Hmmm." She tapped her lips, thinking. "Let's have our cakes. Come, come to the living room."

He followed her and sat down on the tiny, shabby couch which made him feel like a giant. He stared at the painting of her as a little girl jumping with hair on either side of her head. *Ponytails, that's what they are called.* It was a joyful picture. Nessa passed him a plate with a little cake with a flower on it. "Thank you," he said politely.

"These are the best." She dug into her little cake with her fork and made sounds of delight with each bite she took. She ate it like she was having sex with it.

In frustration, he took a big bite of his cake. It was so delicious that he made a soft *mmm* sound. His grandmother would have enjoyed this cake.

She paused eating and lifted her fork to make little stabs

with it along with the words she wanted emphasized. "Mmm. I'm going to make *sandwiches* for the car for tomorrow—obviously we'll stay overnight so pack a bag. Shoot, I don't have hotel reservations. I usually sleep in Olaf's car or we camp. Do you have a sleeping bag? I know the woods around there. I lived on a farm up there for several years." Her eyes grew distant and her face was suddenly still, all the dancing expressions, eyebrows, mouth smiling or pouting, the nose wrinkling, all gone.

He shook his head. "We will not camp. I'll get a reservation at an appropriate hotel. We'll leave early in the morning."

She blinked and smiled. "You and your fancy hotels."

He walked over to her drawing of the two people running in a forest with birds swooping around them. "I like this one very much."

She came and stood beside him. "Thank you. It's my current favorite."

They stood silently, side by side, not touching but close enough to feel each other's body heat in front of her painting. This quiet Nessa was different from the talkative one.

She whispered. "I'm glad you are coming with me." She squeezed his fingers quickly and then pulled her hand away.

Next to this delicate woman, he was like a beast, huge and black, peering down at her, aching to take the shiny jewel with his mouth. *Control*—he needed to calm down around her. She was a test of his willpower, of his discipline, to be around a temptation and not yield. "Yes. It's better I come with you. Safer," he said more for himself than for her.

"I suppose so but mostly it always nice to have good company. Now I need to call all the people worried about me including my father who doesn't know what happened to me. Then Olaf wants to come over to bring me dinner. I have to pack. I've lots to do. You need scoot along. Meet me in the morning—we leave at six sharp." She smiled at him.

The whirlwind known as Nessa snatched his dessert from his hand and Maelcom found himself at the front door with a half-eaten cake in his hand, wrapped in a napkin.

She rose up on her toes and kissed both his cheeks. "Yes. Yes. I'll see you soon."

He walked downstairs wondering how she would taste if he kissed her. He would make her say *yes, yes*. But he was on a job. *Focus. Work.*

Maelcom texted Naberius about following Anders, and walked back to his hotel with his mind whirling with idea of Nessa. But the phone rang. He tapped to pick up and held it to his ear.

"Maelcom, what the hell?" his commander asked. Naberius's voice sounded confused.

"What is the point of texting information if you just call me to ask details?" Maelcom said.

"An EDM music festival?" Naberius said incredulously.

"What? I can dance," he said seriously. He hadn't danced in years, since he was young. "The woman I rescued is coming with me as cover and guide. She knows where

Anders went either to a farm or the concert. I'm to be the reluctant boyfriend dragged to the festival."

Naberius made a choking sound. It was disconcerting as Maelcom knew Naberius was laughing at him.

"I might be able to resolve it before the concert. We are first going to the family house of the soldier who started this. Anders told his roommate he was going there. I'm driving Nessa and I will claim she wanted to stop to say hello. I will tell him about a job offer from an intelligence subcontractor who is a friend of mine. The position comes with no security access and lets him write reports in a back room for a couple of years. But if he isn't there then we meet him at the festival."

"Clever. I like this plan," Naberius said seriously.

"We have to pay the salary since he won't be producing useful work but it is a modest amount, and I have to help if they need more information or intelligence gathering without billing them. But it will work out for us in the long term as information will flow both ways."

"Good. Do you really need to accompany this woman?"

"Yes. I do."

"Okay. Stay in touch," Naberius said.

"I'll try. Later." Maelcom ended the call. Naberius simply did not understand the situation. If Nessa was going to go to this EDM concert, she needed a bodyguard. She needed him.

CHAPTER 8

Nessa

NESSA RELAXED INTO THE SOFT SEATS of the Mercedes-Benz and rubbed the buttery soft upholstery of the armrest with her fingers. It was like sitting in a leathery cloud. Her father was well-off, but he drove regular cars, not super luxurious cars that cost as much as a house. She fiddled with all the buttons that adjusted her seat. Lying flat was interesting. So was raising the seat level. Maelcom looked over but said nothing as she played with the controls.

"I could live in this car. I love it. I don't own a car right now. My friend Olaf lets me borrow his car because he works all day but it's very old and the seats are stiff." She was chattering again so she pulled on her lip to remind herself not to talk so much.

Maelcom was more silent than the average man, just as she was more talkative than the average female. A very private man.

He made her feel flushed and breathless. Ridiculous—she was not one of those giggly, silly girls. Well, she might be giggly but she wasn't silly. She tried to rationalize that it was because he'd rescued her and she'd developed some messed up adoration for him. But it didn't feel like that. She was grateful to him, but mostly she was fascinated by him, by the contradictions of a soldier with a hard past and the man who let bakers hug him.

"Are you tired? You can sleep. There may still be trace elements of the drug in your system," he said with his usual quiet rumble.

She should be honest. "I don't feel one hundred percent, and I guess I'm nervous. You know these festivals can get kind of crazy. I guess what I'm saying is that I feel so much better going with you to the festival. It's totally selfish of me, but anyway, I'm sorry and not sorry. It will appear more casual if we are together but I just wanted to be honest. You've been very sweet to me. Blah—sorry, I babble a lot."

His hands tightened on the wheel, his knuckles whitening, and she noticed he wore a thick gold ring with an insignia. *Maybe from the army?* He looked like he wanted to say something.

"Nessa," he said, "it's my pleasure to accompany you. Whatever happens, you will still get to enjoy your festival. As you said, if we go together, meeting Anders will appear natural since we already know each other. It's a smart idea because I don't want him worried. Clever Nessa."

She blushed. Not a lot of men called her smart except her father and Olaf. Cute, funny or talkative—all of those adjectives. Never smart or clever. "Thanks. I think creatively. Maybe you intelligence guys can't think outside the box. That's why I'm here. Ta-dah. Saving the day."

His mouth quirked in a funny way—it wasn't quite a smile. She'd seen it a couple of times when she talked a lot. More like his face slightly relaxed, but it made her happy.

"Can I ask you some questions, Maelcom? Not about intelligence stuff but about you."

"Yes."

"Where do you live normally? In Denmark?" she asked.

"No, near San Francisco in the US."

"Why there? You tired of our winters?"

"Actually, yes. I work for a company that does extreme wilderness survival training in Europe and the US. Our first location was Greenland but no one wanted to live there full-time, so our CEO opened a headquarters in California as we conduct many training programs on the West Coast. I run a separate investigative division which is focused on intelligence efforts, which is why I'm here."

"You trained soldiers?"

"I still do on occasion."

"I don't get what you do." It sounded like he was a businessman-soldier-intelligence spy. Which a crazy combination, but she wouldn't tell him she thought that.

"Investigations and Consulting for intelligence efforts. Someone recently told me I was a Special Projects Manager."

"I'm a special project for you?" She asked jokingly, but it felt serious at the same time.

He was silent for a second while he drove. "Yes, I think so." He glanced quickly at her. "Is that okay?"

She grinned because it was the closest thing to flirting that he had said to her. "Yes. If that includes your bodyguard service. Unless you're pissed about me using you?"

"No, you need a bodyguard. You are physically at a disadvantage, although you're a good fighter. A natural. But I'm still concerned for your safety."

Probably he thought that because of his training. Rescuing people, teaching people how to survive and stuff. She made karate hands. "Yes. Yes. I need to learn more self-defense."

"Okay. I'll teach you. When you were attacked, you showed an intuitive ability to fight. You were drugged but managed to kick the man who attacked you. You immobilized him."

She narrowed her eyes at him quickly to make sure he wasn't teasing her. He was sincere. "It was like an instinctive reaction, which is good, right? I think I just got lucky. I need some better fighting moves. I took a self-defense class last year but I quit because I ended up covered in bruises."

"I can teach you some tricks which will take advantage of your agility. But Nessa, it is always better to run if you can. You're light and fast. You'll be able to outrun most men," he said with confidence.

"I *am* a fast runner. How did you know?"

"You have running shoes at your apartment by the door because you run regularly and the soles are worn in the front which means you run fast."

"Hah. That's clever you noticed. I guess that's your training," she said.

"For your size, you have to be strategic. There are simple ways to protect yourself and incapacitate an attacker."

"Kick him in the balls? I got that one down." She smirked and punched the air.

"You risk them catching your foot and pulling you off-balance. You actually knee him in the crotch at the perfect angle. Starting low and moving up."

"I know all the basic self-defense moves. Kick him, knee to crotch and fingers in the eye or nose."

His mouth turned into a frown. "I can show you how difficult it is to try that on someone of my size and skill level. You need to practice in situations that aren't optimal."

She saw them practicing in her mind. His arms wrapped around her in some fighting move, his face close to hers, and it made her feel warm. "Umm, yes. Yes, let's do that." She darted a nervous look at him, hoping she looked cool about the suggestion and not excited.

He tapped his fingers on the wheel. "I know a woman who carries a Taser. They're very effective and rarely kill."

"Really? Rarely kill? I am not sure about using something that could kill. It's against my personal beliefs."

"Would you have used it against Thorsen?"

"Yes! Okay. I get it," she said. The idea of tasing that creep made her happy.

"I know. Tasers are very unpleasant," he agreed. "I hate them, too."

Despite appreciating his commiseration, she decided not to ask any more questions even though she was curious as to how he knew Tasers were unpleasant. Probably during military training, she imagined, he had been tasered. She shivered at the idea of training where you were hurt on purpose.

They were driving through farming country a couple of hours northwest of Stockholm. This was the area she grew up in. There weren't lots of good memories, except leaving. She shivered involuntarily.

"You okay?" Maelcom asked.

She stared out the window with a twist to her mouth. "I lived around here on a farm when I was a child. A fundamental religious commune. My mother divorced my father and took me to live there without telling him. He searched for me for years before finding me and rescuing me," she confessed.

It was a sad, pathetic story. She hated telling people because they all got freaked and looked at her funny. How did you explain abuse? *Yup, starved and beaten but I'm fine now, really all good.* She was the lucky one—her father came for her and helped her recover. The other children at the farm had no one.

When people heard about her life at the religious commune, they generally changed the subject, sensing her discomfort. But Maelcom simply listened carefully.

"Were they cruel?" he asked in his low rumble without any inflection of weird curiosity or pity.

Oddly, she was comfortable explaining it to him. "Yes, they were cruel. They thought they could beat Jesus into our hearts. But mostly they just didn't feed us. Starvation was a method of control. Adults ate first and children ate whatever was left over, and there wasn't ever that much. The farm grew everything we ate and they were terrible farmers. I was malnourished—severely. It affected me permanently. I know you think I'm skinny now. Hah! I'm fat in comparison to how I looked when I left that place."

"How old were you when your father rescued you?"

"I was thirteen," she said. "It took me a long time to realize that I'd become accustomed to violence. I had to figure out how to live peacefully."

Maelcom was silent for a while. "I understand."

She stared at his profile. There was so much in the simple, plain way he answered. She asked him the same question he had asked her. "Were they cruel? In the army?"

"No, it was me who was cruel." His face was unreadable but his voice had a tight edge like he was talking with a clenched jaw.

It was odd, but she understood. Living in that kind of mad world made you do things you later realized were terrible. "Sometimes I saw things at the farm I couldn't do anything about. I felt cruel at times."

Mostly it was food she hid for the children—she'd worked serving food. The men always ate first and then the women and then the children. So the safest group to steal from was the women, even from her mother. But she always had to pick which child to feed. The eyes of the children not selected for her stolen food had haunted her for years until she'd met one of the children who'd told her that her visits with the stolen food gave them hope even if they didn't get any.

They both exhaled at the same time. Had Maelcom must have experienced some trauma from his time as a soldier?

"Do you want to eat the sandwiches you brought?" he asked.

She knew he was changing the subject and that was fine with her. "I know you want to get to Anders, but we are about to pass a beautiful lake up. Can we stop quickly? It's right off the road, and we have to stop somewhere to eat lunch."

"We can eat while we drive. I need to go to the farm," he said stubbornly.

"Please, we can eat fast. I'll just quickly swim for five minutes and then we can be on our way." She added the swimming at the last minute. It was a lake after all.

He looked unhappy but agreed with a brusque nod.

She told him to turn off the main road, and after driving

down a dirt road, they ended up in a little clearing in front of a large lake. It was perfect for swimming, cold but refreshing. She grabbed the bag and a blanket from the back seat.

"Come on, Maelcom. We have to swim first and then we eat. No eating and swimming, which I actually think they have disproved that as being a bad thing but I avoid it anyway. Right, why risk it?"

He scratched his head and didn't respond.

She pulled his arm. "Follow me." She headed down the small path that led to the water's edge. The lake was a deep blue circle with the forest trees up against it. It was like swimming in a bowl edged with green.

"I'm swimming first." She placed the lunch bag down and pulled off her dress. She heard Maelcom suck in his breath. "I'm going to swim in my underwear." She quickly pulled off her bra and remembered she had bright red underwear with the words *Cherry Pie* on her bottom. Whatever, it was on sale. "I'm not one of these people who are shy or ashamed of my body. It's not much to look at but see, I have muscles. Are you okay? Us Swedes, right? We are always getting naked. You Danes are much more proper." She was just teasing him a bit, to see what expressions moved across his face.

Waiting for him, she stood there hugging herself to stay warm because of the slight breeze. He grunted and started undressing. He was not a man who showed a lot of emotion, but he was cool. Maybe it was the wars he'd fought that had stolen his smile.

She intended to wait for him, but half naked, his body was already so beautiful that she started blushing. She walked into the lake so she wouldn't stand there gaping like an idiot. The water was cool so she splashed her arms and dove in. When she popped up, she saw Maelcom diving in, all glinting copper skin, big, blocky muscles and strong arms as he swam out to her.

She swam out some more. The water was cool so it was best to keep moving. Treading water, she laughed. "It's wonderful, isn't it?"

With his hair slicked back, his face was all hard edges. "It's very cold," he said tightly.

"Well, there aren't any hot springs in Sweden, which is why we love saunas."

"My toes are numb." His voice was mournful. This enormous ex-soldier who taught wilderness survival didn't like his feet cold. It was ridiculous. But she didn't laugh because she was staring at his powerful shoulders with sharp, defined muscles. She wanted to draw his body or touch him or something. He caught her eye and she looked away.

"Poor, cold Maelcom," she teased. "Come, let's swim to the other side and back."

She set out at a fast pace and Maelcom matched her. She trained to swim this fast so it was impressive that he kept pace. Of course, he had those powerful arms. They were almost at the other side and she turned around, treading water so she could talk.

"You're an excellent swimmer."

"But you, you swim so fast. Did you compete?"

"I was on my school swim team when I was fifteen, but I never grew tall and strong enough to compete at the national level. I did mostly to build strength, but by sixteen, all the other girls were so fast, and I came in last, so I quit. I was too skinny and not enough muscle mass. You swim very well."

"I have always enjoyed the water. Recently, I learned how to surf with a friend in California. You would like this friend. He is a musician, an artist."

"You surf? I'd like to try that. It looks like flying down waves."

He nodded looking cold while swimming slowly around her.

"Let's head back." They swam back at a more relaxed pace.

At the shore, she ran out of the water, grabbed the blanket and wrapped it around herself. The pleasant breeze she had noticed before now seemed like an arctic wind when she was wet. "Brrr, so cold."

He stayed in the water.

"It's chilly in the breeze." While he watched, she turned away and slowly she started to dress. Exaggerating every move, she bent over to retrieve her bra and stood up. She could feel his eyes on her. Carefully, she pulled her bra on. She slipped the dress on then pulled off her wet underwear and wrung it out. She heard him exhale. *Hah.*

"I'll get lunch out. If you are shy, I won't look." She held the blanket out for him and peeked up at him from under her lashes. She wanted another long look.

"I'm not shy." He rose up out of the water and she stopped breathing. All hard muscles and strength—he was a mountain of a man. It would be fascinating to draw him, so many interesting lines. She would need such a large sheet of paper and a ladder.

She blushed again, imagining naked Maelcom, and started looking in the picnic bag as if there was something very fascinating at the bottom. She was accustomed to nakedness with ordinary bodies. But he was like an amazing sexy good-looking artwork; it was hard not to stare at him. He probably had crowds of adoring, beautiful women around him. Thin, flat-chested Swedish artists were probably not his thing.

He watched her with those strange eyes while he dried himself and put his clothes back on.

"That was refreshing? Yes?" She handed him a sandwich.

"Yes. Thank you." He sat in the grass next to her and took a bite of the sandwich.

"I made two for you. Cheese Sandwiches." She nibbled on her sandwich as she cast a side glance at him.

"*Ja?* Thank you." He caught her eye and almost smiled.

It felt like sunshine peeking out from the clouds. She realized she was staring again and looked down at her cheese sandwich. She wondered if she liked him because he was sexy or if he made her feel safe. Maybe both. The truth of it was she'd been attracted to him the night he'd walked into the bar.

He finished the first sandwich and opened the package for the second.

"So why did you retire from the military?"

He chewed before answering. "Tired, old. Old men do not make eager warriors."

"You are not old. What are you, thirty-five?"

"My ID says thirty-three."

"Whatever. You're not really old but I guess most of the guys are in their twenties. So then you worked for this military survival training?"

"My commander was asked to run a training program and I went with him. I had served him for years and we are close. It's more peaceful than the military." He scratched his chin. That was a lot of words for him.

"And now you do intelligence work. It's really amazing what you have done in your life."

Wrapping her arms around her legs, she lifted her face to the sun. A rustle and thump. His warm body right next to her, not quite touching her. Leaning over to him, she placed her hand on his shoulder. "I'm glad you're here. And I think…" Her brain just stalled. Scared that he would touch her, scared to tell him to touch her, scared that he wouldn't touch her and scared that his touch would change her.

He lowered his head for a moment then lifted it to look

her square in the eyes. "Nessa," he said and with his index finger traced her jawbone like he was drawing her portrait. "Can I kiss you?" he whispered, hot breath pushing the words against her ear.

Her heart was beating crazy fast. "Please, yes," she whispered while nodding.

Maelcom scooted back, leaned forward and pulled her between his legs. Relaxing back in his arms, she turned her face and he kissed her sweetly like he was tasting her. He smelled clean but with a hint of smoky fireplace. His lips were warm against her still-cold lips. As she tilted her head, her mouth opened and he kissed her with hungry ferocity. She held on to his shirt and pulled herself closer while the blanket slipped off her shoulders.

Can you feel a person through a pair of lips, through a tongue? He sent a stab of heat through her. She grasped his shoulders to pull him closer, and he responded by gently holding her head while kissing her, tasting her like he was telling her something. A secret told with his lips. Her breasts ached, and she was wet between her legs. All itchy hot.

He growled while their tongues tangled. He tasted warm. And then he was gone.

"I should not." His expression went stern and distant.

Her lips were puffy and tingly from the kiss, and she grinned at him. This mountain of a man sat next to her looking guilty for stealing a kiss. "I said yes. I liked it." She licked her lips. "Very much so. I'd like to kiss some more." Hopefully he did too, so she pushed her hair back to be ready.

Standing, he frowned and brushed his hands. "We should go. I need to focus on my responsibilities."

"No more kisses?" She jumped up.

"I—I don't think it's a wise idea. My time here is limited. N-Nessa, I don't kiss and flirt with women, I just sleep with them," he said plainly. "That sounded wrong. I am not good at this."

His stuttered confession was so honest that she burst out laughing. He wanted to discourage her or maybe himself. She covered her mouth to stop the smile. "You're very honest but I think you are missing out. Kissing is the best. You should kiss more, it's fun. I've a lot of theories on kissing which I won't bore you with. But that kiss was really great."

He looked at his watch. She waited with her hands on her hips. He finally sighed. "It was nice."

"Nice? Ouch." It had rocked her world. She wanted to kiss him more. It sure seemed as if he really liked kissing her as his hard cock had pressed against her while they embraced. They should try to kiss with clothes on to make sure it wasn't just this particular moment that made the kiss amazing and mind-boggling. An official kiss test should be done in a neutral environment. Swimming half-naked probably skewed results with horniness. Perhaps.

He pulled on his jacket. "It was better than nice," he said just loud enough for her to hear.

She gave him a big grin and winked at him. "Let's go," she said. "We have to find Anders."

CHAPTER 9

Maelcom

HE DROVE STARING at the road with focused intent, pretending that he wasn't in a state of shock. Nessa—half-naked on the beach, her warmth, her soft lips and breathy exhales—had made his cock hard. *Shit.* He liked her. She was funny and sweet. But that kiss. Like eating little cakes. He wanted more.

"The seats in this car are so cool. Oh my god, I just found the button that heats the seat. I love this. My bottom loves this," she said, wiggling in a distracting manner. She leaned forward and proceeded to play with the buttons on the stereo. Switching through the channels, she asked, "What music do you like?"

He shrugged noncommittally to all her inquiries. If it

made her happy to push all the buttons, he didn't mind because it gave him time to calm down. She commented on every station, why she liked that music or what she didn't like about it. It seemed she barely had time to breathe, she talked so much. He memorized the names of the musicians she loved.

Eventually she settled on some throbbing electronic music. Her head bobbed along to the music as she danced in her seat. It reminded him of some ancient Pale Daimon songs that he had heard once, strange percussion and some simple lyrics repeated and repeated. They had a Pale Daimon who worked for Naberius now and she loved music.

"These guys are going to be performing at the festival. I love them so much. It's music that just sort of blows my mind. It's sort of moody and spiritual. You like it?" she said.

"Not really. I prefer acoustic."

She laughed but not at him. Somehow her laughter was light and happy.

"Maelcom, you're the most honest, straightforward person I have ever met."

"Me? Most say I'm too quiet."

"No, you are not. You only speak when you mean it. Kind of the opposite of me."

"I like your talk."

"It's so relaxing being around you."

"It's because there is no threat or danger. I mean, you are not threatening so I can relax."

"That's the first weird statement you've made. If we were on a date, I would call that a red flag," she said frankly and changed the radio station again.

Why did she think it weird? His friend Bobby once told him to try to put himself in the mind of the other person. It was a basic military strategic exercise he understood. He tried to imagine what Nessa would think. She would think that he said she was weak, that he intended to use his strength against her. Of course she would. Anyway, she had just been assaulted. He was stupid. "I apologize. My statement implies a threat since you are weak and I am strong."

She wrinkled her nose. "A little bit. Glad you figured that out. But I'm really good at reading people, so I knew you would. The fact that you would consider the level of threat as a normal part of how you interact with people is not healthy for *you*... I don't know, it implies that you're normally in a lot of dangerous situations. It's not a positive way to live your life. Somehow you seem to have put that aside, mostly, and you're very centered. Well mostly, besides the threat obsession."

Threat obsession? "I don't have an obsession."

She snorted.

"Situational awareness and threat assessment are habits ingrained in one in the military. I'm attempting to not act like a soldier but I'm not always successful. It is an attempt to increase the level of chill in my life."

"I respect that," she said honestly. "Did a friend say

that?"

"Yes, my friend Bobby has many theories about being chill and the positivity of that. He is not completely incorrect."

They drove on in silence. She so calmly accepted his weirdness. Who told attractive women that he didn't consider them threatening? Idiots like him. She made him feel out of control. His level of chill was not high—Bobby would laugh at him.

Nessa didn't ask a follow-up but she darted several quick side glances which he studiously ignored. She stared out the window. "So, we're just going to stop by, right? Quickly. Because it's another two hours to the concert and I don't want to miss the opening band. What are you going to do? Arrest him, or do you take him into custody?"

"Sort of a custody but he hasn't committed a crime. I've arranged for him to talk to a friend. He is being offered a job in a private firm where we can be assured he won't be talking about top secret information or be able to write up unauthorized reports and send them to allied countries."

"That's what he did? I thought you were arresting him? Now you are going to help him get a job? I wasn't expecting that."

"It would be embarrassing to drag this through the courts. He really only disobeyed Swedish Intelligence regulations. I don't think a criminal case is warranted in Anders's case. But we need to ensure he doesn't give away more secure information while he is obsessed with his conspiracies. So we give him a job where we can keep an eye on him."

"So it's a way of controlling him?"

"Yes. We need him to stop running around with his crazy ideas and using sensitive information to try to prove his theories. We don't think people will start believing the government is making monsters in secret laboratories in Greenland but we don't want locations of secure facilities to become common knowledge."

"Oh my god, he tried to tell me about that but I just cut him off. *Ridiculous.* You should be grateful that he isn't a social media genius. That kind of story on Twitter would go viral."

He frowned, because if Anders had been on social media that would have been a disaster. Obscure Reddit forums were not a problem. Anders operated in fringe groups that were ridiculed on social media and lumped in with the space-aliens-kidnapped-me people. He needed a social media intelligence expert to work on this. Gusion would be the logical choice. In fact, he had suggested seeding some fake stories about Daimons so if real ones surfaced, they would blend in with the crazy stuff.

Nessa rummaged in her bag and brought out a tin of hard candy which she offered to him. He took one red candy and popped it in his mouth. Raspberry. He liked that flavor.

Sucking on the candy, Maelcom pondered. If Anders was at the house, he needed him to go to Stockholm. If

Anders refused, then he would have to forcibly escort him back. But he had promised to guard Nessa at the concert. His friend would have to send a pickup van for Anders with a couple of guards—they would manufacture some crisis for Anders to work on. He didn't care what it was so long as Anders was off the street, working on meaningless data no one ever saw.

Nessa sucked on candy and made a loud smack with her mouth. "I love these."

Her tongue darted out to lick her lips, wet, dirty thoughts raced through his head. The car seemed hot and stuffy. A bead of sweat rolled down the side of his face as he punched the air conditioning on. "Are there any lakes near the concert?" A completely stupid question. Why did he ask that?

"Oh, I know all the swimming places up around here. I wish I had packed towels or a bathing suit. Some of the places are more public than the one we went to." She stretched her arms.

"We'll stop and buy you a bathing suit," he said abruptly. The idea of her swimming in the nude annoyed him. He didn't want to have to beat people up who ogled her because anything that created an unusual amount of scrutiny was undesirable.

"Okay. I like swimming with you because you make me go faster. But it's also safer to swim with someone else."

"You swim alone normally in those mountain lakes? Naked?" he growled.

She snorted. "Actually no, not naked, because a swim-suit helps provide some heat. If I plan on swimming alone, I wear a swimsuit, red cap and tow a little inflatable buoy so I can be seen."

"That is wise."

She leaned over and blew into his ear softly. "But if I swam alone with you, I would be naked."

A wave of heat exploded in his chest and he growled softly. Her laugh came out husky and low, full of promise. She sat back in her seat with a triumphant grin, and he had the sinking realization that he was not going to be successful in resisting her flirtations.

CHAPTER 10

Nessa

SWIMMING WITH HIM HAD BEEN AMAZING. Maelcom's comfort in the water showed in his movements, relaxed and powerful. *Shit.* Not to mention his mind-blowing, beautiful body. Built like a Norse god.

In art school, she would draw the broken Roman statues. Beautiful torsos with one leg or just arms, but she would always finish what was missing or broken on the statue. The arm, the head, the leg and even the occasional penis that had been chopped by some zealot in the Middle Ages. Once, half a face was missing and she filled it in. He reminded her of those statues, but the missing parts weren't visible. The missing parts were things about him which he kept hidden.

And oh, that kiss.

The sign for the town of Bergson appeared. "You have to turn at the next intersection. That road will take us to the farm."

He nodded as if that seemed entirely logical. "I know. I memorized the map," he said with a shrug. "I have a photographic memory."

"I've a terrible memory for numbers and exact memorization of words but I'm really good at remembering names and faces." She twisted her fingers together. "It's useful when you are a salesperson in a gallery. People like it when you know their name, and if they like you, they want to buy something from you. Or sometimes they do."

"You're a talented artist. You should be making more art, not just selling other people's work. That painting of the woman with wings. It's amazing."

"Maybe that's the drawing you want?" she said. Her heart pounded eight million miles an hour.

"I would, but it must be worth a lot more than the hotel room. You should not undervalue your art."

"I don't. I just want you to have the best."

He turned his head for millisecond, catching her eye with a searing glance, and her mind blanked. "I would like that drawing," he said as he turned away to drive.

All she kept thinking about was how she was going to get him to kiss her again. She could ask him—he was nice and did things for her all the time. *Can you kiss me more?* It was a reasonable question. Maybe.

A sign appeared, listing towns and the various distances to them. The town where the religious community had been located was listed on the sign. Mindlessly, she stared at the fat and healthy cows in the fields and remembered how hungry she used to be.

Maelcom turned the car down a road. "You seem unsettled," he said. "Something is making you...sad."

She pointed to the cows. "When I was young, I used to sneak to the neighboring farms to steal milk. Drank it right from the udder. Didn't stop until my stomach was so full it hurt," she said.

Maelcom grunted. "Hunger makes one's stomach shrink. When you put rich food like fresh cow's milk in an empty belly, it hurts. I teach occasionally at a wilderness survival school. Every soldier I train must understand the effects of hunger."

She grimaced. "Like trying to digest a brick."

"You were a kid. The pain was temporary and the calories were important," he observed.

She nodded. "Yeah." His empathy for her experiences overwhelmed her, and his acceptance of the terrible facts of her past.

He turned the car down a driveway and up to a box house with a steep roof. There was a barn a little farther down the driveway with empty paddocks and fields. "I'll go and see if someone is home."

"Hey, that car belongs to Anders." She pointed to an old Volvo parked by the garage.

"Let me park and check the area out," he said.

"Don't be ridiculous." She jumped out of the car before Maelcom could say a word. "Anders!" she yelled out. If they could find him fast, they could make the first round of performers playing today.

Maelcom parked and slipped out of the car, closing the door softly behind him. "We should be more quiet about our arrival."

"What? They heard our car pull up. What did you want to do, sneak up and surprise them, all secret-agent-stealthy? Come on, you said you wanted to talk to him," she said. Strange—why was he acting as if there might be danger?

She marched up to the front door and knocked hard. Nothing. She pulled out her phone and called Anders. Nothing.

"He isn't picking up," she called out to Maelcom. The call went to voicemail.

Maelcom put his hand on her shoulder in a comforting way. It tingled slightly and he pulled her away from the door. He put his finger to his lips for her to be quiet. "Shh," he said while he breathed in deeply like he was trying to smell something. Like he actually could scent the air.

As she lifted her face to thank him, he suddenly picked her up and threw her over his shoulder. It surprised her so much that she laughed. Like she was a duffel or a bundle. She tapped him on the back while hanging upside down. "What are you doing?" she squeaked but he moved fast, almost running to the car.

Somehow he opened the car door and she found herself buckled in her seat. The back of his hand gently grazed down her cheek, his eyes blinking. "Please, there is danger. I can smell it. Lock the car doors." He sounded so deadly serious that she obeyed him. She watched him walk around the house and disappear.

He didn't lie. If he said there was danger, then there was danger. But what? She knew it wasn't a joke because he didn't joke, other than a dry observation or an eyebrow raised. She hadn't actually seen Maelcom laugh because he wore that constant mask of seriousness on his face.

Maelcom reappeared at the front of the house and held up his finger. *One minute.* His mouth became a hard, flat line while he sniffed the air. She jumped out of the car and ran up to him. "What is it?" She knew something bad had happened.

He grabbed her by the shoulders to stop her motion forward. "I found Anders out back. He's dead."

"You're joking."

"No."

"I want to see him."

"No," he said firmly. "You shouldn't."

"Don't be ridiculous, Maelcom. What happened? How'd he die? I need to see him." She pulled away from him and stomped around to the back. A weird sense of responsibility weighed on her.

Turning the corner, in the bright light of one of the last summer days, she saw Anders lying on the stone path that wound through the back gardens. He might have been sleeping. His eyes were almost closed, as if he was in a light sleep, his pale face relaxed and the normal frantic look gone. She reached down to grab his wrist to feel for a pulse but Maelcom held her arm back.

"No, don't touch him. I already checked."

She held her hands against the side of her face like she could hold off the horror of the dead Anders from seeping into her head. "How did he die?"

"The back of his head is injured. It appears he fell or was pushed. I'm guessing pushed. Someone else was here." He waved to a stone path that led to the back door.

Nessa stared at a fly that landed on Anders's nose. This was like a dream, where everything moved slow and details were all important. Look, his shoe was untied. Here she stood in front of a dead man. Anders, the most boring person she knew, had died in some tragic way. Shit, she'd been kind of mean to Anders. She had thrown him out of the apartment and lied about her cousin. If she hadn't lied about her cousin, he would have been on a train with her, going to the concert. Maybe if they hadn't gone swimming they would have been here earlier. Her brain just spun through all the maybes and possibilities.

It was quiet out here. The only sound was a distant low gurgling croak of birds and the trees rustling in the breeze.

She crossed her arms tightly across her body and bent her head. "Anders, I'm sorry that I found you so annoying as a roommate. I tried to be as friendly and accommodating as possible but I was unfriendly at times. Please find peace and serenity," she whispered to the dead body. Blood soaked the side of Anders's head and dripped down his neck. She covered her mouth with her hand and looked away.

"Did you say a prayer?" Maelcom spoke softly into her ear while he touched her shoulder lightly.

Was he aware how much he touched her? They were always quick touches, not groping or anything. Guiding or concerned gestures, almost like that was how he told what he was thinking or feeling. A ridiculous idea. She always overthought things.

"No. I don't pray. Just some words for whatever reason. For karma." She reached out for his arm to steady herself but he had wrapped his arm around her. She buried her nose in his chest.

In her brain, she associated prayers with pain. The worst part was that she could remember whole Bible passages and verses by heart, beautiful poetry made ugly by the hunger and deprivation of her childhood. So hungry that she used to suck on her hair because it was salty. Why were all the memories popping up now?

"Are you religious? I don't mean to offend," she muttered into his shirt.

"No. I like the stories but the gods have not proven themselves to me."

A bead of sweat ran down her neck while spots danced in front of her eyes. "I feel dizzy."

"Nessa," he said softly as if that said everything.

She pulled her lip nervously. "You think it was an accident, or you think someone killed him? That's a big difference. Is this some counterespionage? Or assassination?"

"Someone killed him. See, his shirt is torn where someone strong grabbed him." He held his hands over the ripped areas. "It is conceivable that they were struggling to subdue him during questioning him and he fell. Yes, I think that's it. They would not have killed him like this." He pulled her away and led her back to the car.

"How do you know that someone else was here?" she said mournfully while walking beside him.

"Training."

"I forget sometimes. All the soldier spy stuff. You know, I didn't even like him much and that makes me feel horrible. I kicked him out of the apartment. Maybe I'm responsible?"

He walked her to the car, leaning over her to listen carefully to her words. "We're leaving. I'll call on the road to inform the authorities."

Awkwardly, she climbed into the car, all numb and confused. "I think you should call now. I don't know. It's horrible. You shouldn't wait."

A dark car pulled up in the driveway and a young man jumped out. "Hello, can I help you?" he called out.

Maelcom turned to her and said, "Stay in the car." He walked up to the young man. "Harald, let us talk," she heard him say.

How did he know the name of the young man? She couldn't hear clearly as they turned away from her. There was a lot of fast talking and hand waving. An expression of horror came over Harald's face as Maelcom talked, explaining something calmly. Harald started to shout and point at Maelcom who shook his head, his hand held up in a gesture of *stop*. But the young man kept shouting. Maelcom called someone on his phone and passed it to Harald, who proceeded to converse with this mysterious person. Harald calmed down but appeared scared as if he was in a lot of trouble. Finally, he looked embarrassed and gave the phone back to Maelcom. The young man sank down on the stoop, resigned and pale.

Maelcom glanced at the car and held up one finger. *One moment*, he needed a minute. She nodded quickly at him and Maelcom took off running, disappearing into the forest. It was impressive how gracefully and smoothly he moved.

She locked the car doors and kept an eye on at the slumped young man. Maybe this guy killed Anders. Flipping up the hood of her hoodie and putting on her sunglasses, she scooted down low in the seat and waited. A couple of minutes later, Maelcom appeared, running from the opposite direction than he had started. Stopping, he talked to the young man. The young man spoke slowly, nodding in agreement to something, and he shook Maelcom's hand.

Maelcom got back in the car. "You okay, Nessa?" He turned the car around and drove back down to the road.

"Maelcom, that guy was all freaked out. And why we are leaving the scene of a crime?"

"It's been approved. I have called the appropriate intelligence people who will investigate the murder correctly. Not local people. Harald is just a young man from a prominent family caught up by Anders's conspiracy theories. They'll send a team to deal with this."

A shiver went through her. "I feel strange."

"It's adrenaline and shock. Drink some water and eat something sweet." He reached and held her hand briefly. It made her feel better.

She dug in her purse to find a chocolate bar. "So where are we driving?" she mumbled with her mouth full of chocolate.

"I found this on the ground next to him." He held out a paper sleeve for a concert ticket holder. It had the graphic of a flower that was the symbol of the EDM festival. "Someone took the ticket."

"Why would they? They murdered him for a ticket?"

"No. The person who took the ticket is not the murderer. I found one set of distinct footprints indicating that they looked at the body, edged forward and plucked the ticket from Anders's pocket, and then they left fast, running. Like this person was being followed. I found other tracks confirming that suspicion. I believe he ran to the road at the side of the property where he entered a car and left. Another vehicle was parked at the entrance to the property. People who wanted to approach carefully."

"So Anders was killed, his murderer left, some other guy came by and took the ticket then rushed away when the murderers came back?"

He furrowed his brow. "Perhaps. The sequence of events is not clear. I believe we have stumbled on several people in some sort of chase of their own that inadvertently involved Anders. The one who took the ticket is being hunted."

"I don't understand why he would want to go to the festival."

"He is meeting someone there. Or more likely, he wants to meet someone there. Perhaps a person Anders was to meet."

"And how are you going to find this guy among thousands of people?"

"Easy. This person will be like me—someone who does not normally go to this type of event. He won't fit in perfectly. He will stick out. And someone will be chasing him."

"In thousands of people? I don't know. Are they dangerous? Like terrorists? How were they going to find Anders?"

Maelcom wore a confused expression while she talked. "Terrorists? You thought that? No, they are not terrorists. These people are more like spies and I will find them at the Daisy concert. I have their scent."

"Flowerdance," she corrected absentmindedly. *Scented* must be a metaphor for being on the trail of someone. She grimaced. "I was thinking we wouldn't go. Poor Anders." She was determined to help find justice for her poor, deluded, dead roommate.

He nodded. "You don't have to come, I agree. I can drop you off at the train station. I must try to investigate further."

"Isn't that the police's job?"

He tilted his head to the side and pursed his lips. "Military intelligence takes precedence over civilian police."

"I don't know what you mean by that. I don't want to argue but…" She peeked at him, feeling nervous. "I'm coming with you to the festival. I can help, I want to. I think I owe Anders that. I'll help you get around because it can be crazy confusing at first. Sometimes I can barely find my friends there and we're both on the phone talking to each other. The layout is always the same every year, so I can show you the best place to watch for people. The main performance tent is at the center and the side venues spiral out from that."

She would be his guide, or he'd get lost at the festival and not know where to go. Well, maybe not but it would be faster if she helped. She knew the flow of the crowds at the concert, and she knew how to move through dense crowds. It would be useful, her knowledge.

"You can come with me because you'll just talk until I relent," he grumbled.

She grinned. "You're getting to know me well, Maelcom. You need my help, just admit it. It's going to be hard to find this guy."

"I'll find him. I have his scent," he said again with a quiet seriousness.

She pursed her lips at his grandiose statement. "Hah. I get your meaning. Yes. Yes. We are on his trail."

It must be some secret technique that he doesn't want to talk about that they use in military intelligence. That she liked him and thought about kissing him more—well, she wanted to see if they could figure something out. She'd flustered him in the car with her teasing about swimming naked with him.

She twirled her hair around her finger. Wow, she was beginning to really obsess about him. Imitating him, she inhaled deeply and decided he smelled like a thunderstorm before it rains.

CHAPTER 11

Maelcom

EVEN IF ANDERS WAS DEAD under suspicious circumstances, at least he had the instigator of the cluster fuck contained. Harald had seen Daimons sparring with their swords in their Daimon form when he was hiding from a difficult training exercise, and had told Anders all about it.

Harald had recognized Maelcom immediately and accused him of being in on the effort to hide these abominations called Daimons. Maelcom had simply lifted his eyebrow at the sputtering young man, told him to calm down and call his commanding officer. The commanding officer told Harald that he had suffered snow hallucinations. He was given an opportunity to take a new position if he would shut up, and the vague threat that his father would be publicly embarrassed took the wind out of the young man's bluster. Harald's commanding officer was a good man and promised to take care of the young man.

A team was en route to clean up and someone would take Harald to his new unit where trusted people would keep an eye on him, with the promise of a promotion on the condition of silence so that his father, the ice hockey legend of Sweden, would not be seen to have a crazy son. A reward and a threat. It had worked.

When Harald called Daimons abominations, it reminded Maelcom of the great exterminations when religiously inspired zealots burned Daimons at the stake. A shiver ran down his spine. Things had not changed that much in a thousand years.

But his mission had changed. He needed to find the Ice Daimons he scented around the house. One of them had killed Anders. The other had stolen the ticket. *Shit.* They had clearly missed at least two Ice Daimons. Probably minor players left behind but they were doing something—fighting each other, perhaps? He knew where to find one of them at least, and hopefully the second would not be far behind.

Nessa turned on the radio but kept it low. There wasn't much to say but she snuck little looks at him and pulled her lip while she thought. He appreciated her quiet so he could think.

As they approached where the festival was held, Nessa directed him to take a shortcut. The traffic built the closer they got to the festival area until they slowed to a crawl for the last few miles.

Nessa shifted in her seat. "Anders's death has left me feeling strange. Freaked out. I don't feel sad up about his death and that makes me feel terrible. And I feel guilty because I told him to move out. It's brought back some old memories. I haven't seen a dead body since the farm."

"That farm. It was a bad place." He was a soldier but she had been a child.

"It was." She closed her eyes then opened them. "But I'm okay."

"Do you want to go back to Stockholm?"

Her phone pinged. "No. I'm sure. I'm helping you, plus I'm meeting up with Olaf sometime. He's arriving later this afternoon. I think seeing my friends might be good for me."

"Your choice. If you change your mind, I will escort you back. I'm sorry if I startled you at the farmhouse. I moved quickly because I didn't want you in danger." He was worried that she was angry that he'd picked her up and carried her to the car.

She touched his arm lightly. "I know that." Her eyes darted around his face as if searching for clues, and only stopped briefly to look him in the eyes.

He wasn't sure what she understood but her touch calmed him.

When they finally arrived at the parking for the festival, a deep thump from warm-up acts reverberated out over the cars.

She rubbed her face and blinked rapidly. "I have to

change. I brought some clothes to change into—festival appropriate. Blend better with the crowd."

Maelcom cleared his throat while he tried not to think about her getting undressed.

She rolled her eyes at him. "You don't have to watch me. I'll crawl into the back seat."

Nessa was different from the dancers he usually took home. Stupid to think of that. He felt a tremor inside but assumed he was simply tired.

Instead of getting out of the car, she crawled over the seat but slipped. He pushed her up and took a little energy from her. He felt guilty, like he was stealing from her.

"Thanks." And she scooted over the seat into the back, providing him an eyeful of her bottom. Small but round.

She was teasing him, he decided as he studied her in the rearview mirror. But she ignored him while she rooted through the large carryall bag she had brought. Pulling out a lacy white dress of some sort, she laid it out on the seat and started undressing.

He pulled out his phone. "I'll call my contact to make sure Anders was taken care of properly and his family notified," he said.

Confirmation came in a text that the team had removed Anders's body, transferred it to Stockholm and his parents would be notified. The young soldier had gone willingly to his new post, believing that he had experienced snow hallucinations. And if he hadn't, his father's reputation was on the line. The human mind conformed to find an appropriate solution to his dilemma, and that was believing in snow hallucinations.

Maelcom checked the rearview mirror to see Nessa sitting in white leggings that ended at the knee and small, white lacy bra which looked more like a small shirt. Pulling a flowery dress over her head, she smiled. "There. Done! I need to do my hair now."

Always her smile emerged even after terrible things, not foolishly but genuinely. She pulsed with energy, but she had layers and a past. That he could understand, but she had taken the blows in her life and become a creator of beautiful stories and images. He was simply someone who had retreated.

She started to braid her hair, many small braids plaited and pinned up in groups. Her hair looked complex, all interwoven and shimmering blonde. The color reminded him of moonlight. Finally, she pulled on tall, clunky boots that she laced with a frown of intense concentration on her face.

A ripple of energy started deep inside him—just a tiny disruption in the center where his shift always began, but he contained it quickly. Now he understood how Naberius had struggled with inadvertent shifts during his depression and madness. It had been deeply embarrassing for Naberius. Maelcom had experienced one drunken inadvertent shift and he really didn't remember it because he was so far gone. It was disconcerting to feel on the brink of shifting to his other form without specifically making it occur. Unnerving.

His space-outs were different from an unintended shift of form. He was triggered by events or images which brought him back to many terrible memories and he would become lost in his mind. He experienced long space-outs where he couldn't react to anything around him. They'd occurred less and less over the years. He was no longer the brutal Fist of General Naberius's Daimon Army.

He suspected Naberius's brother, Ephraim, had orchestrated their exile to get Naberius away from the pressures of life as the ex-general and heir apparent to the ruling family of the Daimon Realm. That Naberius's personal guard chose to accompany him was not entirely accidental. They all had benefited from being in a new place without pressure where they could start fresh. Maelcom had worked for Ephraim, the head of Daimon Intelligence, and he had orchestrated the "exile" to the Earth Realm. To be sure, Naberius's behavior had been irrational and threatened the fragile peace between all the Daimons and created political tensions during a highly charged transition from an oligarchy to a democracy. His exile to the Earth Realm was a release and a chance for all of them to start fresh.

Nessa tapped his shoulder, her energy tickling him. "I'm done." She climbed headfirst into the front seat, her body in her tight leggings and semi-transparent flowery dress passing close. She brushed his arm or perhaps he had moved it slightly.

"Let's go," he said.

She leaned forward with her brush. "Hold on. Can I fix

your hair?" She bit her lip, waiting for his answer. "Your clothes are perfect—black is appropriate. But your hair could be fixed."

He froze. When she asked him in that husky voice of hers, it sounded like an intimate question. A voice like that should be asking him to do other things. She touched him a lot while she talked. Come to think of it so did he. It was like they were opposite magnets pulled together. She gave him a tap on his arm or a little playful punch when she made a joke. Usually, he disliked people invading his personal space and altering his energy, but for her, he made an exception.

Keeping his expression neutral, he nodded yes.

"I'm good with hair. Don't worry," she told him and pulled herself up on her knees and gave his hair a critical stare. He worried. The brush went one way and then the other, like she was trying to make his hair stick straight up.

Normally he kept it short but he had been busy or surfing at the beach all summer. His hair was now thick and wavy, long enough to reach his collar.

She fussed, using her hand to push his hair into some desired state that she deemed appropriate. Her little touches were like small kisses of energy. While she fixed his hair, she evaluated him with heavy-lidded eyes. He tried to repress a groan by turning it into a throat clearing.

She grinned. "Oh, sorry. You're done. I just didn't want you looking so proper and stuffy. It would make our investigation difficult if people worried you were with the police."

He checked himself in the mirror. He could have stood out in the wind to get the same effect—it was messy. "This will help me blend?"

"Yes, yes. You cannot look so tidy. Your hair is beautiful, you know, but no one sees it when you brush it back so flat. You should grow it long," she declared.

Like Daimon soldiers who let their hair grow long enough to wear it in one long braid. His brother Muli used to have fine straight hair, down to the middle of his back. His own hair was slightly wavy and wild—he cut it short like all military men here but had not bothered this year. Maybe he would grow it as a tribute to his brother.

"Come on," she said, tugging at his sleeve, her little touches making him obey.

She even seemed to be able to chase away the thought of his brother, which always made him lose control.

As they walked, Maelcom noticed how people turned and stared at Nessa. She was pretty, but it was something else about her that made people stare. People grinned when she smiled at them. She bounced along in her black combat boots and small flowery dress. The dress appeared very short and he was glad she wore the leggings underneath because he didn't want to have to hit people. Looking around, she pointed to the enormous sculpture that was ten feet tall and standing on a pedestal. It was a creature holding a sword.

"Those are trolls from a local fairy story. I loved those stories when I was little."

He looked again. The trolls had horns. Damn. "I think those are supposed to be giants. Jotun," he said. Jotun Daimons still lived in the local fairy tales. These artistic interpretations had horns and long teeth. Not very realistic at all. And Daimons were handsome, not monsters.

Nessa squinted at the sculpture and thumped his arm with her fist. "Oh yeah, the horns. I think the artist got carried away with the teeth, don't you think? The Jotun were brave and noble, right? Weren't the gods themselves Jotun? I haven't read those stories since I was a child."

"Yes, they were. I was just thinking that." Would she like his horns if he shifted? Crazy. It was stupid to think that. He did not shift in front of humans.

"You're a very visually perceptive person. I didn't think soldiers would have opinions about art. But I forgot that you collect art, which is very cool. Oh, smell that." She sniffed the air.

He breathed in deeply. "Sausages," he said. He breathed in again, looking for the scent of an Ice Daimon, but he failed to find any scents of the Ice Daimons, only meat cooking on a grill.

She grabbed his hand and pulled him through the crowds. "Grilled. They are so good. You will love these. They're made locally with meat from pigs who are treated like princesses until they slaughter them. Because the pigs are raised humanely, it makes the meat yummier. I sound very bloodthirsty, I know, but these are the best sausages."

At a food stand, they bought two sandwiches stuffed

with sliced sausages and then stood at a tall table eating them. Nessa looked delicate holding her gigantic sandwich, but she ate like a soldier, ripping off big chunks and chewing enthusiastically.

"See, I told you. So yummy. I love meat. I have vegan friends who lecture me all the time. But for me, it gives me energy, and I love the taste. Veggies are good, but I have to have meat." She took another big bite.

"You eat a lot but you are thin. Can you not gain weight?"

She held up a finger so she could finish chewing and then she started talking more. "Messed up metabolism." She swung her leg back and forth as she talked. "My girlfriends hate me. But you know the grass is always greener on the other side. I wish I were curvy. And my curvy friends think they're too curvy. Crazy, huh? Our society is body crazy in an unhealthy way." She tapped his arm and pointed to his sandwich. "Are you going to finish yours?"

Her touches sparkling with her bright energy caused him to twitch. "Yes, I'm still eating." He held out his hand to protect his food and raised an eyebrow to tease her. That was unusual for him. Joking was something he did with people he trusted. Like Naberius, Gusion, Bobby and a few Daimon soldiers. They were like family. Why did he think of her like that?

Her eyes twinkled as she chewed and she gestured to him that she would talk as soon as she finished swallowing. "You have to eat fast around me," she joked while wiping her lips delicately.

"We'll just buy more food." He said it in a soothing manner.

She tilted her head and gave him a funny look. "The night I was attacked—I was terrified because I couldn't move. You calmed me down. I knew I was safe. You told me you were going to take care of me and I believed you. You were steadfast. That is probably what made you a good soldier."

"And you, Nessa, you are the one who is steadfast. Your remained calm after you were attacked. Today, finding Anders. You are strong."

"It was hard, finding him," she said in a low voice, "dead."

"You were very calm for a civilian."

"You know, I've seen dead bodies before. I suppose that's something we have in common."

"I was a soldier, Nessa. It's part of the job."

She pulled her lip nervously. "At the farm, it was my job to wash the babies that died, before they were buried."

He reached and took her hand between his, stroking her fingers. "You were a child."

"And easily intimidated. They were all boy babies. The girl babies never died." She chewed her lip in a worried manner. "I never tell anyone about that. I mean, I told the police and my therapist but no one else. I knew I could tell you."

"The people who ran that place were monsters. You

were and are a good person, Nessa."

She shrugged. "Just normal, it's just next to monsters, being normal looks extra wonderful. Anyway, I guess seeing Anders made me think about it. I feel better. Thanks for letting me talk. You need to talk to me more." She casually punched his arm with her clenched, bony fist. She did that a lot.

"You remind me of my friend, Bobby. The chill guy. He taught me to surf," he confessed. That sounded stupid but that was all he could think to say. She must think he was an idiot.

She folded up the paper that the sausage had come in. "I read an article once which said you're attracted to the same energy of people. You know, the essence of them. The author was a well-known psychologist and it's not just bullshit. She had data," Nessa said with several affirmative nods.

He wondered if there were always humans who were aware of Daimon energy or just her? Energy in the Daimon Realm was traded back and forth in a social way, part of basic manners and integral to family relations. He would take a human's extra energy flowing off them through handshakes and casual contact, although sometimes by having sex. Because if he was naked with a beautiful woman, why not take a tiny bit, a taste of energy?

He rarely shifted into his Daimon form here in the Earth Realm. Once, he had inadvertently shifted when he was very drunk with Bobby. They were alone camping by the beach. Bobby had laughed and covered him with a blanket as he passed out. Good friend that he was. And Maelcom had decided to stop drinking the next day. Bobby had winked at him and said, "Smart idea, friend. Or that shit would be a world of trouble." So Bobby became the only human friend who knew about Daimons, until his sister and Naberius met. Except, of course, certain earth families who had pledged loyalty to Daimon families.

Nessa tugged his arm and pointed to the main stage. He took a little sip of her sweet energy because he couldn't resist. Her energy made him feel horny, which was distracting. Was she addictive? That should be impossible.

"So what are you going to do now? Sniff him out?" she asked jokingly.

To tease her, he made an exaggerated show of inhaling deeply. *Shit.* He caught the scent, so he pretended to look around and actually spotted the Daimon in the crowd. But he didn't linger—he kept looking all around. "All I can smell is sausage but I think I just saw someone who appears suspicious." He pointed where he had smelled the scent of the Ice Daimon.

Nessa nodded. "Too bad. It would be cool if you were like a hound dog. But being tall is also very useful in a crowd. You see everyone."

"I can scent in the wilderness." Maelcom had no idea what Nessa imagined trained Special Forces soldiers could do but she seemed to think he had "secret agent skills." If she chose to believe scenting a trail was a plausible skill for people here, it wasn't really a lie. He'd trained soldiers to survive in the wilderness, watched while they struggled through an advanced orienteering course. They couldn't smell their way home like Daimons.

CHAPTER 12

Nessa

THE IDEA OF HIM SCENTING the trail like a hound dog made her chuckle. Trust Maelcom to make her laugh right when she needed it. He, of course, was talking metaphorically about scenting to find people. He had lots of super-secret-agent tracking skills. Scenting was probably spy slang for tracking people down.

Maelcom held her shoulder lightly, barely resting his fingertips, and his other arm was held out in front of him to clear the path. She was in a protective circle of Maelcom as they walked together. No one even bumped her—he somehow angled himself slightly forward, causing the crowd to part before she even got there.

She knew he enjoyed her touches—he was hesitant and

restrained, but his breath had come out fast and shallow as she'd fixed his hair in the car, his eyes slightly closed.

Flirting was fun with him. Hell, the kiss at the lake had been an impulse. But after the kiss, everything changed in her head. All the things she thought her kiss test evaluated he passed with flying colors, but she was more confused. Her childish test was not the ultimate end-all for a possible relationship. It couldn't be. Maelcom was complicated; he had a history, maybe a broken heart or an ex-wife and she thought his life as a soldier must have left some emotional scars. Perhaps he'd been alone so long that he wasn't sure how to be with someone. She understood that.

Maybe she was crushing on him simply because he'd rescued her, and that made her feel stupid and shallow. Sexual attraction always had a component of ridiculousness that was inexplicable. But he did kiss like a god and that was a fact. His eyes and his voice were like his secret weapons. Certainly, they were her personal kryptonite. They should just sleep together so she could get him out of her system. Great idea. She would volunteer for that. Thinking about him naked made her deeply happy.

"Come," he rumbled.

They made their way through the crowd of dancing people toward the right side of the stage. A small beer garden was set up and people were having drinks while watching the show.

She pulled him toward the stage. "Come on, let's go up front and listen to this guy. I played some of his music for you in the car. You said you liked it."

He let her tug him forward. The DJ on stage was mixing up a crazy beat, and the audience was bobbing and swaying to the music. People had their hands in the air and rolling heads and hips. Most were wearing wild and extravagant concert outfits, with colors and ribbons and unusual combinations with a dash of steampunk and hippy chic thrown in. She started dancing and ended up backed against Maelcom. Dancing, she rubbed her butt against his thigh. He didn't move. She did it again until she heard him growl her name. It was fun.

The crowd kept surging closer to the stage. A laughing man fell and sprawled toward them. Maelcom picked him up easily, like he was a fallen child, and asked if he was all right. The guy thanked Maelcom and danced off.

She was getting into the song, swaying to the beat. Everyone was dancing or jostling for a better viewing spot and their motion pushed her toward the front. She became separated from Maelcom, so she spun around and found him behind in the crowd, but he was looking in the opposite direction.

He was sucking air in through his nose like he was trying to smell something. He turned and locked eyes. Boom. Boom. Boom. The bass beat throbbed. She danced back toward him. Suddenly he whipped around as if he caught another scent. That was fucking crazy, she was imagining things. She grabbed his hand so she wouldn't lose him again.

His thumb rasped over the top of her hand and he pulled her close to talk in her ear. "You meet me by the bar. I'll be back," he spoke loudly in her ear so she could hear above the loud music.

Dancing the entire time, she nodded and gyrated her hips. He frowned slightly before disappearing into the crowd. The next song was the huge hit for this DJ. Lights started flashing on and off, strobes hitting the audience. Nessa scrambled up onto a raised platform where people were dancing and spotted him right away. Those broad shoulders, dark hair, and the way he carried himself, powerful and graceful.

The lights flashed. He grabbed a tall young man and said something to him. The man's mouth moved fast, talking at Maelcom, explaining something as he put his hands up in surrender. Maelcom kept his grip on the man and looked around till he found her eyes. He jerked his head to the exit.

Yes, yes. She understood so she gave him a thumbs-up. Was that the man they were looking for?

Maelcom spun around and pulled the man out the gate at the back. Nessa scrambled down and had to push her way through the crowd, but without the benefit of her body-guard Maelcom it was slow going. She ducked and weaved. It took her a couple of minutes to get to there.

The security guard stood in front with folded arms. He gruffly informed her, "No reentry through here."

"Yes. Yes. No problem." She ran through the exit gate

and right into a dense crowd pushing her in the wrong direction. Everyone seemed to be much taller than her and it was hard to see. She moved to the edge where an emergency ambulance was parked and hoisted herself up on the side step to look out over the crowd. Up ahead, she caught a glimpse of Maelcom dragging the man toward a tent that appeared unused.

Maelcom and the stranger walked up to the security guard guarding the tent. A sign next to him said 'Closed". The guard held up his hand in a motion to stop. Maelcom put his hand in his pocket then shook the guard's hand while talking to him calmly. The man nodded, slid his hand into his pocket after the handshake and walked off casually. Maelcom jerked his head, and the other man ducked inside. They weren't fighting anymore, it was like they had agreed on something.

She beat her way through the crowd to the tent. Quickly, she looked around for more security guards before slipping inside, hearing Maelcom's voice. Maelcom and a tall, handsome man were intently staring at each other, having finished some unknown discussion.

"We need a guard on the door," the stranger snapped.

Maelcom shook his head. "She is helping me. But she is not one of the earth families and knows nothing," he spoke in a serious rumble, with a glare at the man.

What was he talking about? Earth families. Was that a back-to-nature thing? A hippie thing? Maelcom could explain it to her later. "Hello. I'm Nessa Gustafson. I'm with

Maelcom. Do not mess with him, he is ex-military."

"Nessa, this is Leal. He knows who I am, has heard of me. This is the one who took the ticket."

The man gave her the once-over and lifted his eyebrows. "Is she Små folk?" he asked.

Maelcom snapped, "No, just a woman."

Nessa pointed at the stranger. "Did he kill Anders?" she asked Maelcom.

"No. By the time this man got to the house, Anders was dead. He found the ticket but left quickly when the assassin returned."

"Are you sure this guy isn't lying?"

Maelcom shook his head. "I believe he's telling me the truth."

The tall man nodded curtly at Maelcom. "As I told you, I thought Anders was part of a false flag plan masterminded by Naberius as a way to ensure secrecy. I assumed Anders worked for you in some capacity so I followed him, hoping that one of the Jotun would find me so I could turn myself in, make a bargain—amnesty for information, although mostly everyone is dead. I am tired of hiding out."

Nessa lifted her eyebrows at Maelcom and mouthed *What*? And twirled her finger near her temple? He could be crazy.

Maelcom ignored her and nodded like he understood what the man said. "A false flag? It is safer for all to exist under the radar. You know, you could have simply called Naberius on the phone."

"Really? Just called?" His shoulders sank. "That idea does not come easily to me. Just call Naberius, the Mad General of Armies, slayer and defeater of my people, he'll help," he said, grimacing and shaking his head.

Nessa was at a complete loss as to what they were talking about. It must be code for things she wasn't cleared to know about.

"We don't discuss secure intelligence matters out in the open. Everyone has different levels of clearance," Maelcom snapped at Leal. She had never seen him be annoyed with anyone.

"Oh, I see." Leal darted a quick glance at Nessa. "I'm sure they followed me and they are coming to kill me. I saw them here by the gates. I don't know how to leave. Maelcom, you might consider raising the security clearance of the people you are with."

"What the hell are you guys talking about?" Nessa demanded.

"You don't have security clearance. I can't go into detail," Maelcom said.

"He said you can change my clearance. And if people are watching to find people, the gates are perfect to stake out." She pouted. They were talking crazy stuff. The stranger was hot and handsome, with a scruffy beard and sorrowful eyes, sharp, high cheekbones and dirty blond hair. "Who are you?" she asked.

He bowed. "Leal Thrapp."

The bow was cool and courtly and so she curtsied clumsily back. "I never had anyone bow to me so I figured I better curtsy," she said.

He laughed at her but made her feel like he was complimenting her with his laugh. And his smile took her breath away. Jesus, he could model with those cheekbones.

She realized her mouth had dropped open. "You're beautiful. Are you a model?"

He blinked his eyes and darted an anxious glance at Maelcom who stepped forward, putting himself between her and Leal.

"Nessa is an artist," Maelcom said. Like he was explaining her.

She didn't need someone to make excuses for her. "Sorry, I didn't mean to make you uncomfortable. I draw people all the time and I was just thinking about you visually. I didn't mean to be rude. Like Maelcom said I am an artist."

Leal gave a gracious nod. "Please, do not let it trouble you."

That man was dangerously handsome. She smiled back until Maelcom touched her arm. "Nessa, we need to leave."

She blew out a huff of air. "Hold on." She went up on her toes and whispered in Maelcom's ear, "Are you sure about him? Just because he's pretty doesn't mean we should trust him."

Maelcom gave one of his almost smiles and nodded. "Yes. I'm sure. We need to leave without being seen. I believe someone has followed Leal here."

"I spent seven hundred kroner on those tickets." She

moped a bit because she was going to miss a lot of great performances.

"I'll give you back the money."

"What? Why? No, no, I'm helping. Where do you need to take him? And why were you manhandling him if he surrendered to you?"

Maelcom turned and growled at Leal. Leal shuddered slightly.

"I wanted to make sure he was motivated to tell the truth. Leal said our suspects are trying to kill him as well," Maelcom said.

She put her hand on top of Maelcom's. "Are you angry?"

"I was," he said softly, taking her hand. "But not when I hold your hand."

She squeezed back. "It makes me feel good also." Maelcom stared at her, stunned. It seemed to happen to her a lot. It's what came from being honest. "What does Leal do?"

"I'm scribe and a writer," Leal offered.

Maelcom sighed and scratched his jaw. "Nessa, he was the assistant or secretary to a criminal called Rayme. Rayme is dead but we need to learn about who funded him and what alliances he made."

"Rayme didn't like to deal with writing and communication so it worked in my favor. Kept me safe, because no one else was as good as me and I had a lot of responsibility," Leal said.

Nessa was confused. "Who is Rayme?"

Maelcom narrowed his eyes in thought. "The bad guy that Leal worked for. The head of a fringe group working to destabilize the government."

"What government?"

"Nessa," he said unhappily.

"Maelcom." She raised her eyebrow back at him. Two could play the silent stare. She was not going to back down. Here she was, assisting with the security of Sweden and greater Europe, and he wasn't telling her much.

He brushed away a curl of hair that had fallen into her face. "We need to get him away. He has turned himself in to us, so he needs protection because he has information. Please, that is all I can say."

"Really? I know you're a super-secret intelligence guy but I just wanted to know some details. After all, I'm helping out. I'm your partner in this effort."

He considered her words for a second before answering. "I'm working with a European and American effort to resolve an issue with the man Leal worked for. It is a separate issue from Anders but there is some overlap."

She clapped her hands and shimmied her shoulders in excitement. It sounded important but it also sounded vague. "And Leal is important because he knows all the secret inside information of this criminal guy he worked for?"

Maelcom nodded.

"Can we speed up this discussion? I don't want to die," Leal snapped. "I've an assassin on my trail. He has my scent and without a doubt he will find me. If I had been minutes earlier to the farmhouse, I'd be dead also."

Maelcom grimaced. "Fine. I'll use you as bait. Wait till the assassin attempts something and then I'll kill him."

"I don't like that," Leal said. "It sounds risky."

"Perhaps working for Rayme was the real risk," Maelcom growled.

Nessa realized that there was some underlying animosity between them. "I agree with Leal, that sounds risky. How do you know you can stop the assassin before he kills Leal?" Nessa asked.

Maelcom's expression was incredulous. "I am—" He snapped his mouth shut and took a breath. "I can keep Leal safe. Although maybe I could catch the assassin. He might be a better intelligence asset than a scribe?"

Nessa's mouth dropped open. "Maelcom, that is rude. Don't threaten him. He is standing right here."

Leal's expression was serious but not threatening. "Maelcom, I had full clearance on all matters and on who was financing Rayme. I have important information. The assassin is just a robot on a mission. I can provide vital intelligence on various groups. I simply want amnesty like all of my kind received at the end of the war."

Nessa listened with growing confusion, which seemed to be a constant state for her lately. "Wait, so the guy who killed Anders is some kind of an assassin and wants to kill Leal? Which war? Which side are you on?"

Both men nodded as if that answered her questions.

"An assassin followed you here to the festival?" she

squeaked this out. This was a lot stranger than she had imagined.

Maelcom said, "Yes. When the assassin returned to the farmhouse, presumably to clear the scene, he almost caught Leal. Leal says the assassin is here. He saw him enter but lost him."

"We need to get out of here. You explained it badly, Maelcom. We probably shouldn't be here using innocent people as bait. We should leave," Nessa said.

Leal went pale. "The assassin will not stop until I'm dead. His own life is inconsequential. I know who they sent for me." He sniffed. "I was going to try to kill him first but I don't know, he's a better fighter than me. He will be watching for me. I kept hiding in the crowds watching music."

"What about your car?" Maelcom asked.

"I left it in the nearby town and took a bus here. It easier to hide in a big group and they were looking for a man in a car."

Maelcom frowned. "You need to tell me more about how you know this man tracking you. But first we need to get you to safety, then I need to capture him. This is too public. Too much risk of exposure."

"I can't believe I'm missing Dead Haus. You owe me," she grumbled. "We need to leave without anyone seeing us." Her phone buzzed in her pocket. It was Olaf. Maelcom opened his mouth to speak but Nessa waved her hand at him and a brilliant idea popped into her head. "We need to leave in disguise so no one recognizes Tall, Blond and Handsome here and you, Maelcom, Mr. Dark and Dangerous. Hah that would be a good nickname for you."

Maelcom nodded. "No nicknames. How do we disguise ourselves?"

"My friend Olaf is here with his performance musical group. They put on a show in a side venue. In drag. Very ironic, sort of self-aware, artistic take on drag. They have a lot of costumes that just happen to fit men. Leal, you'll look fabulous in a dress. Maelcom, I'm praying someone has a cape for you."

"You want us to dress up as women to leave?" Maelcom asked in a soft but incredulous voice.

"Maybe. I don't know what costumes he has. The idea is to leave the concert in disguise."

He narrowed his eyes as he considered her preposterous plan. "Can he bring the clothes here?"

She already had her phone out and was texting at the speed of light. "Oh, I'm telling him this is an intelligence operation so no talking to anyone about this. Cool?" She gave a big, exaggerated wink.

Maelcom stared at her with an expression of concern. "You can't tell people."

"He's my best friend, Maelcom. I'm not telling him all the details but we need to get out undetected. He doesn't need specifics but he needs some information."

Leal smiled at her. "You're very clever."

She grinned back. "Well, I've been telling Maelcom that

intelligence people should hire artists. We think in interesting ways."

Maelcom said, "It's not a perfect plan. They can still scent us."

Leal nodded but Nessa just laughed. "No way. It will be fine." Really, he had pushed this scenting metaphor too far.

Later, after Olaf arrived with an armful of dresses and a big bag, Maelcom stood behind her with his hands over her eyes while Olaf dressed Leal. He was sort of funny about being concerned about Leal undressing in front of her. She decided to humor him and she liked being close to him.

"It's not proper," Maelcom grumbled. He took hold of her shoulders and pulled her back close to him. He leaned to whisper, his lips grazing her ear. She shivered. "I will cover your eyes," he said.

She looked over her shoulder, up at his beautiful mouth, wide and generous. Lips for kissing.

"Didn't we go swimming together without bathing suits? You're so uptight," she half-heartedly complained, just to make it look good.

He cupped his hands over her eyes. It was not a perfect shield—she peeked and could see tiny strips of the world between his fingers. She rubbed her bottom against him and he froze.

"Nessa," he sighed deeply, all please-don't-torment-me evident in his tone.

She sighed and stopped. She wasn't touching him any-more but almost, so barely an inch separated their bodies.

His hands rested lightly on her face but she could feel all of him. The physical intensity, like her skin was alive with the presence of him. She blushed and she knew he could feel the heat of it through his fingers.

"Can I watch while you undress?"

"I'm wearing a cape. It goes over my clothes, so no getting undressed."

"Damn," she said.

She heard Olaf squeal excitedly. "Oh Leal, you look beautiful in this outfit. It's really more you than me. I'm a failure of a drag queen. I look better in a conservative men's shirt than I do in a dress," Olaf sighed dramatically.

"Maelcom, I'm done," Leal said.

Nessa leaned back slightly against Maelcom, stealing his warmth. His rough hand was lightly held over her eyes like he didn't want to let her go, so she pushed his hand away. "It's fine, Maelcom. You know I wouldn't turn to stone if I saw a guy half-naked."

Maelcom's eyes crinkled in worry. "I apologize," he said.

Nessa melted a little. She'd just meant to tease him. "No, I'm sure you were protecting Leal's tender sensibilities."

She turned to Leal and gasped. Before her stood a beautiful woman. Leal could walk the catwalk as either gender. The long, blonde wig that Olaf had given him complemented his pale skin.

"Voila! I present Glinda, the Good Witch of the South," Olaf said.

"Leal, you make a beautiful woman," Maelcom said

solemnly. "Like a Valkyrie."

"Valkyrie were not my kind," Leal said.

"It matters not. Relax, life here on earth is not as old-fashioned as our home," Maelcom answered.

Nessa was confused about the conversation. Were these veiled comments about Leal being gay, or a comment about the terrorists? What did he mean by "our home"? Denmark or where he lived now?

Olaf started carefully packing up the costumes they hadn't used. It was really wonderful that he let them use them because they were all custom, handmade clothes.

"Maelcom, can the government compensate Olaf for the costumes? Shouldn't they pay expenses on this type of operation?" Nessa asked.

Olaf sniffed at the idea. "I'm a patriot. I want terrorists and troublemakers stopped. This man will provide intelligence, correct?"

"Yes," said Maelcom. "I'll pay for the clothes. Here." Maelcom took out his wallet, peeled off a number of large bills and handed them to Olaf.

"If you insist. You take care of my Nessa. I don't know what we will do for the performance. We'll do the Disney extravaganza instead." He sighed dramatically. "All Disney songs to a club backbeat. Half-naked, oiled men. It's very hot. Wait, this is too much money."

"Keep it. Thank you, Olaf." Maelcom bowed slightly. "I need to talk to Leal about something. I'll be right back," he said.

Nessa watched Maelcom and Leal step away. She and Olaf looked at each other round eyed and amazed. "Wow. Thank you so much. You're the best friend. Who else could I trust?"

Olaf whispered in her ear. "He gave me 3000 krona, that was generous. If you don't jump on Tall, Dark and Handsome, I will slap you."

Nessa bit her lip. "Shhh. Don't joke. I like him."

Olaf kissed her cheek and whispered, "I could tell." But of course, he could.

She elbowed him. "I don't know. What if I'm suffering from just-been-rescued syndrome? He's like my Stockholm syndrome boyfriend, except we really met in Stockholm."

Olaf grimaced. "I dream about being rescued by a man like him. Maelcom is all yummy and stern. I want to be a bad boy with him but don't tell my boyfriend. All that intense smolder. Sex with him will help you recover from the trauma of that asshole in the bar." He sighed heavily.

She nodded enthusiastically. Sex with Maelcom was a great idea. "I'm going to try not to worry. I think he may be worried too, so I don't want to freak him out," she whispered and darted a look at Maelcom talking to Leal. "Do you have the Dorothy dress for me?"

"Oh, it's perfect. Blue gingham and the red wig with pigtails and big blue ribbons. No ruby slippers, none in your size. I think just wear your black boots and carry the ruby slippers in your hand like you are saving them for later. No one will realize they're not your size."

Nessa grabbed the dress Olaf handed her and held it up

in front of her. It was cute but it was big, cut for a young man and not for her.

She put the dress on over her clothes because it was three sizes too big for her. The dress had a built-in belt which she tightened as much as possible. It worked. No one would be looking closely at little Dorothy when she had a gorgeous blonde lady on one arm and the Wicked Witch of the West on the other.

"Maelcom, come here. I need to secure the wig and the hat to your head." Olaf held up a long black wig with a witch's hat and shook it. "It's a theme. Maelcom, with your height, you will make a perfect Wicked Witch of the West. We were going to do songs from 'Wicked,' the best of sort of thing but weirder. The key for this outfit is the green makeup pulled all together by the long black cape."

Maelcom scratched his jaw. Nessa tensed, expecting a complaint, but he said, "Green makeup will be a good disguise."

Olaf shook his head. "We're going to need to slap a pair of sunglasses on those beautiful eyes of yours. One in a million, that color."

Nessa was delighted with everyone's disguises. They were so outrageous, no one would consider they were anything but performers. If someone was checking people who looked like Leal or Maelcom, no one would take a second glance at them.

Nessa took Maelcom's arm and whispered, "Let's go, you wicked witch."

CHAPTER 13

Maelcom

A BEAD OF SWEAT TRICKLED down his neck. He had meant to simply turn her away but touching her gave him an idea so he covered her eyes. "No peeking," he said. His palms were tickled by her eyelashes. Her breathing was shallow and fast. It had felt like holding sunshine—blinding, burning but wonderful.

Leal thought she was Små folk, a long-disappeared people from their realm. A kind of wood sprite. He understood the mistake. She had a different energy from most humans.

Maelcom turned his head to look at Olaf making a final fix to Leal's wig. Leal, of course, made a beautiful woman. Nessa had slipped on her dress and was distractingly sexy in her little farm girl dress and pigtails. She made it hard for him to stay focused and he was annoyed how she cooed over Leal's beauty. He watched her and Olaf whisper to each other. He heard his name.

He'd achieved his objectives. Located an important intelligence asset. *Check.* Managed to avoid killing asset. *Check.* First time he had taken an Ice Daimon prisoner, mostly used to kill them. *Check.* Protect an important intelligence asset by not killing him. Damn, the last two items were the same thing. The idea of Nessa was like a splinter in his brain, disrupting him. He could never pretend the feeling wasn't there.

He talked to Leal briefly about the promise to protect him. It was lucky for all Jotun Daimons that Leal was trying to turn himself in as they desperately needed more intel on Ice Daimons or the hard won peace would not last. Leal worked for Rayme under threat. He had come to the Earth Realm with the Ice Daimon rebels, and while the main group went to be slaughtered in battle by himself, Naberius and Gusion, Leal had been hiding at a remote cabin in Sweden's north country, waiting for their return. Leal had found Anders on a Reddit chat group chatting about Daimons. They really had to do something about those groups.

Olaf had given him tiny round sunglasses to hide his blue eyes, slapped green makeup on his face and given him an old-style broom to hold. He could pass as a convincing witch. He was hot wearing a long black satin cape and the pointed hat with the wig attached to it. Hot from having held Nessa and covering her eyes so she wouldn't look at Leal.

Once he had been a mighty warrior with thousands cheering his name. Now he was sneaking out of an EDM festival dressed in a cape with green makeup all over his face. Olaf had given him tiny round sunglasses to hide his eyes, and an old-style broom. He could pass as a convincing witch.

Gusion would be howling with laughter. He would have to make sure none of the Daimon soldiers learned about this or they'd laugh about it for years. *Years.* Particularly Gusion, who adored cosplay.

Nessa buzzed like a live wire standing beside him.

"Oh my god. I want a picture. Olaf, here take my phone. Take a picture."

"No pictures, Nessa," Maelcom said. She would probably post it on social media.

"Can I take a selfie?" she asked. She didn't wait and held her phone out, pouted and took a picture of herself. Her hair was in two long pigtails with ribbons framing her face. She looked like a doll come to life with her blue gingham dress and white blouse with puffy sleeves.

"Let's go now," Maelcom said.

She grinned at him. "Okay, so we should leave via the east entrance. It's the closest to this location and it's a little quieter because it's farther to the parking lots, but Olaf can pull the car up to the drop off area there," Nessa said.

"Good. Olaf, take the keys. It's in row G11. Black Mercedes SUV—just click the key until you find it."

Olaf nodded. "Give me five minutes." And he slipped out of the tent.

Maelcom pulled Nessa close to him. "Are you ready?" She nodded.

Leal frowned. "It will be hard to walk." He tugged at the dress around his legs.

"Walk carefully, then. We need to head to the gate." Maelcom turned to Leal and poked him with his broom. "You stay close to me the entire time."

"Do not poke me with that broom. I gave you my word."

Maelcom looked at his watch counting down the time.

"Can we go?" Nessa asked.

"Wait."

"I'm walking slowly in this dress," Leal said petulantly. Nessa snickered.

Maelcom stuck his head out of the tent, breathed in and smelled nothing. "All clear."

Nessa slipped her hand in his. "Let's go."

He led the way, taking little sips of energy while Nessa chattered about music with Leal on her other side. Most people ignored them or simply laughed at them.

"Oh look, the Wicked Witch has Dorothy!" someone exclaimed.

Leal tripped and had to stop to straighten the dress with Nessa assisting him. They continued on at a relaxed pace.

At the east gate, Maelcom breathed in, searching for a new scent of a Daimon, and caught a distant hint of something. They were being tracked by their scent alone.

Leal whispered, "Hurry, he's coming."

Olaf was already there, waiting by the car at the drop-off area. "Be safe," he whispered and then loudly said, "Be back for our performance. Don't be late."

The scent grew strong and Maelcom hissed. "I think the assassin is moving toward the gate. I need you to move quickly." Nessa and Leal scrambled into the car and Maelcom slid into the driver's seat. He was forced to drive slowly out of the maze of parked cars until they got to the main road where he sped up, heading south where there were plenty of alternate routes back to Stockholm. He kept checking the rearview mirror but no one followed.

Nessa tapped his arm. "You said you have to go to somewhere with Leal but maybe we should lie low for a day. We should go stay at my dad's place, it's empty while he is in New York putting up a retrospective exhibition of his work. It's on the outskirts of a small town halfway to Stockholm."

Maelcom pressed down on the accelerator because he wanted distance from the Ice Daimons. "What town?"

"Vasteras. You know it? Southwest of Stockholm."

He opened his mouth then snapped it shut. Naberius *Vasteras* would be amused. *Shit.* This would be interesting. The ancient home of Naberius's family a thousand years ago. "We will see. I will head in the general direction. But I need to touch base with my people."

She beamed at him. It warmed him, that smile. He drove silently until they were a couple of miles away from the concert.

"I'm taking off this hair," Leal said and pulled off the fluffy blonde wig.

Maelcom glanced in the rearview mirror. Leal's makeup was smudged all over his face and his hair stuck up from the static electricity of the wig. "Leal, did you see anything as we drove away?"

Leal nodded. "I think I saw someone running just as you turned onto the main road."

Maelcom pulled off his wig and scratched his head while had turned in her seat to look at him. "There is no way he could follow us. Right? He doesn't have his car. We are way ahead."

Maelcom grimaced and shot Leal a look in the rearview mirror. Leal nodded at him. They were in agreement, an Ice Daimon can track in situations most would consider impossible.

Nessa stared at Leal. "You know, if you are all done with the criminal world, you could become a fashion model. Oh, there was a famous criminal who put his picture on Instagram and is now a model. My friend Olaf could help you if you are interested. You would be an awesome front man for a band. Can you sing? I love to sing but only at karaoke."

"Nessa, he does not need you to pick out a profession

for him. He is hiding out from bad people who he used to work for, not figuring out what he wants to do with his life," Maelcom grumbled.

He disliked her mentioning Leal's good looks. He had found her first—she was his. His *something*. And Leal had better step back.

She looked at him from under her eyelashes. "Your green makeup is smudged." He grabbed a cloth from the dash and wiped his face. He only removed half of it but he felt better.

"If I had to pick a profession, I would be in rock and roll," Leal declared. "I have a phone full of amazing music. I can sing as well as these people on my phone. I love David Bowie the most."

"And David Bowie would have loved you," Nessa said with enthusiasm.

"Would have loved? What happened?" Leal demanded.

"Cancer. Harsh. He was brilliant."

"Nessa, what's the address?" Maelcom demanded before they started discussing singers who'd died recently.

"Yes, yes. You're headed the right way. When we get near, I'll tell you where to go."

Maelcom didn't like that kind of vagueness. He liked to know exactly where he was going. "Nessa, please, the exact address."

"Twenty-four Billson Road, Vasteras."

He input the address in a GPS map which estimated they would arrive in under two hours. Nessa naturally found some David Bowie on the radio. She and Leal sang off-key versions of Bowie's songs.

"*I wish you could swim, like the dolphins, like dolphins can swim,*" she sang with Leal in her low voice.

He struggled with the need to kiss her again and the tremor in his energy. Like he was losing control.

They got to the outskirts of the town of Vasteras and Nessa pointed to a road on the right. "Turn here. It's on the outskirts of town to the south."

Farms and small wooded areas lined the roads, green and pastoral. All neat and well kept, a prosperous area.

A millennium ago, Daimons had lived here, almost as many as in the Daimon Realm. They intermarried, but violence against their kind caused them to retreat. Daimons had not taken a human as a mate for a thousand years until Naberius met Jessalyn Weiss. Perhaps the sense of losing control and this kissing urge meant he was experiencing Venskat, the Daimon mating urge. Was he on the same path with Nessa?

He took a left down a curving road to an old house with a huge porch wrapped around it, nestled among the trees and overgrown pastures. Nessa leaned forward eagerly. "You lived after your father rescued you?" he asked.

"No, my teen years were spent in a suburb of Stockholm. My father wanted better schools for me. My father bought this when I went to university, but I'd come on all my holidays here. I've many happy memories here."

There was a catch in her voice. Nessa gave the appearance of being resolved with her past, but pain as a child was never forgotten. Hell, pain as an adult was hard to forget. Her mother had allowed her to be starved and that was a harsh legacy. Nessa had hinted at an atmosphere of terrible violence and privation. No socks. No food. Dead babies. He gripped the wheel hard. Children were to be protected—that someone would hurt an innocent was difficult to understand.

"Park here," Nessa ordered, and he stopped the car. She jumped out and ran to the front door and lifted the mat. Picking the key up, she waved at Maelcom.

Leal laughed softly. Maelcom glared at him in the rearview mirror. "What?"

"You are experiencing Venskat," Leal said smugly.

Shit. Leal had sharp eyes. "You're fucking crazy," he said stubbornly.

"I'm very good at reading energy. And that wasn't a denial."

"You can't read Jotun Daimons."

"Our energies are the same. In fact, I believe all Daimons are genetically identical except for differences in Daimon forms. Puts a whole new spin on the Daimon Wars." Leal rubbed his forehead. "All the men in my family died in the idiotic wars. Only me, the librarian, survived. Someone had to write all the dispatches, ensconced safely behind the lines of battle."

"What does that have to do with Venskat?" Maelcom growled but deep inside, he smiled at the idea of a mate.

Shit.

"It means I, a disgusting, vile Ice Daimon, can read and understand your energy and you are showing signs of the mating urge known universally amongst Daimons as Venskat."

Nessa had unlocked the door and gone inside. She came out to wave at them to come in.

"Let's go inside. *Stop* saying Daimon out loud," Maelcom said angrily. It might be that killing this Ice Daimon was the best course of action. *Hah. Venskat.* Nothing out of the ordinary with being horny—all that teasing and kissing from Nessa had simply got him all worked up. She was sweet. That was all. Or not.

The center front yard had many beautiful flowers and roses instead of a lawn. The house was from the early 20th century with high ceilings, beautiful wood trim everywhere and a huge foyer in front of a large sweeping staircase. It was the type of house in the old days that would have had a fleet of servants. Really, it was a country estate of a wealthy Swede before the great wars. He followed Nessa into a big, open living room with paintings hanging everywhere.

Nessa stood in the middle and gestured to the walls. "The portraits are done by my father. The other works are by friends of his. What do you think? His artwork is everywhere. He said he bought this house so he would have room to hang everything. But really, it has three floors. My father…" she rolled her eyes, "…he can be extravagant."

The paintings were energetic portraits of people in

movement, laughing, talking and dancing in strange landscapes with strange lighting. He stared at them, studying each one carefully. "I have seen one of these before in a gallery."

She punched him lightly on the arm. "Yes. You do like art. His paintings are incredibly dynamic."

Maelcom nodded slowly. "I like them but I like your drawings more."

Her cheeks turned pink. "Thank you. Come, I will take the green makeup off with some cream."

She led him to the back of the house. The spacious kitchen area and dining room and breakfast area took up the rear of the house. Right off the kitchen was a large bedroom, he knew these old houses had the cook or the housekeeper live right near their domain. He pointed to it. "I'll stay here. I want to be on the first floor as security."

She twisted her hair around her fingers. "Sure. It used to be the housekeeper's room in the old days but now she only comes during the day. People don't have live-in servants so much anymore. My Dad usually has a houseful of people staying here, anyone who needs a place to stay or vacation, he tells them to come here."

"Will anyone come while we are here?"

"No. The house is closed while my father is out of the country. When we leave, I will call the housekeeper to come clean."

"Good. No other near neighbors or people doing work on the house?"

"The gardener just came. See the short grass and the rose bushes have been clipped."

Maelcom strode into the bedroom and dropped his bag. She went into the bathroom and opened up cupboards until she found a jar from amongst the other bottles.

"Come in here. Sit, please, because you are too tall. I'm going to take the green off." She gestured to the edge of the tub.

Obeying her command, he sat and she gently smeared some cream all over his face. She wiped his face in smooth motions, like she was painting him clean, while standing between his legs with the same expression she'd had on her face as when she combed his hair. He liked to have her so close to him, to have her touches with her sweet energy as she cleaned the makeup from his face.

"It was itchy," he said while she smoothed with tissue, dabbing at stubborn areas. Finally, she took a warm washcloth and wiped it over his face. The heat made his eyelids droop. It was pleasant.

"All this cream has made your face very soft. You might consider moisturizing now and then. The cold weather is hard on skin, dries it out." She chattered on. He could feel a slight tremble in her hands. He could feel her nerves and understood that they had come to a point where something had to be said.

He had thought Venskat would be a disruptive feeling, something like an explosion. But there was this other odd sensation. It gave him butterflies in his stomach. The feeling could be stress, or a space-out. Or it might be joy, although he had no experience in that.

She balled up the tissue and pitched it into the wastebasket. "I'm glad that is done. I've been wanting to kiss but the green makeup stopped me. What do you think, Mr. I-Don't-Usually-Kiss-Women-Just-Sleep-with-Them?" She put one hand on her hip and gave him a serious stare, complete with a little furrow between her eyes.

"That was before I met you. We'll kiss, Nessa, and more. I'll be kissing your whole body."

Her mouth opened a little. "Really?"

"All over," he said, dead serious.

"Shut up." She punched him on the arm and then winced, shaking her hand in pain. "You'd better. You're making me mental."

Leal's voice called out. "Where are you?"

Nessa rolled her eyes. "Later," she whispered and slipped out of the bathroom. "We're here. Would you like some coffee? I think there is food in the pantry. Let me look in the freezer for something for dinner. Nothing fresh, but my father's housekeeper always keeps homemade canned vegetables and lots of frozen meat."

Maelcom came up behind her, touching her lightly on the shoulder. "I'll walk around the outside of the house for a security check," he said. He would want to take her clothes off if he stayed in the bedroom any longer.

Leal was sitting in the living room with his arms on the back of the couch. Maelcom could see a silver bracelet with an odd-looking gem on his right arm.

Maelcom frowned. "You take an upstairs bedroom. Right at the top of the stairs."

"You think the Ice Daimon tracking me has been shaken off our trail?"

An idea came to Maelcom about these supposed assassins' seemingly flawless tracking ability. Maelcom looked at the thick gold ring on his finger. It was given to him as a token for his service to Lord Naberius. But Ice Daimons didn't wear rings, they wore bracelets of silver with inlaid jewels.

"You wear the bracelet of your fealty to Rayme?"

Leal looked at him, surprised. "Yes. I suppose I have no lord now so it is meaningless. But I kept it nonetheless. Foolish, I know. He gave these to us when we came to the Earth Realm. I probably should take it off." He pushed back his sleeve and showed it to him.

"Can I see it? Give it to me."

Leal handed him the bracelet from around his wrist. Maelcom examined it very carefully. The bracelet was made from embossed silver with an elaborate pattern and a jewel in the middle. Out came Maelcom's knife, and he popped the red jewel out.

"Leal, this isn't a jewel. It's a tracking device." Maelcom placed it on the table and poked it with the butt of his knife.

"Shit, no wonder I was only one step ahead."

"There is a GPS chip in the bracelet. For someone who wasn't tech savvy, this is interesting. The reception isn't perfect and the battery dies."

Leal put his head in his hands. "That is how the assassin keeps tracking me."

"It is fine. I know this technology. It has a chronically weak signal which is why you have eluded them for so long. Ice Daimons obtained this technology from the Earth Realm a while ago."

"What will we do?"

"I need to get rid of this and send it far away. You stay, or help Nessa in the kitchen."

Maelcom stomped out of the house. He sniffed the air. Nothing. Walking around the house, he checked possible approaches. The property backed onto a hill and then there were overgrown farm fields with young trees and saplings. There was an old fenced-in pasture to the side of the driveway where a flock of geese pecked at the grass, hunting for grubs.

Walking quickly back to the house, he grabbed two shoelaces from a pair of boots, an envelope and a roll of duct tape. He tucked the tracking device in the envelope and taped it up.

Outside, he circled the geese till he came upwind of them. He walked straight at them and they scattered with a casual, resentful pace. Lunging at one, he grabbed it by the neck and clamped his hand around the beak, and in the same motion, sat down and threw his leg over the squirming goose. He tied the beak closed with one shoelace and then proceeded to tie Leal's bracelet loosely to the body of the goose while ensuring the wings were free.

Finished, he released the beak and pushed the goose away. The bird ran a few steps, flapped his wings and hissed at him. Maelcom hissed back and transformed into Daimon form. A hot ripple spiraled through him and he adjusted his clothes.

Eyeing the birds, he shook his horns at them and growled. The birds began honking and squawking, flapping their wings and taking off. They could scent a predator. He stood and watched them fly off northeast to an area with many lakes. *Good. Maybe the device will fall into the water.*

He had tied the envelope with the tracker loosely, with a knot that would slip open if the goose plucked at it. Rubbing his horns, he sighed, thinking how Nessa's hands would feel stroking them. He was vain about his horns—they were considered magnificent and fierce among Daimons. Nessa stroking them would send her sweet energy right to his brain. His breathing came fast. He had the real thing at the house. He didn't need to stand out here and dream horny dreams like a young man. He closed his eyes to still his thoughts and transformed back to his human form.

Entering the house, he stared at the forlorn pair of boots without shoelaces. The sound of Nessa's giggle and Leal's voice came floating out to him, and he felt an eruption of jealous anger. Why could he not make her giggle? Storming into the kitchen, he glared at Nessa and Leal who were sitting at the kitchen table with mugs of coffee and a plate of cookies in front of them.

Nessa gave him a sweet smile. "Coffee is ready and I found a tin of delicious ginger cookies."

He bounced his gaze from one to the other. They sat close, as if they were communicating secrets. A low rumble came from his chest.

Leal rolled his eyes and stood up. "Nessa, I must go and shower. All this makeup on my face." He smirked at Maelcom as he walked past him, muttering, "Venskat."

Maelcom hissed back. "Fool."

"*Maelcom.* Why are you hissing at Leal? And what is Venskat?"

He shrugged at her as Leal walked up the stairs. "Nothing. Why were you flirting with him? This is unadvisable."

She narrowed her eyes at him. "You know he plays on the other team."

"What team are you talking about?"

"I mean you should worry about him flirting with you. He thinks you are very handsome." She picked up the coffeepot and poured a cup then held it out to him. A small smile lurked at the corner of her lips.

He took the cup. "Shit. He's gay?"

"Scared? Nervous?"

"No. I'm never scared. I know several Da—, um, friends who prefer their own gender. It matters not. In the army, all that matters is how well you fight."

"Okay, you surprised me. Which means I'm the one with rigid ideas and that sucks. I guess I thought military guys are all very uptight and super straight."

He sniffed. "I'm not uptight. I enjoy sex," he said. "Very much."

Nessa gave him a naughty smile. "Stop flirting with me. Now, sit down. You take up so much of the kitchen. I need to cook dinner. Can you peel some potatoes? I'm making stew."

"You want me to peel potatoes?"

Maelcom had cooked out in the wilderness, but in civilization, people served him. His Daimon rank was similar to a colonel. On earth, he employed people to take care of the humdrum elements of human life, like potatoes.

He sat down at the kitchen table. "I'm capable with a knife. I will peel your potatoes."

CHAPTER 14

Nessa

HE PEELED THE POTATOES with lightning speed, somehow spinning them fast in his big hand and producing peels in one continuous strip. *Show-off.* Nessa cut the meat in chunks while trying not to stare at Maelcom.

When he said he enjoyed sex in that deep rumbly voice, she almost grabbed him and dragged him into the bedroom. She had lied to him about Leal finding him handsome. She was the one who thought that. All sweet and hard at the same time.

Maelcom's reaction to Leal's sexuality seemed genuine and relaxed, which made her feel happy. It surprised her but it shouldn't have. That was Maelcom: very real and straight forward.

"Is there anything else I can do?" The bowl was full of peeled potatoes.

"Can you cube the potatoes? Then I will toss them in. The stew has to cook on a low heat for several hours."

He nodded and started chopping. Damn, she sure as hell would enjoy sex with him.

"Why you staring at me?" he asked.

"Oh, um, shouldn't we hand Leal over to whatever authorities?"

"Tomorrow we'll head to the place to do that."

"Right, you mentioned a gate. And that is…"

"Southwest."

"Aacch…super-secret stuff again. Lucky I trust you." She flapped her hand at him.

"You shouldn't." he said as his knife flashed, cutting up the potatoes quickly. She caught the concern in his voice.

"Listen, I was staring at you because I like you. And *you* flirt with me one second and then the next you are all *stay away*. It makes me a little confused," she said with the hurt clear in her voice.

"I'm sorry. I'm restless. He stood up and brought the bowl of potatoes to her. She poured them into the pot and set it on a low fire to cook. He watched her intently while she added some spices. Finally, when she wiped her hands, he pulled her so she stood inside his arms. "I'm trying to put you off because I think about kissing you all the time. Are you still thinking about kissing me?"

She froze and swallowed hard. This man did not make

jokes or flirty statements often. He spoke with heat in his voice. She could leave—his arms rested lightly around her— but instead she ran her fingers down his chest. It was best to be honest. "Yes, I am. And it better be more than a kiss. I like you, Maelcom. All our kissing and flirting is making me crazy and itchy," she confessed.

His forehead wrinkled. "Are you sure? You were just attacked."

She leaned her head against his shoulder and inhaled, breathing him in. "Totally sure. You are sweet to ask. Don't I seem sure?"

He hummed a *yes* deep in his chest. "Hmm. I'm not all I seem to be. You might not like me so much if you knew everything. You, Nessa, only see the good in everyone." His nose grazed her cheek and he breathed out, the air tickling her.

"First, you need to respect that I know my own mind. I lucked out in that attack and I'm okay. If I choose you to sleep with you should respect that."

His eyes glittered and his mouth curved into his almost smile. "You won't be sleeping. Can I find the place where you're itchy and crazy?" He whispered her words back to her, lips against her cheek, and laid his hand on her thigh, his fingers grazing between her legs.

She inhaled and pushed herself against his fingers. He made her breathless. Where he touched, her skin tingled. He was electric.

His other arm pulled her close while he captured her

mouth like she was air or water or something he desperately needed. Slanting his mouth over hers, he tasted her deeply. Her lips tingled as she kissed him back then moved her lips to his jaw, his cheeks, like conducting an investigation with her mouth. Each kiss she pressed to his face, he hummed. He felt like an obsession; she wanted more.

He pulled away and stood up with her in his arms. Like she weighed nothing. It made her laugh. And he remained still for a second, watching her smile. Then he walked with her into the bedroom, kicking the door shut.

She blushed as he laid her carefully on the bed. He picked up her leg and placed her foot on his chest to take her shoe off. Her feet looked ridiculously small, even in her chunky big boot with a thick sole. One giant hand wrapped her calf and the other unlaced her boot.

"I can do—"

"Shh. Let me, Nessa. I want to undress you."

She lay there and spread her arms wide while he gently unlaced her shoes.

"Now, Nessa, put your hands above your head," he said in a firm voice, and waited till she nodded and stretched her arms above her head.

She felt reckless and slutty, laid out like a feast for him. She lifted her hips as he removed her leggings. Lying there with her dress hiked up and lacy white underwear on display, her arms above her head, she became an odalisque. A slave to his touch. A shirt was thrown to the floor. His eyes were half closed as he unbuttoned his pants, pushing them down quickly.

"Sit up," he commanded. "Lift your arms." She sat up, stretched her arms above her head while he pulled off her dress. Her bra was thrown to the floor.

All she had left were her lacy white underwear. He pulled her to the edge of the bed and knelt down in front of her then grabbed her underwear with his teeth, making her fall back with a laugh.

She pushed the panties down with her hands, the movement causing her to raise her bottom so he kissed and licked her. Her brain couldn't handle all the sensation— rough tongue, her liquid reaction to him, the way her breasts ached. No words came to her, only tingling throughout her body.

"Beautiful Nessa," he said with reverence. She must be dizzy because he seemed to pulse slightly. Nessa covered her eyes with a hand. His voice rumbled out. "Let me see you."

As she removed her hand from her eyes, they stared at each other. His pupils were huge, surrounded by a ring of electric blue. His glinting skin seemed reddish gold in the light for some reason. All hard, beautiful planes of rippling muscles, his hip bones drawing straight lines to his cock, with hardly any body hair, only a dusting of black hair from his chest leading downward.

His hands flat on either side of her head, he held himself over her. Trailed kisses on her neck till she grabbed his shoulders and pulled herself up to kiss, lick and make small, tasting bites on his neck, his ears, his jaw, his mouth.

"Nymph. Sorceress." He whispered the words over her nipple.

"Maelcom, will you make love to me now?" she asked because she needed him so much, ready to scream and beg. She trembled, unable to explain in words her desire for him.

CHAPTER 15

Maelcom

LUMINESCENT AGAINST THE DARK BEDSPREAD in the back bedroom, she glowed, with her white-blonde hair spread halo-like around her head. Her face flushed with pleasure, and her eyes smudged with dark makeup and heavy with desire.

The moment she'd asked him to make love to her, visions of sucking, licking and biting blossomed in his brain. Her sucking him off, licking his chest, his cock, his balls and his ass. He almost came. Jerking away, he palmed his cock to calm it or at least contain it.

He had never experienced such an erotic connection to a woman. He usually felt more removed. But this talkative sprite—it was more than needing to fuck her. He wanted closeness. He wanted to hear her constant stream of chatter, observations, and realizations. God, her laughter, her ass against him while she danced. He liked her but also wanted to fuck her hard. *Shit.* This really must be Venskat.

That naughty Nessa crawled over to him while licking her lips, intent like a small kitten about to pounce on prey. Like she knew what he wanted, what he desired, what he craved. Her, all of her.

The first touch of her lips, he surrendered completely. Like everything fell into place, he was connected to her. He tasted her energy, so sweet, and sent some energy into her while she took him into her mouth. His ability to think fractured into bright light. Her mouth on his cock became heaven, became home.

His fingers sparked with energy while his brain froze in a bright ecstasy of wonder. The need to shift burst forth—he wanted to fuck her as a Daimon. Damn Venskat. He pulled her up from her knees and she gave a soft laugh. Her eyelids were heavy but she looked him straight in the eye and nodded.

He fumbled on the night table where he had stashed condoms earlier. He found one, ripped it open and rolled it on. He lay down on the bed and let the whimpering, sighing woman crawl up over him, the brush of her skin and hair creating an electric tickle. He grabbed her hips and slowly pulled her down onto his cock.

Hot, wet, beautiful. That was perfect. The gods had favored him, an unbeliever. Daimons prayed for a mate like this. He saw himself telling her about Daimons, and he knew that she would accept it. Without screams, without accusations. She was a little wacky like that. Unique like no other.

He put his hands on her bottom and shoved his hips forward. She moaned. And so he kept up the pace and let her ecstatic whimpers guide him. She shifted herself over him with a wiggle.

"Yes, now, close," he rasped out.

"Me, too. Yes. Yes," she whispered hoarsely, slightly out of breath.

They moved together until she exploded. He could feel her spasm and tighten on his cock. *Damn.* He couldn't wait. Shouting her name, he exploded and came hard, deep inside her, long shivering waves of come. Burying his hands in the sheets to hide the sparks, he arched his back in ecstasy.

More kisses, whispered sweet words, and touches. He wrapped his arms around her, taking some bit of her energy, bright bubbles of her. Putting his index finger on her ribs, he gave his energy back. The time for pretense had passed.

"Oh, you're tickling me."

"You are mine, Nessa," he said firmly. "I need you."

"I am? What does that mean?" She wrinkled her nose and stretched like a cat on her back.

He stared at her small, hard, rose-pink nipples, spacing out and forgetting what they were talking about.

She whistled at him. "Hello? Are you asking me to be your girlfriend?" But she didn't cover herself, her arms over her head like a reclining nude statue. Pale white, pale blonde. Almost disappearing in a cloud of whiteness but her luminous brown eyes brought solidity to her appearance.

"Hmm, yes, I suppose. My girlfriend. Is that the right word?" He would woo her slowly. An idea he had no idea how to execute. Make love to her all day? What else? He could take her to the beach in California, give her presents. Damn, he wasn't good at this.

"It's an okay word for us right now." She wiggled up to kiss him gently on his lips. "I accept. I like it. Being your friend."

First step. Second step, he would tell her about Daimons. "Yes? You are mine. That is the only important thing."

"Friends talk to each other and you need to talk to me more. I mean, I understand you're not a chatty man which is great because I talk a lot but I need you to talk to me because I need to know more about you. It's important, I think, you know, for getting to know each other." She blinked rapidly. He could feel her nervousness. "Is that cool?"

He would talk if she wanted that, he wanted to please her. "Yes, I can tell you more about me. I must. I have promised myself to tell you all." But he was drowsy with contentment and joy. She snuggled up against him and his eyelids closed as he sipped a little energy. Everything seemed right. "So much to tell. I'm not who I appear to be…" And he fell asleep.

He dreamed of home in the Daimon Realm. The enormous house of his family, Skov-Baern. Before the wars, it was full of his immediate family and cousins. Now, in his dream he walked through the empty halls. Weeping women drifted by him. Ghosts of their husbands, sons and daughters drifted behind them. His mother sat in the middle of the great hall, her face cold and determined as she still was. The ghost of his father sat behind her and his brother, Muli, laughing, with pale blue eyes sparkling. Muli was the handsomest Skov-Baern in a generation; Daimons wrote songs about his looks, which always made Muli roll his eyes. He was killed in an ambush by Ice Daimons. He and his best friend had fought heroically, killing four Ice Daimons before being taken down.

Maelcom reached out to touch his brother but his brother shook his head and whispered, "You found your mate. Tell her your heart. Leave nothing hidden."

"Muli," he shouted in his dream and opened his eyes to find himself holding Nessa tightly in his arms.

Nessa raised her head and stroked his chest. "Bad dream?"

He remained silent, but closed his eyes briefly in a wordless *yes*.

"I sometimes dream of not having anything to eat. I had terrible nightmares for years about sitting down before food and then having it taken away. The weird thing is, when I was living with my crazy mother, I never dreamed—too hungry to dream. When my father rescued me, then I started dreaming. My therapist said it was healthy because I was unconsciously working through my issues. So, you see, even bad dreams are good. I'm sorry if I sound like a know-it-all. You shouldn't listen to me. I just yak-yak." She made a talky puppet with her hand.

What did she intend to communicate with her wall of talk? It was something he was accustomed to, even liking the sound of it. Her voice was low and raspy. Being with her would be a life busy with bubbling happy noise. "I like your talking. You should not feel like you should not talk."

He could see her swallow nervously, and her eyelids fluttered. "Thanks." Her little husky voice rasped across his heart.

She always asked for him to talk to her, not that she wanted to change him but because she was interested in hearing his thoughts. He would try. "I never used to dream. When I served in the army, I slept like the dead even if I did terrible things. It is only here, I mean, it is only now that I dream."

Her eyebrows rose high on her forehead. "You did terrible things? I mean, I know war is terrible. But weren't you just a soldier obeying orders?"

"*Ja.* But one has latitude. At a certain point, I gave the enemy no quarter."

She was silent for second. "What was your reason?"

"At first, like any soldier, I did my duty. I was loyal to my lord, followed orders, did what was needed and no more than that. Whatever they asked me to do and I did it well.

But my brother's death at the hands of the enemy changed me, made me ruthless. Unforgiving."

"You called out a name in your sleep."

"I dream about him. His name was Malti. It is a strong name, a warrior name, but my brother was a shining light, laughing and joking, so handsome that women and men would fall silent when he entered a room." He played with her hair while he talked, tangling his fingers into it. Beautiful white-blonde hair against his darker skin.

"Hey, stop pulling my hair. Listen, I thought you said 'Muli' while you were dream-talking."

"A stupid nickname. I nicknamed him Muli because it sounded like a cow and he had cow eyes. Stupid. But he loved it and insisted everyone call him by that name because his big brother called him that." He sighed. "That was Muli."

"He was in the army with you. Where did you serve?"

He squinted his eyes. "Can't tell you."

"Ahh. I understand. All that Special Forces and intelligence work is so super-secret, I guess so the baddies won't find out what you are up to? It's for your or other soldiers' safety so I'm okay with it." She pursed her lips. "How many brothers and sisters in your family?"

He had been worried she would ask more about Muli, which was hard because the memory of his brother was a badly healed wound. A fear ate at him that the memories and the sadness would cause him to go into a walking dream or fugue-like state and she would think he was crazy.

Recently, he saw a dead body of a boy who looked like Muli and completely tuned out. Naberius had taken care of him but he did not want to appear weak in front of his mate, his love.

"My father married my mother and died in the early days of the war. She remarried a good man and I have one brother and three sisters. My sisters are Katya, Olga, and Kara. Olga and Kara were shield maidens."

"Shield maidens? You mean they joined the military too? What war was this?"

"It was a terrible war, long and fierce. I meant that they were fierce and strong but yes they served in the army, also. They now serve in the government."

"Cool. And Katya?" She tucked her legs up against her and wrapped her arms around them.

"She loves the land and runs the farmlands with my mother. My family grows corn and oats but mostly, cattle."

"No way, really? Ugh. And I told you I hate farms." She sounded upset.

He gently brushed the hair away from her face. "*Ja.* I'm the same. It is why I joined the army. All that endless manure." He could feel her energy go jangly. She really hated farms.

She giggled. "It's true. So much shit to shovel."

For some incredulous reason, he could feel a laugh emerging out of him like a low, rusty rumble. "Fucking piles of it."

"Hah. We are like manure refugees." He had his arm

tucked around her and he smoothed her hair while she threw her leg over him. "I like your laugh."

"Nessa," he hummed.

"Hold on, I need to check the stew." She grabbed a throw that was on the chair. It was loose and open knit. It didn't cover much. She flicked her long hair over her shoulder and slipped into the kitchen.

He hadn't told her much. Or he had told her too much. He never talked about his family with anyone but he'd told her about his sisters, even their names. The only other people who knew his sisters' names were the squad of men with Naberius. He had never even told Bobby, his closest human friend, about his sisters. If they were here, they'd shout at him for not writing more often, for being stupid, for staying away.

Nessa reminded him of Bobby. How accepting he was, how he shrugged and exclaimed to Maelcom that it all made sense now and told him not to worry.

She slipped back in the room and dropped the blanket throw. "I call the shower!" she said as she skipped to the bathroom stark naked with her clothes clutched in her hands.

His breath caught in his chest. She made him feel light, mad, horny and happy. After so many years of cool removal, the actual proximity of joy unnerved him. He covered his face. "Shit," he muttered. She was his mate. This was Venskat and he had to tell her about Daimons.

CHAPTER 16

Nessa

NESSA SERVED LEAL AND MAELCOM DINNER, insisting they sit while she served them huge bowls of stew with knäckebröd—round, crisp crackers the size of a dinner plate with a hole in the middle—with a thick spread of butter.

She liked to cook—it was part of her obsession with food. She wanted to gain some weight but it seemed impossible for her. She cooked normal food, she just couldn't eat enough. Like her metabolism was revved up so high.

Maelcom scraped his bowl clean with his spoon. "Thank you, Nessa, for the dinner. It's like something from a restaurant. Delicious."

She grinned at the compliment and took his bowl to

refill it. "I like to cook."

Leal nodded also. "I eat mostly fast food here in"—he coughed—"while I have been traveling."

Nessa shrugged. "Don't bother, Leal. I know I don't have clearance. You both lie terribly, which is shocking because I had imagined that you'd be better at it, considering your profession. I mean, doing super-secret work for intelligence, you'd think they'd train the both of you in lying."

"Leal is—Well, he was part of a criminal organization." Maelcom narrowed his eyes at Leal in a mean way. Or least that's how it appeared. Maelcom really had a problem with Leal's people, whoever they were.

She snorted. "Maelcom, when you lie, you roll your eyes upward. Every time you talk about Leal or where we are going, you do that."

"It's just something I normally do," Maelcom said stubbornly.

Nessa could feel Leal watching their interaction. He had probably guessed that they'd slept together, which was slightly embarrassing for Nessa. She liked her personal life private. Tatianna would have draped herself over her lover without any worry and laughed at Nessa's hesitation. She was comfortable with him but she was nervous now about what came next with Maelcom, how to act in front of other people.

When Maelcom was finishing his second bowl of stew, Leal wiggled his eyebrows at her and slid a pointed look at

Maelcom. She, of course, could not help grinning happily back. So much for playing it cool. Maelcom glared when he caught them both grinning at each other.

"Don't frown, Maelcom. It's bad for your digestion. Leal, would you like seconds?" She put her hand lightly on Leal's shoulder. Leal gave that killer-hot, male-model smile again which was like a straight shot of vodka, unless one was already hooked on dark and surly. But she appreciated it. Maelcom growled something in a weird language; it sounded like some old Viking dialect to Nessa's ear.

Suddenly, Leal's expression became very serious and he gave a little bow. "Thank you, Nessa," he said, and handed her his bowl. "I will go watch some movies. Your father has all of *Star Wars* on DVD."

They were her movies. She nodded vigorously. "Start with *A New Hope, Part IV*. Okay?"

He nodded and disappeared toward the living room. There were dishes to be cleaned. She'd filled the sink with warm water when she felt Maelcom come up behind her. She pretended she didn't hear him until she felt the press and heat of his body behind her. He gently kissed the side of her neck as he wrapped his enormous arms around her. She could feel his erection against her bottom.

"Psst. I must clean up. I'm a neat and tidy person." She wiggled against him.

He groaned. "You're a torment."

"What did you say to Leal?"

"I told him to leave the room."

She turned her face up at him, her hair tickling her face from the breeze coming in the window. Everything seemed light and pure. Any sorrows in her heart were muted, like he was something warm chasing the chill away. He looked her straight in the eye and she could feel a click of rightness, like this was how everything should be. "Your eyes make me think of water," she said.

"Yours remind me of chocolate, which makes me hungry. Come here."

She was not going to complain that he was looking at her hungrily so she let him pull her into the bedroom and she kicked the door shut. "What do you want?" she said, teasing him because she knew.

"You naked. Now." His voice sounded rough with desire. He pulled off his shirt and threw it on the floor. "Please?"

"Yes." She pulled her dress up over her head and stood there in her tiny floral underwear with her hands over her breasts. "You need to make love to me." Turning her face up, she kissed his chin, his neck, anywhere she could reach. "Please." *Kiss.* "Please." *Kiss.* She could not get enough of him. She wanted him to fuck her hard. Should she say that? She didn't want to freak him out. Whatever she didn't care. "Fast and hard. Please."

He groaned, turned and grabbed another condom from the night table. His eyes grew heavy. Suddenly he picked her up, lifted and pushed her up against the door. "I'm mad. Completely insane for you." He was like an oven of heat against her. He held her up with one hand, and rolled the condom on with his other hand.

Letting her down slowly, he pushed into her gradually. "Hold on to my shoulders, sweet Nessa. Is this good?"

"Yes. Yes," she panted. She hoped he wouldn't stop. His smell was all musk and soap. He fucked her against the door. Long, hard, door-banging sex. In the distance, she could hear *Star Wars* playing extra loud. Her bottom squeaked against the wood. One big, hot hand of Maelcom's gripped her ass, keeping a rhythm, pushing and pulling. A scream started building deep down so she put her mouth on him, biting him as she came. Then he grunted hard. Slapping flesh, a steady beat, and he came in her, hot and hard, deep inside her.

He leaned his sweaty forehead against hers while he tried to calm his breathing. "Are you okay? Was I too rough?"

"Oh my god, that was perfect, you are a beautiful beast," she slurred as her head fell back and she giggled.

Rumbling a hum of agreement, he carried her to bed. He tucked himself around her, cuddling her. She would not have guessed that. Maelcom liked hugging and cuddling after sex.

They lay together, dazed and getting their breath back, until Maelcom kissed her head. "I'm checking on Leal. Be right back."

She nodded sleepily and curled into the blankets. Some-time later, he climbed back into bed and pulled her close, nuzzling her neck, giving her a sleepy kiss, and they fell asleep in each other's arms.

THE SUNSHINE WOKE HER UP as they hadn't pulled the curtains. Maelcom wasn't there but she heard voices—Maelcom and Leal, talking in the funny dialect—drifting in from the living room. She was going to grab the first shower.

After the shower, she dressed rapidly as she smelled bacon coming from the kitchen.

"You made bacon?" she said as she walked into the kitchen.

Maelcom stood in front of the stove, poking at the bacon with a fork. "I can make a decent breakfast and that is all."

"I love breakfast. That's a great selling point, you know that?"

He looked at her with his almost smile tugging at his mouth. "Yes," he said.

She remembered all the dirty things he had said to her in that rumbly voice of his and she felt herself get hot. Her body had become tuned to him and hummed to his words. "I'm full of excited butterflies being with you. I loved last night, you know, but we're very different. You okay with that?" Her voice trembled slightly. She was asking him if he liked her, but even if it made her feel uncool, she needed to know.

"Nessa, you are perfect." He turned off the stove and put the bacon on a plate. "I like you very much."

They stood there and stared at each other in the silence of the kitchen. The song of morning birds was faint from the outside with the tinny distant sound of Leal watching television. Looking hard at him, she knew Maelcom was telling the truth. "Me too," she said breathlessly, then she coughed. "It's too smoky in here." She opened the kitchen window and the back door to get the smoke out of the house.

Maelcom breathed in deeply and froze.

He leaned forward and whispered in her ear, "Danger. Just relax." He grabbed her and threw her over his shoulder and ran into the living room like a maniac.

She thought she had made her feelings clear about being carried around like a package. It was great that he was strong but it was a little weird. "Hello! Man-handler? Just because you can doesn't mean you should."

"Leal, the assassin is here," Maelcom said completely ignoring her.

"What assassin? The guy chasing Leal? The one who killed Anders? That assassin?" Nessa said over his shoulder. His voice sounded deadly serious. He put her down. Her hair was crazy, all swirling around her head. She pushed it away. "Wait. The guy after Leal? Does he have a name? Just calling him assassin is weird. And you gotta stop with hauling me around and put me down."

Maelcom put her down. "I don't know his name. Leal is his task for now and he is dangerous."

"Leal doesn't know his name? Anyway, we're going to take this guy, right? Are you going to kung fu him or shoot him? Oh, oh." She jumped up and down a little. "You distract him and I can sneak up and hit him on the head. Or Leal can."

Maelcom looked doubtful. "Those are good ideas but he's very strong and I'll not fight well if I know you're at risk. I'll be worried. This is what will happen: I'll go out the front and draw the assassin away from the house, you and Leal need to leave. I don't want you around."

Her mouth dropped open as Maelcom flipped a knife from hand to hand. He was ambidextrous, she realized.

"Leal, can you use a knife?" asked Maelcom.

Leal snatched the knife. "Adequately in hand-to-hand. Perfectly if I can throw it. Need the car keys, too."

"I don't get a knife?" she asked forlornly. Maelcom tossed the keys to Leal, grabbed Nessa and kissed her hard.

"I thought you were a pacifist. No violence?"

"But you said an assassin is coming after us. I mean, yay peace, but I don't want to die." Her heart pounded and her mouth went dry. This was crazy exciting.

He took her hand and kissed it. "You'll not be harmed. Leal and I will die before I let that happen."

"Thanks for offering my life but I will protect Nessa. I promise that. Let's not talk about us dying. Let's kill that assassin," Leal said.

"I need him for intel. I prefer not to kill anymore," Maelcom said.

The way he said it made her shiver, so dark and painful, like he had killed a lot. What must his life have been like when he served? But they were out of time for talking. "Okay. I'll text you where we are."

"Leal, leave twenty-five seconds after I go out the door. He will be fully occupied with me. Take care." Maelcom gave a quick look and ran out the front door.

Leal counted the time out softly under his breath. She considered showing him how to do that on her phone but she didn't feel like talking so she grabbed her purse and put it crossways across her body. "Ready?" she whispered to Leal.

"I drive. Now." Leal flung the door open and sniffed. "Run to the car. They're *close.*"

Nessa ran fast, got in the passenger side, slammed the door, snapped her seat belt and turned to the driver's seat. Leal was already there starting up the engine.

"You are super-fast," she said. Her hands were trembling and she turned to look for Maelcom but saw nothing.

Leal was intent and race-car professional while peeling out of the driveway with gravel spraying out as they took the turn onto the main road.

She was thrown to the side. Her hand gripped the handle on the passenger door as she pulled herself upright. "He's going be okay, right?"

"Maelcom is a legend. The other guy is in trouble," Leal

said as he expertly spun the wheel, down shifted to pick up speed and raced off down the road.

She wrinkled her forehead. "Wow, Speed Racer. You drive like a professional."

He checked in the rearview mirror and slowed the car down to the speed limit. "Driving is fun. It's one of my favorite activities here. My dream is to drive the Alps in a Lamborghini." He smiled at the thought. "I took classes at a race car school." He sighed. "The idea being that I was to be the getaway driver for my boss. I told him I needed to be trained by the best. It was an excuse to spend time away from him. He was terrible and cruel. I'm glad he's dead and I didn't drive him to safety. I'm glad I'm helping you instead."

"I've a million questions right now. You are weird. Your boss was a gangster or some kind of terrorist? Right? Do they often send their assistants to race car school? I mean, I can see it could be useful in a pinch but really—" She blew out a puff of air. "Can you slow down?"

"I'm not driving fast, simply driving aggressively and using the road. There is a difference. My boss didn't know how to drive so he needed me to learn."

"Maybe we go back to check on Maelcom?" Her heart was pounding thinking about Maelcom fighting and being hurt.

Leal smirked and arched an eyebrow. "I don't think there are many who can stand up to him. Least of all when he is in Venskat. It makes one fierce and maybe a little crazy."

"What's Venskat? Is that some kind of a euphemism?"

Leal waved his hand. "Umm…when a man like that finds a woman he likes and becomes obsessed with her. Like Maelcom is with you."

She put her hands on her hot cheeks and a million thoughts raced through her brain. "Are you joking me? You think he's obsessed with me? I'm the one totally obsessed with him. I admit it. Not in a weird way, but a good way? Is there a good obsession? I think there is. He's amazing, he rocks as a lover, he doesn't mind me talking, he listens which is really rare in a man, and he's sweet even though he sometimes looks a little scary. But that's, you know, that's his mask. A girl doesn't get that combination of hot and sweet often. What do you think? He's a keeper, right? I really like him. I love him maybe, although maybe it's early. It's like a mad love." She chewed her fingernail while pondering love.

She was used to talking about her relationship issues with friends and she hoped Leal could provide some guidance. Her history was a mixed bag but she had decided it was her issue, she never really fell in love.

"Nessa, Maelcom is complicated. You should not commit to Venskat until he tells you everything about himself."

"I really don't understand the meaning of that word. It's like love friend or something? Is that like soldier slang or something? I'm not committing except spending more time together. *And* finally, what the hell does he need to tell me that you know and I don't?"

Leal shrugged. "Only he can tell you."

"Is he going to beat up the guy who has been trying to kill you?"

"He might. Maelcom has a reputation for being unforgiving to his enemies."

"What? Oh shit, is that like a sanctioned thing or is he going rogue?"

"Where do you get these ideas?"

"I watch a lot of movies, and I love spy thriller books. So I'm up on the whole vibe of your world. And I like how in spy movies and books they ultimately have to think their way out of the situation. I don't like movies with lots of senseless killing, but I love the whole 'brave agent fighting the baddies for justice and honor.' Personally, I'm a pacifist. Like Gandhi. But I believe in defensive action."

"What? Who?" Leal asked, looking completely confused.

"You're kidding, right?"

"Me? Oh, you said Gandhi. Of course—he believed in defensive action?"

She rolled her eyes. Leal's looks were such that he could almost get away with dumb statements. He had a slippery way of talking, vague and weird like he'd just landed here from outer space. Hot, ripped, rocking alien—as if such a thing existed. He was simply dumb and beautiful.

"Where are we headed?" she asked to change the topic.

"Southeast. Larger and faster roads, more cars and there

are a couple of big towns with more people where we can stop and blend in."

"Great secret agent thinking. Wait, I thought you said Maelcom could take him. Why are you worried?"

Leal took her hand and gave a squeeze. It tingled a bit. "Just cautious. This man hunting me might have a partner."

"Did you tell Maelcom that?"

"No. It's just a guess. You're a good woman for a warrior to love. Brave. Just taking precautions and so is Maelcom. He can take this assassin, no problem."

"Let me look at the map. Oooh, let's go to Norrköping. Turn here!" She pointed to the turn to head for the bridges that linked this part of Sweden together. "It's a busy town."

They drove through Uppsala country and it was beautiful. Nessa pointed out all the scenic points, the historical points and the places she had been. Leal sighed heavily after she told him all the extensive history and detail about the inlets in the area.

She shrugged. "I know I talk too much. My father calls me a chatterbox. When I was a child, I lived with my mother on a religious retreat farm. Children were expected to be seen and not heard. I got beaten with a switch a lot because I talked so much."

Leal looked shocked. "Even my people do not beat children. The war was hard on us. So many lost, so children are a gift. Why did your father allow this?"

"My mother stole me and didn't tell my father where I was. It took him four years to find me."

She couldn't remember her mother's face anymore. Her therapist said that was normal. Once she found a couple of old photos that her father had forgotten to throw out and had studied them carefully to see if she looked like her at all but she didn't. Nessa looked like her paternal grandmother who said Nessa looked like all the women in her family. But next to her father and all the Gustafsons, she was the odd one in a family of hearty giants.

"Nessa, this is why you are so tough. You are like a soldier forged in hard training. This is why you are good with Maelcom. You understand him and you smile. He needs to smile," he said seriously.

"You're a romantic, Leal. I thought we might be too different but you're right, we connect just naturally. We click even though we shouldn't. It's the whole opposites attract thing."

She pinched her lip nervously. Could people just be meant for each other? Like what the French called a *coupe de foudre*, a bolt of lightning with crazy in love thrown in. Yes. Yes. That was how Maelcom made her feel. Just saying his name in her brain made her feel light and happy.

But what did she know about love? She'd had only two serious boyfriends and handful of short lovers but they all had been very blah and sort of boring. Nice guys and nice sex without a lot of emotion. It wasn't that she was sexually uptight, but she'd just expected more from her physical relationships. Or hoped for something more exciting. Olaf teased her, and called her "the slutty virgin." Her girlfriends admired her because she was free of the heartbreaks they were dealing with. They came and wept with their men trouble and she patted them on the back and had no idea what to tell them. Tatiana told her to take more lovers. But now here with Maelcom, he made her physically so happy—everything but cool. This was what she had thought sex would be like. It was more than sex though, it was his kisses, how he listened to her, how he understood her and his gentle, considerate touch.

They passed over the long bridges going south as the water sparkled in the sunlight. Nessa relaxed with Leal. For once, she didn't talk to fill the space.

Leal didn't seem relaxed now though. His lips were thinned and his shoulders hunched. He rolled his window down and stuck his head out into the wind. Was he sniffing the air? "Nessa, what is the town like?"

"Norrköping? Big town. Right now, there's a huge arts and craft fair there. It's a week long. Carving, furniture, clay, fiber craft. People come camp out. A friend of mine will be there showing her art."

Leal pursed his mouth. "You didn't mention the craft fair before."

She snorted. "Shhh, I'll buy you a handmade woolen scarf."

"Thank you?" He sounded doubtful. "We're supposed to stay safe until Maelcom joins us and you want to stop at the Norrköping craft fair so you can buy me a scarf?"

"Come on, there'll be crowds of people there. No one

will notice us. Anyway you said Maelcom will take care of the guy. And you are right, Maelcom is like super Special Forces dude. He eats assassins for breakfast. He's a beast," she said airily with a wave of her hand.

CHAPTER 17

Maelcom

WHEN MAELCOM STEPPED OUTSIDE THE HOUSE, he intended to catch the Ice Daimon and interrogate him. Amnesty would be offered in exchange for information and names. He needed to discover how many other Ice Daimons remained in the Earth Realm and their exact location.

Nessa was away from danger and he simply needed to get this annoying Ice Daimon in custody. He would bring him to the gate and send him to the Daimon Realm where Ephraim, the head of Daimon Intelligence, could deal with him.

Nessa still lingered as a memory on his lips and in his body. The sweetness of her energy made him feel strong and centered.

The breeze hit his nose and he scented the Ice Daimon. The breeze was fickle, changing directions all the time. It made it difficult to stay upwind.

Where was the Daimon? He sniffed. *Ahh, there he is.* Spinning to his left, he ran full sprint. A blur moved from behind the trees. Automatically adjusting to the left, he moved to head off the Ice Daimon.

There was old pastureland around the house, farmland left to go wild. Smooth grass that obstructed visibility. He ran hard and gained on the Ice Daimon. A weak assassin. It was an insult. Really. Daimons usually pissed themselves at the thought of fighting him. This fucking sneaking-around-bullshit assassin ran from him.

He grabbed the top of a fence and easily swung himself over it. Running smoothly across the pasture, he jumped over the farthest fence and headed toward a small stand of woods with young birch trees.

Finally, he caught a glimpse of the Ice Daimon, all in black, holding a sword in his hand while he ran. Carrying a sword would slow him down which would let Maelcom catch him. Maelcom was gaining on him. The Daimon glanced back as he tried to run faster while dodging trees and fallen logs.

Maelcom heard the sound of hard breathing from his quarry. Within an arm's length. He sprang, launching himself in the air, and landed on top of the Ice Daimon. As they fell, the Daimon's sword flew from his hand and landed in the grass to the side.

Maelcom wrapped his hands around his throat and growled at him.

"I yield," the Daimon muttered from underneath him.

"You tell me quickly why you're here," he said harshly. He pulled the Ice Daimon up, shook him hard and pushed him away from his fallen sword.

In order to show dominance, Maelcom shifted to his Daimon form while holding him. He let the transformation slow slightly to exaggerate the shift. He forced the shimmer to blast some extra light in a burst and transformed in a spiral outward from the center of his torso. The air around him appeared distorted from heat or energy as he kept his eye on the Daimon. His horns burst from his head and curved down toward his shoulders, and a tiny crackle of energy sparked from his finger. Sometimes showing off was necessary.

The Daimon held up his hands in surrender but his eyes were flat and blank, his mouth a hard line, which made him look defiant. A young Daimon with a narrow face and large nose.

"My name is Villus. My squad is gone, all dead at the hands of Naberius and you. I was left behind to secure our retreat." He spit the words out angrily.

"Your squad fell in battle. They fought bravely."

"I was to complete the last orders from Lord Rayme," Villus said.

Maelcom said what he said to all recruits in wilderness training. "Be glad to be alive, let that give you hope." He pushed him away and drew his gun.

Villus shifted into his Daimon form, elegant, lean and larger than the average Ice Daimon. His transformation was an awkward slow pop with a tiny shimmer. Not very controlled, but he was young still.

"You use the guns here? So much for warrior tradition," Villus sneered.

Young know-it-alls with attitude always annoyed him. "Fuck tradition. I'll shoot you in the kneecap if you make the wrong move. It'll hurt a lot. Why do you want to kill Leal?"

Villus flinched at the threat. "I was ordered to terminate him if Rayme died. He did all the correspondence for Rayme and had access to important information."

"Are you alone?"

Villus shrugged. "Do you see anyone else?"

That was not a definitive answer. Something bugged Maelcom about this Daimon. He narrowed his eyes at how the Daimon looked away and fidgeted when talking. It was obvious Villus was lying. "You must come with me to the gate," Maelcom said brusquely.

Villus sneered at him. "No. I think not. You will kill me. You're Maelcom, the Smashing Fist of Naberius, Killer of Ice Daimons. You destroy and kill all in your path, you have no mercy, you take no prisoners."

Shit. Villus had been fed the whole myth and scary stories of the Smashing Fist's exploits. Maybe most of them were true but he never killed everyone in his path.

Maelcom shook his head. "Bullshit lies. If asked, I give mercy in battle. And I'm taking you prisoner which proves the lies. Is this the tale Ice Daimons tell of me? I fight hard, and yes, I've killed many in war. I'm a soldier like you. But the war is over and I abide by the peace. Your leader, Rayme, was the one who worked with treasonous Daimons to destroy the peace. He was killed in battle by Naberius's mate when he tried to slit her throat. Rayme is the one without honor."

He didn't mention his work as an assassin behind the lines; that was never discussed. The targets were often political and military leaders. Those missions were best kept secret. They were his burden to carry, and a young soldier would not understand the desperate situations in the darkest days of the war.

"Lies. Lies. You are Maelcom the Fist, vicious and murdering," Villus screamed.

"I swear I will not kill you." He touched his forehead to make the oath, then reached out to touch Villus just lightly. *Shit.* His energy was tainted like a sick person. This Daimon wouldn't be convinced. He needed to incapacitate him—flex handcuffs and maybe a sedative. He had experience in killing Ice Daimons, not in taking them prisoner.

Villus pulled away and started pacing back and forth, talking to himself in a mutter. "No, I do not share my energy with Jotun Daimon. They are killers and destroyers."

Maelcom spread his hands wide. "Listen, I swear I will not harm you. I can bring you home, to the Daimon Realm.

You will be brought back to your people. We do not imprison the Ice Daimons. All Ice Daimons have been granted amnesty through the treaties that ended the war. All live free, only subject to the laws of the land. Do you not miss your family?"

"They are all dead since the early days of the war. I was brought up in an Ice Daimon orphanage and then joined the army as a child."

Shit. How could he convince him? "Is there no one you want to see?"

"Leal. I want to see Leal. He needs to come to me." Villus stuffed his hands in his jacket pockets and stared stubbornly at Maelcom.

Maelcom shook his head. "No. I cannot allow that. You told me you want to kill him."

Villus snarled and pulled out his hands. A Taser and something else in the other hand that he sprayed in Maelcom's face. It stung his eyes. *Fucking pepper spray.* He heard Villus scramble away and a sword hilt crashed down on his temple. Maelcom staggered back and collapsed on his side. Blood ran down his face but he stood up and shouted a battle cry at Villus. Villus aimed the Taser at him.

Shit, this was going to suck. He should have killed him. The Taser hit. It was like all the energy sucked out of him and Maelcom blacked out.

HE AWOKE WITH THE HOT SUN beating down on his face. Pulling himself up, he leaned against a tree. Getting hit on the head should have been minor, but it hurt like hell when combined with a Taser hit. Daimons energy freaked when hit with that device, since it disrupted their energy so much they either passed out or puked. He could heal fast, but he was tougher than most. He gingerly touched his head and felt dried blood. The wound was not serious, but he was as weak as a baby.

He didn't pat Villus down, mistake one. He didn't put restraints on him, mistake two. He didn't assume the Ice Daimon would try to fight back after giving up, mistake three. This whole "trying not to kill Ice Daimons" thing was more complex than he'd anticipated, and prone to danger. Or he was off his game, getting old, thinking about a woman or whatever. In the old days, enemies were killed. Simple, easy, no risk.

He sniffed the air, and under the faint residual smell of pepper spray, he scented the direction of the Ice Daimon but he was long gone. One should never underestimate crazy and this Daimon was touched by some strange madness, with a fanatic gleam in his eye. Maelcom wished he had just killed the Ice Daimon instead of trying to take him prisoner. But he was different now. Enough with the killing. Daimons were going to move forward without war. It was this hope that kept him going. The idea of the Daimon Realm at peace and all Daimons living peacefully together.

In Villus, he recognized that thousand-yard stare which he remembered from war. This soldier was in some sort of intense trauma. The last soldier in a lost battle, trying to find his dignity, his truth, his honor. Which regrettably meant trying to kill Leal. *Damn it.*

He rubbed his head. The clumsy hit with the sword hilt had caught him right at the base of his horn. Taking a deep breath, he transformed back to his human form. He ran back to the house. No scent of Villus there.

He needed two things. A car and Nessa. No doubt Villus was chasing Leal and Nessa and was on their trail.

He texted a high-end concierge service he used here in Sweden. They did everything, quietly, quickly and expensively. He wanted a dark sedan, six cylinders, within an hour.

In the house, he washed the blood off his head in the kitchen sink. He closed the place up, making sure all the windows were shut and the food put away.

Walking through the living room, he picked up a photo of Nessa on the bookshelf. A chubby little toddler with a stick in her hand and a halo of blonde hair. A little avenging angel. Another picture of young teenage Nessa at a swimming pool, thin as a rail but with a shiny, bright smile and her huge brown eyes sparkling, with a medal around her neck. With his phone, he snapped a picture of the photo. That smile made his chest clench a little. From her age, he guessed it must have been soon after her father rescued her. She was a fighter to come out of that experience with her smile intact.

Standing in the driveway, he called Naberius and kept it brief. He quickly told him that he was after an Ice Daimon called Villus who'd attacked him and slipped away. He was experiencing Venskat with Nessa and he needed to tell her who he was.

He could hear Naberius silent on the other end of the phone, and Jessalyn's voice in the background.

"Naberius, I will need to go soon."

"Good luck with your mate and Venskat, Maelcom. Contact me when you've located Villus."

"Yes."

"Maelcom, are you okay? No issues? And I'm not talking about the woman."

Maelcom knew what he meant, that he'd spaced out in one of his unreachable reveries. It was vaguely embarrassing to be forced to reassure your commander that you were capable of the task assigned. "No. I'm good. Except for letting that Ice Daimon get a jump on me. But no, I'm not having problems accomplishing my tasks."

"Good. You're solid?"

"Being tased sucked," Maelcom said frankly.

"So when you said he slipped away, you meant he tased you. You have to always check for Tasers," said Naberius with heartfelt sympathy. Something about Tasers affected Naberius badly. Everyone had their pet peeve, Maelcom hated being cold.

"Yes, I was trying to get him to surrender, and by the

time I realized he wouldn't, it was too late. It sucked, and I passed out. Thanks for asking. My skills are fighting or investigating. Peaceful negotiation with an Ice Daimon? Not a lot of skill in that area."

"Is it Venskat that's scrambling your brain? You let an Ice Daimon get a jump on you. You're lucky he didn't kill you."

"He was crazy, completely insane, so yes, I was lucky. I need to tell Nessa about us, about me." He surprised himself by announcing it to Naberius.

"Make sure you talk to your Nessa about *everything.* Make sure she doesn't have any weapons when you tell her."

That was going to be a problem. "Nessa is a pacifist," Maelcom said as he wondered what she was like when angry. Probably lots more talking.

"You're worried about her reaction to your experiences as a soldier and not the fact you are a Daimon?"

"Perhaps," Maelcom answered. He wasn't sure about anything but his conviction that he loved Nessa and she would run screaming from him when he told her the truth.

"Hmm. Hold on. Jessalyn?" Naberius said.

Maelcom could hear Jessalyn saying something in the background and Naberius chuckled but then he became serious again. "Listen, Anders's death has been ruled an accident officially. There is no more risk regarding that but Ephraim really would like to debrief Leal. And Villus. We can offer them protection if they agree to give us information."

Ephraim was Naberius's twin brother, second in command in the Daimon Realm and head of Daimon Intelligence. "That is what I was trying to do but I think Villus will not be turned. I'll retrieve Leal and bring him to the gate."

"Then capture Villus with force. And what do you mean retrieve Leal? Is he not there with you?"

"I sent Leal and Nessa away when I scented Villus. They are waiting for me nearby." Or at least he hoped they were.

"How do you know Leal will not escape?"

"Because I trust him. Any updates from Gusion? Villus implied by not answering that there might be another Ice Daimon."

"Nothing specific."

Maelcom heard a car engine in the distance. "Got to go, my car is here. I'll text you updates…"

"But when—" he heard Naberius ask as he hung up.

A black SUV pulled up and a young man jumped out. "Mr. Skov-Baern?"

Maelcom nodded and held out his hand for the key. He signed a paper and got into the Mercedes. "You'll be picked up soon?" He did not want to leave this person here.

"I've a taxi coming and he'll bring me to the train," said the driver.

Maelcom gave a brusque nod, got in, and the powerful car hummed as he pulled away. Now to catch up with Leal and Nessa, he'd drive fast.

He dialed Nessa. No answer. He tapped the app which

tracked her phone and location. It was a good thing he had prepared for such a possibility. She would not like the fact that he'd installed an app on her phone and was tracking her. She might see it as intrusive but it was important he be able to find her. On the other hand, as soon as the danger passed, he would delete the app.

Anyway, if she'd answered the phone, he wouldn't have to use nefarious methods—that was his story and he would tell her so. She would scold him with a torrent of words. He would kiss her till she forgave him. Yes, that was a plan. This whole Venskat and falling in love was more complex than he had imagined. She held his heart and he was powerless. He needed to tell her everything; or maybe simply explain what he was and then later, the rest.

CHAPTER 18

Nessa

THE CRAFT FAIR WAS SET UP in a small park on the outskirts of the city, overlooking the fjord. Brightly colored flags and banners flew and a band played popular tunes. Nessa dragged Leal to find a friend's booth of ceramic work.

"Elena!"

"Nessa."

They hugged and kissed. She introduced Leal as a friend and Elena nodded hello. "I was just driving by and decided to stop because I remembered you said you were going to be here. Your stuff looks amazing."

"You told me that you were going to the music festival," Elena said.

"Things changed. I had to leave and head back to

Stockholm," Nessa explained.

Elena's booth had displays of beautiful ceramic bowls and ceramic sculptures. A couple came in to browse and the woman exclaimed over how lovely the bowls were. Elena whispered to her, "Got to go. Need to make a sale."

Nessa and Leal wandered off and toured the entire festival. Nessa bought a scarf in red wool for Leal and he happily wore it casually thrown around his neck, occasionally stroking it with his hand. "I didn't realize it would be so soft."

"It's merino—the wool is imported from New Zealand. Elena taught me how to knit but I'm not as good as her. That scarf is really lovely. Oh, let's go eat," Nessa said and pointed at the food trucks.

They walked over to where trucks were parked and bought sandwiches, but there was nowhere to sit. Nessa remembered there was a park by the lake and suggested they drive there.

"Leal turn here, it's a quiet spot to eat our lunch and then we can call Maelcom again."

Leal turned down the street which ended at the lake. They sat on the grass by the water, eating their sandwiches. Nessa pulled out her phone but the battery was dead. She would charge it in the car.

Leal brushed his hands of crumbs and said, "I'll be right back."

She looked at the restroom building near where they parked. "Oh. Me next." She leaned back in the sun and waited for Leal to return. The thing she loved about the countryside was the silence.

"Nessa."

She jumped and held her chest. "Leal, do not sneak up on me."

Leal widened his eyes and put his finger to his mouth. "Sorry. Hey, how about we hit the road?" He passed her the car key with little nod.

Something was happening. He acted nervous but pretended to be casual. Leal casually scratched his chest and jerked his head toward the car but held her eyes. Someone dangerous was here, ruining lunch and trying to kill Leal. So there were two guys? Or did this one escape from Maelcom? She wrapped her sandwich and tucked it in her purse. Great, another sprint to the car. She nodded at Leal to tell him she was ready. He counted on his fingers, *one, two* and—

She ran to the car. A sprint across the grass. She didn't know why she believed him but she could feel the tension in Leal.

She heard Leal take off running, and looking over her shoulder she saw a person chasing him. He ran in a broad circle like rabbit escaping a predator. She crawled into the driver's seat and started the car. She spun the wheel to drive to Leal so they could escape. Driving slowly, she estimated where Leal would be the closest and aimed for that spot. She squinted her eyes as she saw the man following him was holding a sword. A fucking sword. Well, screw that. She wasn't going fast but it would be enough to stop a man with a sword.

Thump! The body flew back. Putting the car in park, she jumped out to check on the man, but Leal popped up in front of her and grabbed her by the waist, preventing her from going to him. "Wait, I've got to make sure I didn't kill him," she wailed.

"I checked. He's fine." He picked her up and tossed her in the back seat of the car. Jumping behind the wheel, he gunned the engine, backed out and raced out of the parking lot.

"Hey, that was rude." Nessa sat up and looked back. She saw the guy with the sword standing up. "He's okay! He is standing up. I was worried I killed him."

"Shit. You should have hit him harder," Leal grumbled and spun the car around and raced onto the main road while Nessa looked behind them.

"Nobody's following yet. Did you know him?"

He ignored her question and simply tightened his beautiful mouth into a hard line. "Get up front and put on your seat belt."

She slid herself into the front seat and snapped her belt on. "Yeah. No kidding, Speed Racer. And what was that—you threw me into the car? Just cause I don't weight that much." She pushed her hair back from her face and straightened her clothes.

"Had to keep you safe. Maelcom would kill me if you were harmed. And I like being alive."

"Maelcom wouldn't kill you really. He's very sweet. A

growly teddy bear."

Leal looked at her disbelievingly. "Maelcom was known as the fiercest of all soldiers. He might not kill me but he would hurt me if I let anything happen to you." He sped up.

She frowned to herself. Maybe she didn't really know him, or maybe she was blinded by lust. The whole soldier thing was something from his past and she had colored it with a patriotic brush, with the idea of duty and nobility.

Leal sighed and said, "We need to get far away. I noticed him when I went to the toilet. He went to hide near some trees to watch you. While he was busy, I disabled his vehicle then I let him chase me."

"Let him chase you?" she exclaimed disbelievingly. "He was about to catch you if I hadn't hit him with the car."

"I had it. I was going to jump in the car before you decided to hit him with it."

"Well, it helped that the car slowed him down." The other guy had been about to grab Leal when she hit him. She shivered hard, remembering the thump of the body on the bumper.

"Thank you," Leal said huffily. "Where do you think we should go now?"

"Lemme see." She squinted at the map. "This town is not so far away. Go straight then left at the fork."

"What are we going to do, sit around a park? That was not a good idea, Nessa."

"No, of course not. I agree we need to stay off the streets. There is a bar I know of and we can wait there till

Maelcom joins us. It's called Thirsty Bar but it's more like the living room of a good friend, if your friend owned a bar." She wrinkled her nose, trying to explain.

"I'm unsure. A bar?"

"You love your scarf. You thought the craft fair would be terrible."

"We just ran for our lives, Nessa, so the fair *was* terrible despite the beautiful scarf. I have higher hopes for Thirsty Bar."

"I'll text Maelcom." She tapped her phone. "Shit. I forget I let the battery die. Let me plug it in. Okay but still, how the hell did that guy find us? I mean, I know we were sitting outside but it's like he knew where we were."

Leal grimaced. "Shit. We need to pull over. I think we may have a tracking device on the car."

"Shoot. But if we pull it off now, won't they figure out where we are going?"

"Yes. That's why I am pulling over there and putting it on another car." He pointed to small café with a full car lot.

After they were parked on the far edge of the lot, Leal opened the hood on the engine and then crawled under the car. "Let me help," Nessa said. "What does it look like?"

"Like it doesn't belong. New or shiny, round or square."

Nessa pulled out a blanket and laid it down at the rear of the car since Leal was at the front. She shimmied her head and shoulder under the car to examine the underside with her little flashlight. Nothing. "Nothing here," she called out. She reached out to grab the rear bumper so she could pull herself out from under the car and her fingers felt something round and smooth. She plucked it and it came off, a small black round disc.

"Hello there. *I found it*, Leal. I just put my hand on the bumper and there it was." She frowned, looking at it. "It doesn't look like anything. No writing or anything."

Leal pulled himself out from under the front of the car. "Excellent. Go put it on another bumper."

Nessa scanned the cars in the parking lot. She didn't want to draw danger to an innocent stranger. She walked to a local bakery delivery truck parked by the side of the building. It looked like they were inside making a delivery. Her heart slammed inside her chest. She hoped someone didn't see her, so she pretended to tie her boot shoelace while she put the tracker on the inside of the bumper of the truck. Running back to the car, she squealed, "Let's go!"

It was late afternoon by the time they got to town and they pulled up to a building with a big yellow sign declaring it to be "The Thirsty Bar." So quaint and cozy looking. And people were pouring into the place.

She clapped her hands together. "It's karaoke night. I'm so happy right now." Her cell phone was now charged, so she tried to call Maelcom but there was no answer and no voice mail, so she texted him her number. "Let's go in for a quick drink."

CHAPTER 19

Maelcom

HE CLENCHED HIS TEETH and muttered curses while driving well over the speed limit to the location of Nessa's cell phone. If he was stopped by the police, he would give them his Danish Intelligence ID. He was calling in a lot of favors lately. She should answer her damn phone.

His phone pinged. It said missed call but it never rang. He had a weak cell connection. Nessa texted their location as being the Thirsty Bar and said they were in the bar having a drink. She put little kissy symbols on the message.

Heading south over the long, flat bridges connecting the islands, he estimated it would take another hour.

Nessa. They were supposed to remain under the radar and she picks a bar. He didn't want Leal in a bar. Ice

Daimons loved to drink and a drunk Ice Daimon was a crazy beast but she didn't know that.

He drove slowly through the town until he was close to the bar. Parking on the main street, he stood in a doorway to examine the street carefully to ensure no Ice Daimons were watching. He entered the bar and walked into a wall of sound. He scented her immediately, and right after her, he scented Leal.

Suddenly, a familiar husky voice floated out over the loudspeakers. Singing. It was her voice, his Nessa. He moved through the crowd until he could see her on a small stage decorated with colored streamers, standing straight and bold and singing her heart out into a microphone.

She was singing something about a heartbreaker and a dream maker, and not messing around. Nessa swung her hips at the end like a punctuation to the words she sang, wearing a very tight tank top. He could see her goddamn nipples. So could all the people—who seemed to be mostly men—clapping and roaring their approval of her singing and, most likely, her nipples.

The audience roared when she finished and he pushed his way to the front. She saw him and waved like crazy, her face flushed pink and her hair a wild mess framing her face. "I'm going to win the karaoke contest!" And she bounced into his arms.

He sighed and clutched her tightly. She kicked her legs in happiness. Drunk happy. "We need to talk," he said seriously.

Giggles and kissy noises erupted from her. Clearly, he needed to wait until she sobered up. He saw Leal chatting with a man and pinned him with a stare. Leal grinned and raised his glass to him. *Asshole.*

She patted him on the chest. "Okay. Just pick up my beer. I left it onstage or somewhere."

He ignored her and stalked out the back door of the bar and put her down. She started trembling and went pale. He was an idiot. She had been grabbed and drugged by that asshole sexual predator.

"Shit. I'm sorry. Nessa, are you okay?" he said in a soft voice. "I just wanted to talk to you somewhere quiet."

She stood, wavering slightly. "What? No. No. It's not that. I had too much to drink." She held up a finger and her face turned so pale it made his heart clench. "Need to puke."

And she folded over onto her knees and vomited with terrible little moans between several heaves. He bent down to hold her hair out of her face. The vomit pooled around his shoes.

She looked at him over her shoulder with glazed eyes and wiped her mouth with her sleeve. "Umm. I shouldn't have had that last shot. But I was worried about you. And when I worry, I drink. It's your fault. Why didn't you call?"

He opened his mouth then snapped it shut. Her logic confused him. "I did."

She sighed as she took her phone from her pocket and studied it. "Shit. I ran the battery dead and it only charged a little bit by the time I got here. It's dead again. I'm sorry, we were chased and I hit a baddie with the car and I got freaked out."

"Who chased you?" he demanded.

"One of the guys chasing Leal. He had a tracker on the car but after I hit him and we escaped I put it on another car," she announced happily.

He shut his eyes briefly, just imagining what had happened, and decided to hug her instead. Wrapping his arms around her, he gave her some energy. He kissed her head. "I'm glad you are safe. I need to talk to you. To tell you everything."

"I need to brush my teeth," she said miserably. "Later we'll talk. S'all good. Don't be worried, Maelcom."

He kept hold of her while they went inside to get Leal. A glass of ginger ale was obtained from a friendly waitress. Nessa sipped it cautiously and the color returned to her face.

Nessa received her ribbon and the prize was a yellow T-shirt with *Thirsty Bar* spelled out in big red letters. Everyone clapped as the bar owner presented her with the prize. She waved like a queen. The men slapped him on the shoulder and said what a lovely girl she was. Maelcom frowned at them and the crowd quickly dispersed.

Leal snickered drunkenly at him under his breath and blew a kiss at him. "Venskat it is. She's your mate." Maelcom glared at him till he shut up.

The virtual concierge service that Maelcom used directed him to the nearest appropriate hotel in the town. It was a secure facility. He tucked Nessa in his car and she closed her eyes. "Why did you let her drink?" he snarled at Leal as he got in the car.

Leal gave him a sloppy drunk smile. "What? I couldn't stop her. She is a force of nature. It's hard to argue with her and I was busy drinking because she offered to buy. Besides, I love bars in the Earth Realm. Oh my god, I didn't tell you, the assassin found us in another town. I found a tracker on the car after we escaped. Actually, Nessa found it and we put on a local bakery truck."

"She told me. We'll leave that car. It's compromised. Go get the black bags. I will bring my car around and pick you up."

"I'm too drunk," Leal complained.

"It will help burn the alcohol off. Get a move on," Maelcom barked.

"No shouting. You military types are always yelling. All right, it's right down the street." Leal set off down the street.

Maelcom followed him and pulled up to the car. Leal threw in various bags of Nessa's and the large black carryall that belonged to Maelcom, which Leal held up with a raised arm. "What's in here? It's heavy."

"My sword, various weapons, explosives and body armor," Maelcom said honestly. He packed everything carefully in high-tech flexible foam so it wouldn't clank or get damaged. The bags were very heavy but Leal handled them with ease.

Leal rolled his eyes. "Soldiers," he muttered.

They drove to a hotel that was safe and very exclusive

on the outskirts of city center. They were met by the manager who bowed slightly to Maelcom. "Two rooms, sir. A standard and a suite."

Leal cleared his throat. "Make it two suites."

"Next door to each other," Maelcom said. The manager went to get another key and directed them to the elevator.

They all went up to the top floor. Maelcom kept his hand on Nessa's elbow, monitoring her energy. She was very drunk and her energy tasted sour. Their suite was the first door and Leal's was further down. Leal walked past to the next door down. "Night, Leal! You rock!" Nessa slurred. Leal waved and disappeared inside.

Maelcom leaned Nessa against their door. "One second, Nessa." She nodded and grinned. He reached into his bag for a small sensor and walked to Leal's door and stuck in on the handle. If the door handle moved, he would get a text message.

He returned to see Nessa's eyes fluttering closed. Shaking his head, he wrapped one arm around her, opened the door with his other hand and guided Nessa gently into their room.

She stood in the middle of the richly decorated living room, wavering back and forth while looking around. "Oh. It's beautiful. Do you always stay in luxury hotels?"

He thought for a second then nodded. "Yes. Expensive hotels are secure and discreet."

"Another weird and loaded statement. But I need to take a shower. I smell," she said forlornly.

"Let me help," he said gently.

She staggered to one side, trying to get her boot off. "Okay, my balance is off. You're so sweet to me, Maelcom. Your nickname is now Sweetie."

He shook his head. People feared him mostly. His friends gave him shit about his introverted behavior. But sweet? "No nicknames. Let me help you shower."

He pulled her into a spacious bathroom and set her on a bench. She flopped over and wrestled with the laces on her big black boots.

"Stop, Nessa. Let me help." He sat down on the floor and picked up her leg, put her foot on his thigh and quickly unlaced the boot.

"Sorry to make you worry. Hey, how'd you find me?"

"Leal texted me." He untied the second boot. The app he installed on her phone to track her would be deleted later.

He helped her stand up and held on to her while she shimmied in an unbalanced manner out of her little dress. "I got it. I'm good," she muttered, pushed off him and walked into the shower. Underthings were flung out of the shower. Lacy underwear landed on his boot. Leaning against the wall, he watched his mate in awe, this woman, this beautiful creature. His. She giggled and gave him a soapy wave when she noticed him watching her openly. Brazenly.

He watched her wash her hair and rinse it carefully. Long wet strands were plastered against her back. The steam from the hot water started to build and she was hidden from clear view. The water noise was soothing and the bathroom started to warm up. Steam fogged the mirrors and he breathed in the humid air. She put something else on her hair and rubbed more. He sat down on the small bench and leaned back to wait for his drunk lady to finish her shower. The white noise of the water and the heat made him sleepy, made his eyes close for just a second.

He awoke to a pair of lips kissing his forehead, and Nessa's delicate hand rested on his shoulder.

"You drifted off. You must be tired, my Maelcom."

It was good to be called hers. He looked up at her glowing face, which had been scrubbed clean of all her mascara and eyeliner. She wore a white hotel robe and her wet hair was beginning to dry in long curls.

"I didn't get a lot of sleep last night and I might have a concussion," he said. "What about you?"

"Are you kidding?" She petted his head until he winced. "You have a lump there." She peered at his head. "I think it's a little bloody."

"I was in a fight. I lost to the man who was after Leal."

"You want to tell me about it? I feel much better. Totally recovered. I think it's because I don't have a lot of body fat. There is nothing to hold the booze. Anyway, I puked it all up."

He watched at her reflection in the mirror, looked right in her eyes. "I tell you later about my fight. Now I am so happy to have found you. In all ways."

"I think the same thing about you," she said seriously

227

with a tiny blush pinking her nose and cheeks.

It was now he must tell her. He rubbed his face to wake himself up. "I have to explain something about me and I don't know how to say it."

She sat on the bench next to him and leaned against him. Her fingers gently stroked his forearm, making his skin tingle with her touch. Her sweet energy flowed into him. "Take your time. It's okay, Maelcom."

Maelcom stared at the floor. She would think he was nuts. He exhaled all his nerves in a noisy breath. "I'm a Daimon. We share a common ancestry with humans but we are a different species." He looked up at her. "I should have told you before."

Her mouth had opened slightly and she frowned. "What? A what? From where? Hold on. What the hell are you saying? Are you messing with me? Are you feeling okay? Are you drunk?"

"I'm not messing with you. I'm a Daimon, we are part-human and the place I come from is a hidden place, like another dimension. I came to Earth to support my Lord Naberius, who is in exile here. I did serve in the Special Forces in Denmark and I do contract work for the European intelligence community."

"Wait a second. Daimons. That was what Anders was babbling about. He was right? My crazy roommate was right. Oh my god. Are the Russians involved?" She kept her hand on him, he noticed, like she needed to touch him.

"Anders was only correct in that Daimons exist. Everything else was wrong and the Russians are definitely not involved. Anders made up most of what he knew and he was not supposed to send his made-up theories as a report to allied intelligence groups."

She moved away from him and pulled at her lip in her little nervous gesture. "Prove it," she whispered in a low rasp.

"I will but you must promise me that you won't scream. *Please*," he begged. She nodded at him. He took a deep breath and stood up. "I have two forms. I am this, but also this."

He closed his eyes to focus on a clean and elegant shift to his Daimon form. He wanted to show her the best of what he was. The warmth of his transition rippled up from his core, and he held his energy in check to make the change as smooth as possible, like a brush sweeping over his physical presence in a spiral outward from his center. He muted the brightness and softened the effects of distortion. The only tricky part was his horns. It took extra focus for them to smoothly appear as they curved down toward his shoulders, angled in slightly. His horns were ideal warrior horns, they didn't interfere with his movement and protected his neck.

The idea that she would look at him in horror haunted him and he braced himself for the worst.

"Oh my fucking god," Nessa breathed out with wonder in her voice. Not fear. Wonder.

He opened his eyes. She was grinning. Holding one

finger up, she poked him once in the chest like he might evaporate, then laughed some more. She covered her mouth and shouted a muffled, "Shit!"

Her eyes were huge and dilated. She took a deep breath in and then started talking. "Amazing. Mind-blowing. *Excellent.* You just swayed and rippled. You actually shimmered into a transformed spiral outward. Almost freaking fractal. Wild. I mean, the air around you actually distorted. And your horns sort of extruded down to your shoulders. And your skin, it's like burnished copper and feels strange. You're a little bigger, if that is possible, and your hands are crazy huge. Why didn't you show me sooner? How many people know about this? Am I the only one? How many of your kind are here?"

"Very few humans know of our existence and there are only a handful of Daimons here in the Earth Realm. I wanted to show you the other night but I lacked the courage."

She bounced up and down on the balls of her feet looking thrilled. "Your horns are beautiful. They're so smooth. Do you polish them? Can I touch them? Do you ever poke yourself with them? I mean, when fighting. Is this your fighting shape or your always shape? Where do you come from again? And you're really part of European Intelligence? And do they know? Were you born in this shape or in the human shape? How many Daimons are here?" She slapped her hand over her mouth. "Sorry, the shock is making my brain spin and I have a million questions."

"That's a lot of questions." He would answer them all for her, slowly.

She sighed heavily. "You are a beautiful man as a human, but you blow me away as a Daimon. I've never seen anything so beautiful and fierce. Stand up and turn around. Please?"

He frowned and stood up. She made a circling gesture with her finger for him to spin around. He obliged. She hummed a happy noise. Standing, she walked over and put her arms around him and hugged him hard. "Thank you for telling me," she whispered against his chest. "I'm honored."

She was impossible. She should be shaking in fear, screaming, running, but his mate hugged him. It made him feel uncomfortable and strange.

She kept on chatting. "I always knew there were other planes of existence that we didn't know about. I think that's what a lot of mystics have been talking about. This is really mind-blowing." She buried her nose in his chest and squeezed again. "Are you okay?"

"You don't find me horrible or frightening?" he asked.

"Frighteningly hot and sexy," she said. "Stunning and wonderful. Oh my god, Maelcom, you're the most intense, amazing being," she whispered. Her eyes were big and dark with desire.

Maelcom was dizzy with relief. "In this form?"

"Hell, *yes*. Can you have sex in your Daimon form? At all? With a girl like me? Are all the parts the same? No unusual differences? Shape, color, size?" Her brown eyes sparkled while she bounced up and down on the balls of her feet.

He rubbed his face. "Yes, I can have sex as a Daimon. No unusual differences except the horns, my hands, my skin. I am slightly larger all round."

She ran her fingers down his neck and his chest. "Umm, okay. You skin is different when I touch you in your Daimon form. Like it's harder and tougher than my skin. It feels like fine leather but it looks like aged copper. Your hands are twice the size, so you need to watch that manhandling action. I think your musculature changed some, like you are pumped up from lifting weights."

"I don't really know how my skin feels to another. And here on earth I always stay in my human form with women." He looked down, embarrassed to be talking about other women with her.

"How about in your own world?"

"I think Daimon women were frightened of my reputation. We didn't have many intimate discussions regarding my anatomy or the texture of my skin," he said dryly.

"I hate them if they were mean to you and I hate them because they were with you. You trust me to show me, don't you? Does this mean we are official? Like boyfriend and girlfriend?" She looked all starry eyed and amazed.

"I transform into my Daimon form and you want to know if you're my girlfriend? Yes, Nessa. You are that and more."

She lifted her face up. "Please kiss me."

He bent his head and kissed her with all his love. She put two of her fingers on his horns, making him shiver.

One little corner of her mouth ticked up. "Can you please take your clothes off?"

She could command him anything, but he went slow to torment her. One button at a time as he held her gaze. First, the shirt. Then removed his shoes, pushed down his pants.

"My clothes are specially made to accommodate a shift." He flexed his hands.

"I bet gloves are a problem. Your hands are as big as shovels. Do you work out a lot? And do you have to work out in both shapes to get muscles or does it translate? I hate the gym but I would totally go if I can watch you work out." She tossed her hair and stared at him like he was cake.

He considered that idea happily. "You can watch me work out in my human form. I teach occasionally at a military training facility in Greenland. I need to personally set a high standard of physical preparation," he said.

"Very high. Wait a second, Leal is a Daimon also?"

"Yes, a different type of Daimon."

"And he can shift forms?"

"Yes."

"Wow." She stood up on her toes, ran her hands over his shoulders and kissed him on his neck softly. Then his ear. His jaw and finally, his lips.

"Nessa," he breathed her name against her lips. She smiled a wicked smile, dropped to her knees and proceeded to destroy any ability of his to think. His cock was already hard. Her lips on him were wet and hot and he could feel her sweet energy. Her touch became his very breath.

"Nessa," he said in a warning voice. She looked up at him with her shining smile. He jerked his head toward the bedroom and lifted her to her feet.

Shrugging her robe off, she pulled the towel from her head. "Follow me, you crazy wonderful Daimon man." She sashayed into the bedroom. He obeyed and trailed after her.

She lay on the bed, smiling a naughty smile. "So, only two forms? This, and handsome, hunky Mongolian-Swede—just those two?"

"Yes, only two. Why aren't you scared?" he said confused.

"I know you, Maelcom," she said dismissively. "You're a good man. I've kissed you, slept with you, swam with you and talked with you. You saved me from a true-life monster. Why would I be frightened? Your Daimon body is beautiful and so is your human shape, but it's the you inside of your form that amazes me. Maybe I think differently than other people, maybe I'm the freak but I don't think so. Do other humans know about Daimons? Do they all get scared? Have they freaked out on you? And if they did, that's terrible." She looked angry at some non-existent person.

"No, we live in secret here in the Earth Realm. A handful of humans know of our existence."

"Can we stop talking? Can you rub those horns on my body? Can you kiss me?" Her lids were heavy and her mouth open in desire.

He complied with her request. Here he was, the Smashing Fist of the Daimon Armies and all he wanted to do was kiss this beautiful woman all night. The gods had given him, an unbeliever in their powers, a little shining flower for a mate. He knew one thing: do what she asked and worry about the rest in the morning.

CHAPTER 20

Nessa

MAELCOM STOOD BEFORE HER, that blue gaze pinned on her like a laser. The hard lines on his face were softened by his almost smile which made him look mischievous in his Daimon form. He stared at her like he adored her or something which was mortifying and embarrassing and wonderful all at once. She was a weird, skinny, pale artist who talked a lot. He was a wonder, rare and special, glowing copper-colored, with sweeping, elegant horns. It didn't shock her. For some reason, her one thought was "of course." When he kissed her, she could feel the Maelcom she knew: silent, strong and sweet.

Men usually found so many faults in her: too energetic, too opinionated, too little, too intellectual, too skinny, too loud, too talkative. Always too talkative. But he simply tilted his head and listened carefully.

Her beautiful Maelcom was a miracle. She wiggled her bottom against the mattress, happy to be lying naked in front of him like a pagan sacrifice to an ancient god.

Maelcom lifted her foot and kissed it. Then onward and upward. Her calf, her knee, which tickled, her thigh. She threw her head back. "Hmmm. Yes. Yes."

He skirted the area between her legs. *Damn you.* But he kissed her breasts. Oh yes, that was it. Taking one of her nipples in his mouth, he sucked it till she moaned. Her brain dissolved into fuzzy and happy. Each touch left a tingle on her skin until they all added up to pure pleasure.

Looking down, his copper coloring showed bright against her pale white skin. He found the constellation of beauty marks on her belly and traced lines between them. His touch was electric.

"Hey, do you have some electrical discharge or something? It tickles like a low-grade electrical current."

His eyebrows went up. "Umm. Yes?"

He looked nervous. Like he was afraid she wanted details on the specifications. *Not.* Waving her hand, she said, "Forget it. Tell me later. You haven't kissed this breast." She rubbed her lonely nipple, which stood up hard at attention.

The tiniest curve upward of his mouth. An almost smile. Like the holy fucking grail when hanging out with Maelcom. She could wipe that smile off his face. Cupping her breasts with her hands, she pushed them up, making them appear bigger, posing like a sexy model and she bit her lip. His mouth opened in a silent *oh*.

He knelt over and did as she asked and kissed her breasts. Holding the back of his head, she pulled him closer. So huge, he surrounded her. The sky was Maelcom. Then he turned his head and rubbed his horn against her breast, her belly.

She froze. His horns were black and smooth. She'd assumed they would be cold to the touch but they were warm. Like semi-precious stones held in a hand, they absorbed his heat. Suddenly, he let the point rest on her belly, then pulled it down, gently, like a giant fingernail drawing a line down her body.

He picked his head up. His pale blue eyes glowed in his face, framed by his dark hair and horns. "Now I make you happy, my lady."

His tongue flicked out and licked her lightly one way and lightly the other. She shivered. Cupping her bottom and lifting her in his enormous hands, he held her up for better access, open to him.

"This way?" He licked her clit. "Or this way?" He licked in the other direction.

"Yes, both. Try again." Why did he ask questions like that? She grabbed his shoulders. It was like putting her hands on the back of a horse, with the power and strength tangible under her hands. *My beautiful beast.*

He stopped licking and sucked her clit. That sort of stopped her brain—she went liquid as he lapped at her. His tongue was amazing. He hummed and it rumbled into her, the vibration spread up deep inside her. She experienced her pleasure in paint colors like her brain was a palette with cadmium orange, red and yellow, hot colors swirling inside her. A million colors, like a great wave building in her. She shouted. "Maelcom, Maelcom, don't stop. Yes. Yes."

He didn't stop and she exploded, all she could do was feel everything. She was shivering, twisting and arching while he watched her.

"Beautiful," he said.

She lay boneless on the bed, just enough energy to drool slightly onto the sheet. He pulled her up to him and she kissed him hard, feeling all her energy flooding back to her. Her kisses tried to say all the things she felt because there were no words.

She rasped out a command. "Come up here. I wanna be on top."

He crawled up on the bed and flipped over on his back. All that beautiful copper skin, hard stomach and defined muscles.

She thought *Lord of lords, creator of the universe.* A phrase from a prayer they'd had to say at morning services on the farm. It'd always seemed dumb but not now. It was a miracle. He was a miracle.

She crept up over him, mimicking his kisses to her. He groaned in a happy way. His eyes flicked open with that crazy blue, freezing her, then his eyelids closed as she gave little kisses up his hard, flat abdomen, all that beautiful definition rippling under her fingertips. She headed up and stopped at his nipples. They were round and flat, a deep mahogany color with the nipple rising slightly thick and full from the center of the disk. More kisses and sucking.

He groaned and pushed her to the side as he reached for something. He ripped the package with his teeth and rolled a condom on. Then he pulled her back on top of him.

She lifted herself up and gently slipped him inside her. His skin was hot like he had been lying in the sun. She rocked on top of him so she could push him in deeper. More. She wanted more.

"Hold on. Hold on. Let me." Her eyes weren't working but she couldn't stop rocking herself on him. She felt a pressure deep inside her and she stopped to get her breath.

He froze. "Are you okay? I don't want to hurt you."

"I'm just getting used to you." She wiggled a bit on top of him. "Now move. Oh god, yes please move."

He put his huge hands under her bottom, lifted her slightly up and down. They were rough hands, hands that did hard work and hands that controlled of her body. His breathing came hard and fast. She bit her lip. This was freaking perfect and he felt perfect inside her.

He fucked her like that for a while. Somehow he scooted them to the side of the bed and picked her up. He leaned her up against the wall and whispered in her ear, "Do you want hard or do you want it soft?"

"Fuck me hard," she growled at him. She could barely form the words. All she knew was she wanted more and she wanted it now.

He was a man who took orders well. He held her hands above her head, her legs wrapped around his hips, and he slammed into her hard. It shouldn't feel that good but every nerve ending in her body buzzed in ecstasy until she was whimpering.

"Now, my Nessa, I'm going to love you softly." He pulled in and out of her gently.

Each time he pulled away she said, "Come back. Please." She said it over and over. She burned and dripped sweat. Reaching out, she reached high up onto his curved horns and tucked her elbows near the tips. They were smooth and warm in her hands. She balanced herself by holding on to them.

He stopped breathing and obeyed her. Faster. Harder. Then he shouted her name.

She could feel the heat gather in his cock until he exploded inside her, pushing her over the edge. She came so hard she could barely breathe, like she was going to black out. Releasing his horns, she wrapped her arms around his neck and shivered in the aftershocks of her orgasm.

He pressed kisses on her neck while muttering small endearments. Tilting her head up, she sought his lips. She kissed him long and sweet. A perfect kiss.

CHAPTER 21

Maelcom

THEY LAY TANGLED in each other's limbs with the sheet partially covering them. He was stunned, blown away by the intensity of being with her.

His past experiences with women were pathetic, he realized. In the Earth Realm, he would let himself fall into casual relations with women, wrap his cock in a high-quality condom and fuck long and hard for twenty-four hours. No kissing, no amazement.

Shit. Condom. He pulled it off and saw it had a rip down the side.

"Nessa, the condom ripped. It must have been my fault. Are you on birth control? I'm sorry." He rubbed his face and tried to think. All Daimons here wore condoms for protection against disease and against pregnancy. Daimons making babies with humans was the stuff of old and ancient poems but like soldiers, they thought better safe than new Daimon babies on Earth.

She put her hand on her cheek and widened her eyes in shock. "Oh crap. Have you knocked me up with little Daimon babies? Those kids better come out without horns or I'm getting a cesarean." She covered her mouth with a snort.

A rushing noise filled his head. He didn't understand her. What should he say?

"Oh my god. Your face. Where is my phone?" Nessa said. She tried to shove him with her little hand. "Ow. You're like a brick wall."

Her energy stopped the noise and he frowned. "No pictures ever of me in my Daimon form."

She gave a small smile. "Just joking. I'm on birth control pills. Just because I haven't been dating anyone doesn't mean I'm not prepared. I think the problem with sex in your Daimon form is that you rip condoms when you put it on, you've no experience. You actually could use a manicure, just saying." She kissed his shoulder and snuggled up. "Can Daimons even make babies with humans?"

"Yes, I think so because it has occurred in the past but not recently. It's why I look Mongolian and Naberius looks Swedish. It's hard for me to think clearly around you, but when I was with other women, I was in my human form." He rubbed his face, exasperated. "My immune system is strong so I'm not susceptible to most human diseases, but babies…"

She rolled on her side and kissed his ear. "No STDs. That rocks for the Daimon world. Lots of sex and lots of babies."

He shrugged. "We have condoms made from sheep gut. We don't have lots of babies, some say because the wars were so terrible and woman grieved too much. But our science is behind yours."

"If we had a baby, would it be Daimon or human?"

"Daimon, I believe, but it hasn't happened in a thousand years."

She sighed. "I thought I could feel something funny but my horny brain wouldn't let me stop. Thank god for birth control."

"We would make wonderful Daimon babies," he said seriously.

"Slow down. I'm not ready to be a mother," she said firmly.

"No, not yet."

"Is this baby talk because of Venskat? Leal told me about it."

"Nessa, what I feel for you is definitely Venskat. It's a term we use for a feeling that occurs when we meet a possible mate, a partner for life. I think you are my mate."

She leaned her cheek on the side of his chest so her long lashes brushed his skin. "You saying you love me?" she whispered but he felt her energy burst into action.

"Yes," he said with complete honesty.

Blushing, she blinked those huge brown eyes and stared with such intensity at him. "I don't really understand Venskat. This feels pretty intense. It doesn't feel like flirting. Maybe this is just what comes before love." She traced the muscles on his abdomen with her finger. "My recommendation is we hang out together, have lots of sex, as much as possible, till we figure this out. I like you but I don't know about love either. I've never been madly in love. Not really. But I've never felt like this. It might be love." She frowned.

He wanted to kiss her hard. "If you decided to mate with me, you would change."

"The word mate is a little freaky. How about partner?"

He thought about that. Mate probably sounded archaic to her. "Partner is good, better in fact."

She grinned and rolled her eyes at him. "If you stay with me and bind with me, you would become a hybrid Daimon," Maelcom said.

"What's binding? And would I physically be a Daimon?"

"The binding is a ceremony. It is in all ways a marriage. A handfasting. A promise to each other."

"And the hybrid thing?" she asked, wrinkling her brow.

"A hybrid Daimon is a physical change which occurs sometime after the binding. At the cellular level. We don't know much. Only one woman has become a hybrid since before we kept accurate records." He wanted her to understand before she committed.

"No, she turned into a Daimon?" She sat up in bed. "Really? What does that even mean? Like, crackle and snap like you? Cool skin and horns?"

"No horns. A hybrid doesn't take two forms. Jessalyn wondered the same. The change effect is not visible to the naked eye."

"This woman, Jessalyn, you know her?"

"She's the mate of my commander, Naberius. We didn't know because it has been so long, we thought maybe the records from that time were exaggerated. We thought the stories or fantasies were imagined, not real."

"So she was human and then she changed? How exactly?"

"Her energy became Daimon, changed on a cellular level, and aspects of her physicality are Daimon. Strength and more."

"So why'd Daimons stop marrying humans?"

"During a period of great violence against Daimons on earth, Daimons withdrew to their realm. We call it the Killings. Many thousands of Daimons and their families were killed. It changed Daimon society."

"It was like a holocaust?"

"Less organized. The church believed Daimons were evil so there were flare-ups against us wherever the church had a lot of power. And Daimons were too complacent. Entire families and villages were killed. The rest fled back to the Daimon Realm."

"Horrible." She shook her head. "So you don't know

much about hybrids?"

"When Jessalyn changed, we didn't know anything. We have an old poem which describes the change but in vague terms."

"I don't know much about marriage. My parents obviously were a huge disaster because my mother was crazy. My father never remarried but has had a partner for eight years. She is wonderful and she is legally my father's partner but they are not married. They met when I went to university. She was teaching art and he came to visit. It's a beautiful love story. They are like two halves of one, so in sync."

"They sound like mates. For Daimons, two must pledge themselves to each other and that's it."

"So, tell me what happened when Jessalyn became a hybrid. Did it hurt? What does she think of it?"

"It was scary. She became sick and feverish for many days before she changed."

"Should I talk to her? Get the lowdown? I don't know— maybe I hope I'm strong enough? I don't know if it requires physical strength or stamina. It would be good to talk to someone with firsthand experience. I mean, I know you know her but she might have a different opinion of what she went through."

He rubbed her shoulder hearing the anxiety in her voice, in her torrent of words. An irrational burst of happiness exploded in him making his chest hurt as he heard her wish to be strong enough as a sign of her desire for him. It made him want to shout *yes* and make love to her again but he needed to play it cool.

"We don't know if the reaction was just her or if it'll occur in every human. As a hybrid Daimon, she became stronger, healed faster, has an improved sense of smell and gained the ability for the energy give-and-take."

"So a Daimon woman and a human man? How about same-sex?"

He shrugged. "I don't think the process of Venskat is gender-specific. That would be interesting. Daimons are less rigid about genders. Anyway, we are accumulating information to have a more modern understanding of mating with humans but we have just started." He rubbed her arm as he spoke, absently, while he pondered all the things they needed to learn.

She grimaced. "The word *mates* is a little old fashioned. So that tickle thing you did just now. You did that while we were making love. Why does that happen when you touch me? It's a Daimon thing?"

"Yes. I take a little of your energy and give you some of mine. Like a Daimon handshake. Sometimes when Daimons are upset, they become low on energy, and getting some energy from friends is calming and restorative."

"Wow. Can you, like, drain someone dry of energy?" She bared her teeth at him and hissed before breaking into a laugh.

"No. Think of it more like a handshake, but just a sip of energy, like aloha. Right? Both hello and goodbye."

The human vampire myth was weird and reminded him of Daimon stories of the Draugr, the walking dead. Daimons took special precautions with burying the dead to prevent them from returning. The Draugr were not hot and sexy.

She giggled. A light, sweet sound. A warm sense of contentment swept over him. It was like being drunk. Here in this soft bed with a beautiful naked woman, in his Daimon form, dizzy with contentment, he tasted happiness.

"You give me a lot of energy. I feel tickles and sparkles when you touch me. You know when you connect to someone, I don't know, it's like their touch becomes electric. You're pretty wonderful. Deal with it."

"I will deal with it. Now, I'm going to transform back to my human form for sleeping."

She wiggled. "This is very exciting. Which form do you prefer?"

"Here in the Earth Realm, I prefer my human form. It is a personal preference, but often simply practical, like wearing a coat if it's cold."

"Do I have to back up or something? Is it dangerous?" she joked.

"No, stay in my arms." He looked her straight in her eyes with his whole focus centered on her brown irises. Everything shimmered, from his navel outward. Her face became cloudy for a second as he shifted back to his human form.

He could feel her shaking. She was crying, terrified of

him. He was a complete idiot. "Nessa. Please. I'm sorry. I won't do it again. Stop crying."

She lifted her face up, laughing so hard she had tears in her eyes while she made little snorting sounds. She shook with laughter. "That was ultra amazing. Oh my god. Oh my god. I couldn't see clearly, it's like everything goes fuzzy and floats away. Like in a dream when one thing fades into another. That was coolest thing ever. My beautiful Daimon."

The happiness exploded in his chest and he smiled at her, big and wide.

She put her hand on the side of his face with an expression of wonder. "I love you, too."

For a woman who spoke in a torrent of words, sometimes it appeared she didn't need any words from him. He could tell her with a smile.

CHAPTER 22

Nessa

IN THE MORNING, she woke up warm and happy. She stretched like a cat and Maelcom kissed her softly and told her to get ready. He would check on Leal.

She took a quick shower and then slipped on a stretch jersey dress with horizontal stripes, tied her boots and pulled her black jacket over it all.

Maelcom sauntered back into the hotel room and kissed her neck while she brushed her hair. Their eyes met in the mirror and they both exhaled. "Let's go," Nessa said. "Don't look at me like that or we will never leave."

Maelcom shrugged. "I wish. Leal is waiting downstairs in the lobby."

Leal was sipping a latte and reading a newspaper in an

enormous leather armchair. He was talking to a young waitress who blushed furiously as she took his order.

Nessa whispered to Maelcom, "So he how does he look in his Daimon form?"

Maelcom stopped walking and pulled her into a small alcove. "Nessa, we do not say our name in public. Leal is slightly different." He leaned down and whispered in her ear. "He's an Ice Daimon."

"What do you mean?"

He rubbed his chin, thinking. "Like Neanderthals to Homo Sapiens."

"You know, I read most humans have Neanderthal genes in them which is really kind of cool. I want to do a gene test and find out if I have Neanderthal in me. Like I imagine so many beautiful romances occurred across species." She blushed, realizing that they were the same. "Like us?"

"There has been conflict going back thousands of years but it became worse when we withdrew into our realm. Life became focused on the warrior's way."

"But you fought them?"

His face became serious. Before she really knew him, she thought his expression was a fierce face but she could see the subtle nuances of his expression now. She could see the sadness in the tightness in his mouth, the way his eyes didn't meet hers.

"Yes. Too long. We were foolish to think we could accomplish anything with wars. We've moved forward and changed," he said. "We are becoming better. Changing our ways."

As they walked across the lobby, Leal waved at them with a knowing grin. Nessa thought Leal was just goofy enough to temper his handsomeness because otherwise such a man would have made her nervous. Maelcom wasn't magazine pretty—he was a little rough and unusual looking, he was mesmerizing in a truly beautiful way. Beauty was something one could stare at for a long time, and Nessa could stare at Maelcom for hours.

Leal's eyes moved back and forth between their faces while he smiled. "I have to say, you stay in far better accommodations than Rayme used to select. The bed was a cloud. How did you and Maelcom find your bed, Nessa?" he added with a smirk.

Jerk. Nessa stuck her nose in the air. "Don't be rude, Leal. Nobody appreciates your juvenile snickers." She wasn't going to be slut-shamed by some punk traitor turned informer. Maelcom growled beside her. Big points for being a supportive friend.

Leal flinched and bowed slightly. "I apologize, Nessa. I hope you slept well."

She smirked. Bowing to her. *Hah*—pretty Daimon and his snarky remarks. "I know about…well, everything, Ice Boy."

Leal looked visibly startled and turned to Maelcom. "It is? She is?"

Maelcom proudly nodded. "It is, but we need to leave.

Nessa needs to return home and I need to bring you to the gate."

She looked back and forth between the two men. They were weird. "Wait, what are we doing?" Nessa asked.

"You're going back to Stockholm."

"What? Are you nuts? I'm so coming with you. I'm on my official holiday from my job for two weeks. You don't want me to come with you?"

He trailed his index finger down her arm—she shivered at the tingle. "Nessa, I must take him to my home." He lifted an eyebrow.

Oh, he's going to the Daimon Realm. Maelcom had never made her feel annoyed until right then. "You don't want me to come? After everything, you're going home and I can't come to meet your friends, your family, your people? You've met my friends. I want to see your home. Learn more about everything."

She folded her arms over her chest and stared at him, no smile. Right in the eyes, wouldn't let him look away. They had just spent an intense night together. Talked about love and being together. He'd called her his mate and then didn't want to take her to the Daimon Realm with him?

Maelcom shuffled his feet and scratched his jaw. "Oh," he said, furrowing his brow. She hoped those wheels spinning in that handsome head of his would produce the right answer. "If it means so much to you, you can come. I would miss you greatly if you didn't come." He looked at his boots.

In a flash, she saw his nerves and could feel a prickle about him that was the Maelcom version of nervous. *Duh*— she was such a self-centered girl. He was stressed about them, about her, whether she might freak out about the idea of them. "You shouldn't worry about me, if you think I'm going to freak out or something. I really want and need to go with you to see the Da—"

"*Nessa*," Maelcom hissed while looking around.

The lobby had started to fill up with little groups of travelers. A hum of chatter filled the place. Leal put on an ugly cap with the Swedish flag on it, some kind of tourist disguise. A group of women ready for a hike walked by and murmured good mornings. Maelcom straightened up and gave them a little bow. This made the ladies giggle and they bustled away with little glances over their shoulders. Leal had slumped down in a chair and held a newspaper in front of his face but managed a slight eye roll. He was a snarky Daimon.

"Let me get another coffee before we go. I'll meet you by the entrance," Leal said as he wandered off.

It was clear that being with Maelcom would require her talking less. It was going to be hard but she could do it. But she didn't like strange woman giving her man the eye so she threw her arms around Maelcom and kissed him hard. Under her hand, she felt a rumble in his chest and then kissed her back. His kisses were words and they told her wonderful things.

Maelcom pulled away with a smile in his eyes and whispered in her ear. "This is a safe hotel. Run by humans who pledge their loyalty to my family of Skov-Baern, but the guests are just regular people. I will tell you later about the great exterminations. You will understand why we are careful. We do not say the word out loud in public. Sometimes we say whales instead."

Looking up at him, she thought his blue gaze was like the sea on a summer day. "Whales? Seriously."

"Whales are innocuous," he said and lifted an eyebrow as if this was obvious.

He was funny. She snorted a laugh. "I'm going to need more details about the ins and outs of the correct language."

He looked at her like he wanted to kiss her. All hot and intense. "I will give you all the details, my Nessa." He held on to her hand tightly, making it tingle with his energy.

Leal followed them closely, clutching his coffee and smiling at Nessa when Maelcom looked away. A huge black BMW SUV waited for them and a doorman gave him the keys. He bowed to Maelcom. "Lord Skov-Baern," he murmured.

Nessa rolled her eyes. She didn't care that he was from a noble house—she was not impressed by titles. It was interesting, another facet to the complexity of Maelcom. These little moments of discovery would happen a lot. He shrugged sheepishly at her which she took to mean that he agreed with her. She was happy they could communicate so well already.

They drove slowly through the town and picked up

speed on the main road.

She sat in the front passenger seat, and Leal sat in the back. Maelcom asked her if she wanted to drive, but frankly, his vehicle choice intimidated her. He always had huge cars. It would be like driving a truck. The only car she had ever owned was a beat-up twenty-five-year-old Volvo which couldn't go very fast.

Anyway, Maelcom liked to drive. He relaxed at the wheel of a car. He even slumped in a casual way while he maintained a safe and steady speed. Very reliable and safe.

"So where are we headed?" Nessa asked.

"To Slätbaken Fjord."

"It's pretty there." She and her father would go camping around there. They would bring their watercolors and paint landscapes. Those were happy memories. "When my father found me after searching for me for years and took me home with him, I had trouble adjusting. I was a little weird—well, weirder than I am now. I didn't know how to act or talk to anyone. Didn't talk much at all, which is the crazy part, right? Me, Nessa the chatterbox."

Maelcom raised his eyebrow.

She smiled softly. "I know, inconceivable! Me not talking? But they wouldn't feed me when I talked too much at the farm. It was my punishment. I think the elders believed I was too worldly or something. I swear I can't remember what they hated about me so much. I was too hungry to listen to them. When my father took me to his home, I became overwhelmed. They were feeding me such wonderful food, I worried I wouldn't be allowed to eat so I stopped talking. I mean totally silent."

"Oh, Nessa," Leal said from the back seat. Maelcom simply tightened his hands on the wheel but she could sense his pain at her story.

She snapped a look at him but Leal's expression was serious and concerned. "My dad took me camping for like two weeks. We ate simple camp food, sausages cooked on sticks, or even fish we caught. No doctors or psychologists or concerned family friends. Just my dad and me. Fishing, reading, and drawing. It relaxed me and I started talking. My father loves to tease me about my talking but it makes him happy, I know. He struggled with guilt because my mother stole me away and was an abusive parent. This area holds good memories for me. About spending time in nature, getting to know my dad, learning to talk."

Leal leaned forward and patted her on the head. "You must have Små folk heritage. These are wood sprites but they disappeared from our worlds. You could have small folk genes somewhere far back in your heritage. I read stories where they go to the woods to recover from sickness because they have a link with the trees."

Maelcom frowned. "You Ice Daimons and your fairy tales. Små folk died off ages ago."

"Små folk? Wood sprites? I don't know. I have heard of water sprites but never wood sprites," Nessa said.

"Exactly what a wood sprite would say. Tricky, you are," Leal said.

"You're joking, right? I'm not a wood sprite or related to any Små folk. I'm not short, just average."

He waved his hand at her dismissively. "And I'm not icy and neither is Maelcom a giant. Things are never and have never been as neatly divided as the Jotun Daimons would like. You Jotun Daimons chose to forget after the killings that it was some of your own earth families who led the slaughter. Nessa, we were once a seamless world, all related, inter-marrying. During the killings, we retreated to our realm but some hid through magic. My mother said the wood sprites hid through their magic and they still exist."

Maelcom shook his head. "He's telling you tales. He's exaggerating and mixing things up."

She shushed him. "I can see that but I want to hear the story. Who knows, maybe I have Små folk DNA in me? That would be cool."

"According to our historians, all the Små folk people were killed in a town where they had taken refuge. A group of men who were hunting Daimons and folk like them barred the gates and burnt the entire place down," Leal said.

"Oh my god, that's horrible."

"It's not possible she has Små folk genes. That would be thirty-five generations ago."

"Who says they are all gone? Maybe they sneak back occasionally. Sure, most might have died in the flames of tears at Langstrom but who magicked away or hid else-where. Daimons have no magick and tend to disbelieve any magick possibilities."

"Quit telling foolish stories," Maelcom snapped.

Leal smirked and turned to Nessa. "I could tell you some foolish stories about Maelcom, the Right Hand of Naberius, the Mad General. His Fist. Maelcom led the way for Lord General Naberius Vasteras—your axe swinging its wicked way through ranks of young Daimon soldiers."

"At least I served my lord loyally," Maelcom said in a low and angry voice. There was pain in his tone. Nessa could feel it.

Leal fell silent and stared out the window.

Nessa gave Maelcom's arm a squeeze. "Maelcom, making a snarky loyalty comment is not helpful. He surrendered to you and is going to help you with information about Ice Daimons. You said Daimons were changing and peace was important to that future."

Maelcom pinched his nose and took a deep breath. "Leal, I was doing my job and serving my lord as you did. There were no other options. Although I never worked for a murderous bastard like Rayme—"

Nessa coughed loudly.

"I mean, that was then. We need to move forward. I'm sorry for all the lives I took in battle. I wish we never had to fight. I no longer swing my axe and live the warrior way. That's the truth."

Leal pursed his lips as he considered the apology. "Truth. It was lucky that I am clever enough to stay alive while working for such a man."

"What did you do?" Nessa asked.

"I insisted on a quiet room to do all the writing and reading of correspondence, and stayed out of his direct vision. Once I had privacy, I could do whatever I wanted so long as I was productive. If he didn't see you, he couldn't order you to be killed. Of course, initially he threatened my family who live in the main port, to get me to work for him. I had no choice. I couldn't say no."

Nessa turned in her seat. "I understand that. When I lived on the farm, I tried to stay invisible to survive. Sometimes I would see things but I couldn't say anything or it would be my fate, too. I was lucky because even when I was visible, I was so skinny I could hide in little places," she said.

Leal nodded brusquely but his handsome mouth was a severe, flat line. "Nessa, are any of those people still alive? I could kill them for you."

Nessa shook her head and pointed to Maelcom. "He already offered. I'm not interested in revenge. Bad karma."

Leal nodded. "I wanted to escape from working for Rayme. I made copies of correspondence, possibly for my escape or if Rayme tried to kill me. When he died, I thought I was finally free. But apparently his orders transcend death. His faithful still do his bidding. I needed something to bargain with Naberius's Fist and the Mad Dog, if they caught me. If somehow I had no options."

"Fist? Mad Dog?" Nessa said.

Maelcom looked a little embarrassed. "I'm the Fist. Gusion was the Mad Dog. He served with me. Now he's retired and runs a bar."

"As one does after a career as what? A berserker?" Nessa spoke jokingly.

Maelcom nodded. "Exactly." Nessa's jaw dropped.

Leal shivered. "I never want to meet him. My father used to tell me tales of him in battle to frighten me. The stories still haunt my thoughts. Gusion is a true berserker."

"He is like a brother to me. He saved my life, and those of many of the men in my squad, so speak carefully." Maelcom's voice was hard and clipped.

Leal held his hand up and nodded.

Nessa had not heard Maelcom speak with such intensity before. It was best to change the subject before Leal and Maelcom argued. "Can you tell me some details on where we are going and how we will get to the Realm?"

"We go to the gate location and we will travel to the Daimon Realm Gatehouse that protects the gate in the Daimon Realm. Ephraim Vasteras, head of Daimon Intelligence will meet us and he will want to talk to you. We must stay at the Gatehouse as the Realm is closed officially except for Intelligence."

"Where is the information you stole from your boss, or is it all in your head?" Nessa asked Leal.

"Some of both. I bought a computer here in the Earth Realm, and a phone, and told Rayme I was improving his ability to communicate. He was not able to understand how the technology worked. Rayme had ordered all paper records burnt before he launched the attack and my computers smashed. I have all the information on a USB stick and the backup is in a secure location in the cloud." He pulled out a USB stick that hung around his neck. "It's waterproof and holds a hundred and twenty-five gigs." He held it out with a proud smile.

"Give it to me now," Maelcom demanded.

Leal slipped it over his head and passed it to Maelcom. "I was going to give it to you but we have been busy," he said petulantly.

Nessa was impressed. "You're clever. I can barely back up my computer and I have been using computers for years. You don't have computers in the Daimon Realm? Why not?"

"Our isolation is our protection. We've stolen some technology, mostly medical knowledge, but it is strictly controlled. Our technology is what you would consider Victorian but our roads are medieval. I'm not sure if I want to go back. I will miss computers and Earth music," Leal said mournfully. "Can't I come back and work for you?"

Maelcom was silent but then nodded. "I will ask," Maelcom said. "It might be possible. I need someone with your knowledge about Ice Daimons here in the Earth Realm."

Nessa tapped Maelcom's arm. "Psst, I don't have my passport with me. I don't need it, do I?"

"We don't need passports the way we travel. You simply need approval from Daimon Intelligence. I have the authority to give it to you. The gates are closed to all but intelligence operatives."

"Ooo. I'm an operative? So cool. Can I have a code name?"

"You don't need a code name," Maelcom grumbled.

She totally needed a code name. "Plastic Stardust? Artemis? Feral Puppy?" she suggested to get the ball rolling.

Leal started laughing, almost a giggle.

She turned to frown at him. "For a hot guy, you have a girlish giggle."

He stopped immediately and glared at her. "I do not giggle like a girl."

It was fun to mess with him because she owed him for those the snarky comments in the hotel lobby. Maelcom interrupted them before Nessa could argue. "You can be code-named Buttercup," he said to Nessa with an icy blue glance from under his lashes.

"You know *Princess Bride?*" Buttercup was the best code name ever. She was joking about the need for code names. Then he gave her the sweetest code name a guy could ever give a girl? It was like getting flowers.

"And I have a girlish giggle but he can watch *Princess Bride* and no jokes from you," Leal grumbled.

"My friend Gusion likes to go to conventions where they all dress up as favorite movie and comic book characters. He has gotten a bunch of the men into cosplay. *Princess Bride* is a favorite with cosplay people and Gusion loves it. He made me watch it many times. I believe Nessa looks like Princess Buttercup." He nodded at her with a sort of definitive, you-can't-argue-with-me attitude.

She gave him a goofy smile. He might as well have said, "as you wish" which as everyone knows really means "I love you."

"You both can call me Princess Buttercup or just, Buttercup. And Leal, your code name is Inigo Montoya," Nessa said with a snicker.

"You have killed my father, prepare to die," Leal muttered. "That is what Inigo says as he fights to bring honor to the memory of his father."

"Ha. I knew it! You have watched it."

"The mountain cabin I stayed in had an extensive DVD collection," Leal said.

"Inigo is a master swordsman," Maelcom noted. "But Dread Pirate Roberts can beat him."

Nessa laughed. "That could be your code name, Maelcom."

His face completely serious, he shot her a quick glance. "As you wish."

Nessa clapped her hands in delight. "You get extra kisses today."

Leal leaned forward. "We *are* having fun, aren't we?"

Maelcom shoved him back away with his elbow. "We could if I had my gun," he added with a smirk.

"Only if you use it to stun," Leal shot back.

"*Stop*," she demanded. Two men taking the roles of Inigo and Fezzik was more than she could handle. Maelcom's face relaxed, the almost smile lurking at the corners of his mouth.

"We are here," Maelcom announced. He turned down a dirt road and they bumped along it until they came to a small cabin.

Nessa shivered at the dilapidated place. Plastic sheeting covered a broken window. "This is the gate?"

"No," Leal said. "It's on the island."

Maelcom parked the car. "Come, there is a boat in that house there."

They walked down a grassy path to the shore to the waters of Mälaren, an enormous lake with thousands of islands and bays. Nessa saw a low boathouse built out over the water. The walls were painted the same color as the bushes and trees so you could barely see it was there. She followed Maelcom inside and he pulled off a cloth over a boat hanging above the water and then pushed a red button to lower it. With a loud squeal and a clack of pulley wheels, the motorboat slowly lowered into the water.

Maelcom held out his hand to Nessa while she stepped into the boat.

Leal tossed Maelcom their duffel bags and jumped in. Out of her bag she pulled sunglasses and a pink beret with a huge flower on the side. Maelcom stared at her adjusting her hat. "What? Just so my hair doesn't blow in my eyes."

He muttered, "Pink." She blew him a kiss.

They motored slowly out of the boathouse until they were well away from the shore before Maelcom opened up the throttle. They were flying over the water. Nessa sat on a small bench next to Maelcom. The water sparkled in the sunlight, bright and shiny.

She peered ahead and saw several small forested islands. "Which one are we going to?"

He pointed to the farthest one.

They arrived at the island but it had a steep and rocky shore without any dock. "How do we get to the shore?"

"I'll pull up close. Leal will hop out first and take the bags. Then I will get out and carry you so you don't get wet. There is a shallow underwater jetty a foot under the surface right near the shore. It's around fifteen meters long."

"He doesn't have to carry me. My legs can get wet. You Daimon sure like to carry ladies around. Do Daimon ladies like that?"

"No, I think not. They would probably punch me," Maelcom said.

Leal suddenly froze and sniffed the air, then frowned. "Maelcom, you scent anything?"

Maelcom breathed in deeply and then gave little snorts as he scented the air. He'd never told her about the ability to scent. They had been busy in bed, and discussing Daimons' ability to scent had slipped her mind. They weren't secret agent skills. They were Daimon skills.

"Nothing. I'm not scenting anything unusual. Ice Daimons?" Maelcom asked.

Leal shook his head. "Maybe. I apologize. I thought I caught a scent but—No, you're right. There is nothing there now. I'm just feeling jumpy."

"Stay alert. There should be no one on this island. It's

marked as off-limits military property," Maelcom commanded. "Nessa, take your shoes off and put them in the bag. They all sat down, untied their shoes and stuffed them in a backpack.

Maelcom carefully pulled the boat up close to the island while looking overboard. She peered over and saw the flat concrete pier under the water. Leal hopped overboard and the water came to his knees. Maelcom passed him all the bags and they watched him carefully walk the ten feet to the shore and up onto the wooded shoreline. He moved with a grace and coordination that amazed her, considering he had a rucksack on his back and two big bags of Maelcom's, and his messenger bag strapped across his body.

"Yay! Awesome, Leal," she shouted.

"Nessa. He doesn't need encouragement."

"You're wrong, Maelcom. Everyone needs encouragement, Leal in particular. He is a sensitive soul who was trapped working for what sounds like a real asshole. He has scars, emotional. We, as his friends, should always try to keep his spirits up. I mean, people are trying to kill him. That must be extremely hard and emotionally trying."

Maelcom frowned. "I don't think so. People have tried to kill me and I don't need my spirits to be kept up."

"Maelcom, that's so sad. And yes, you need encouragement. Yay, you!" She gave him a peck on the cheek.

He gave her a little of his almost smile. His life as a soldier had been harder and more violent than she had initially imagined. She shivered thinking about what it took to casually state that people had often tried to kill him.

Maelcom slipped overboard onto the jetty and tied the boat off to metal cleats that were under the surface of the water. Secret docks for top-secret islands.

"You ready?" he asked and held out his hand.

She quickly rolled up her pants, swung her legs over and reached for his hand. The underwater jetty was slippery and the water came up to her knees. She moved ahead carefully but a thin film of algae had grown on the concrete making it slippery. Maelcom was right behind her. The water was icy cold, as this fjord was connected to the sea. All she wanted was to get to the shore. She tried to move a little faster but she slipped on the rocks and fell, submerged completely under the water. She surfaced on the side of the jetty, gasping from the cold.

Maelcom grabbed her arm and pulled her up. He picked her up in his arms. "This is safer."

"Ugh. It was very slippery." She shivered in the cold breeze as he moved slowly and carefully toward land.

Leal stood waiting with a blanket in his hands.

"You're freezing." Maelcom wrapped the blanket around her. He stripped his wet T-shirt off and picked her up again.

"I think you're hauling me around again."

"You're wet and cold."

"You say the sweetest things."

He was already walking fast toward the trees. "I know I promised not to haul you around."

"I'm teasing." She laid her cheek on his magnificent chest.

"We need to get out of sight."

She wanted to say something funny. But she just kept thinking about her beautiful, huge man walking through the woods, holding her in his arms. How many times did this happen to a woman? Once in a lifetime, she hoped. A little knot of nerves formed in her stomach.

CHAPTER 23

Maelcom

MAELCOM SET NESSA ON HER FEET, carefully tucking the blanket around her. She had grown quiet while he walked or she might be tired from that quick swim. It made him worried that she had no words. Something about him had silenced her. He stripped his wet shirt off and threw it to the ground.

Leal dumped the bags beside him. "How was the water, Nessa?" He waggled his eyebrows while checking Maelcom out.

"Icy. I don't know how you carried all those bags without slipping. And stop checking out my boyfriend's chest," Nessa said quietly. Leal held up his hands and turned away.

Maelcom looked at her. No one had ever called him a

boyfriend before and it made him absurdly proud to be a boyfriend, but he covered up his reaction by dressing quickly. Nessa remained quiet, wrapped in her blanket. Like a glowing candle in the dark green forest. "Nessa. Are you okay? Tell me. I'm the quiet one, not you."

She looked at him, her huge brown eyes watery. A tear rolled down her cheek and he wanted to howl and rage.

"I didn't know being in love would be so scary, so crazy. I mean, beyond you being a Daimon and the whole other dimensional realm thing which is awesome. Very cool."

"What's wrong? I'm sorry. But talk to me. You say we should talk."

"What I'm saying is that I love you. I had to tell you," she said hoarsely.

"I know. You told me." The moment she started chattering he knew what she felt. She didn't have to say the words. Still, a weight came off his shoulders, she was right— he experienced the same tickle of fear as he realized he loved her. He was frightened, terrified like a new soldier on his first tour.

"Nessa, I love you." He wrapped his arms around her and tried to calm her worry with some energy. "You are the beat of my heart. Everything else doesn't matter. We can figure it out."

She tapped her forehead against his chest. "I told you that," she said in her husky voice. He nodded.

They were running out of time. He could feel the hum of the gate in his bones. "You have to dress now. The gate will open soon."

"What should I wear? I mean, I don't want to offend anyone. I don't need to wear special clothing or anything like that? Because I might have a problem with that. Are women equal in Daimon society? You haven't told me any details! Can I shake hands? Oh wait, I have the perfect dress, good for all occasions," she buzzed happily.

He knew he didn't have to answer any of her questions. That was just Nessa. She started pulling clothes from her rucksack. She stripped her wet clothes off and dressed quickly in a long, pink flowing dress with a high waist, leggings and a fleece jacket, and she jammed her feet into her black boots that had specks of paint on them. A very feminine yet wild outfit. Nessa always dressed like that, feminine but somehow practical and very unique.

He must be insane to be having thoughts about how beautiful his woman looked in her outfit. Entirely insane. *Fucking Venskat.* He grabbed a black T-shirt from his bag and slipped it on.

Leal waited by the gate. "It should be a couple more revolutions and then it will open."

"Where's the gate? And what do you mean revolutions?" Nessa asked.

"Look again, Nessa. Look harder." Maelcom laid his hand on her shoulder, turned her slightly and sent a little energy into her.

"Stop that, Maelcom. Oh, wait, I see it. Is that it? It's shimmery on the ground in that cleared area. Is it that roundish area?"

"Yes. That's it."

"Hah. It's horizontal. I thought it would be vertical— you know, like a gate. It doesn't look huge. How do you prevent people from just going through? Falling in. What about animals? And bugs?"

"Each gate is guarded on the other side by a squad of Daimons. But you can only transition when it opens. Animals can pass through when it's open but they avoid it. They sense the disturbance. Anyway, we share the same animals as earth, mostly."

"Cool. How did the Ice Daimons get through?"

"They attacked and captured a gate location but it was taken back. We had a traitor on our side who helped them."

She kept staring at the gate. "When do we go? And if we go too soon, what happens?" She scrunched up her face while thinking about this.

"You just bounce back. It hurts a little." He pulled on his clothes and slipped on his boots, down on a knee to tie the laces.

Standing up, he scanned the area and the hair on the back of his neck prickled. He scented the air. Shit, there it was. "Leal, you were right. The assassin is here."

Leal scented the air and frowned. "Yes. He's here."

"Really? You can really smell him?" Nessa asked. "I thought that a metaphor for something." She frowned. "Wow, everything you talked about just clicked."

"Stay next me, Nessa. And Leal, there are two of them."

It made sense that there were two of them. Guard duty was always set in pairs.

Suddenly, Leal went flying backward. Villus, the assassin, landed on top of Leal with a knife to his throat.

"Traitor," he hissed at Leal.

Maelcom put his hand inside his jacket, figuring that he could shoot Villus and the impact would blow him back. But his main concern was where was the second Daimon? He scented another but this unknown Ice Daimon was watching.

Leal grunted. "No, Maelcom."

Villus screamed, "Stop talking."

Leal sagged back into Villus, resting his head on Villus's shoulder like a lover. "Why you? Because I left you? You hate me that much because I didn't want you? We had fun but we are not mates, not made for each other."

Villus froze. "I was told to track and terminate you. I did not ask for this."

"Then don't do it. Rayme is dead. There is no one left who cares if you carry out your assignment."

Villus yanked Leal up, holding him by his shirt, and spat his words at him. "I have honor. Loyalty to the people I serve. Not like you—cheating, lying, hiding information."

"What are you saying? I tried to stay alive and ensure my family wasn't hurt. I was forced into service for Rayme because he threatened to kill my mother and my little cousins. Our Ice Daimon leaders failed to lead us, to take care of our soldiers, our families. When defeat became inevitable what did they do but waste thousands of lives, reject the peace proposals from the Jotun, and now even after they are dead, you are going to follow because of honor? To kill a man who was your lover, a man you claimed you loved?"

Maelcom froze listening to the sad story of Leal's life. He had never thought about Ice Daimons who were simply trying to survive. He wished none of them had to worry about the lives of their families.

Nessa yanked at the arm that held his pistol. "No, don't shoot," she hissed softly.

Leal turned his face up, all steely-eyed and determined. "Villus, go ahead, then. There is nothing left. My family is all dead, all my little cousins, my mother and father. All gone, lost in the march of retreat. They didn't die under the sword of Jotun, they died from cold and hunger because Ice Daimon leaders thought it better to march and die than surrender."

Villus's mouth dropped open. "All of them?" he croaked.

Leal jerked his chin but a ripple moved across his body, not a transformation but disruption. In pain from his memories, his jaw was clenched so hard that the muscle jumped. Maelcom released his gun. This would not be resolved with him blowing Villus's head off, as tempting as that option appeared.

Nessa sucked a breath of air, her face a mask of devastation. Her eyes full of tears. Maelcom sidestepped closer to her so his arm brushed against her.

Leal stepped out of Villus's hold. "I escaped because the Ice Daimon leadership was not the most enlightened. I left because they were cruel and violent. Because they didn't really care about the Ice Daimons, they only wanted power. I cared about you. I left you to protect you. You wanted everything and I couldn't give you that. Rayme would have killed you if he found out. And now, ironically, you want to kill me."

Villus shook his head in confusion and his form flickered. Maelcom didn't think Villus could be convinced. This Daimon was lost to madness. Dangerous, lost and confused.

Leal transformed into his Daimon form. Elegantly. A smooth, rapid transition oddly centered on his right ear, which Maelcom had never seen before. Ice Daimons usually had very even and similar transitions, some sort of cultural conformity thing which Leal clearly rejected.

Villus uttered a cry and transformed himself. The transformation went weirdly slow and full of distortions, from the top of his chest per custom with Ice Daimons. He thinned from his human form into the Ice Daimons' silver skin and sharp features with straight, swept-back horns.

Nessa gasped and staggered back. A transformation of strange Daimons in battle was different, fiercer and more intimidating than her experience with him. Maelcom stroked her arm to calm her but she didn't respond, she was frozen.

Villus face contorted in anger. "When you left everything changed. Rayme mocked and punished me for missing you. He knew about us. He threatened you. I had to obey him. His final order was to kill you. It made sense but now it doesn't. Nothing makes sense."

Maelcom kept checking on Nessa so his focus was fractured and he didn't scent the attack until he heard Nessa scream. He twisted away and pushed Nessa clear as a sword hissed past him in a huge arc.

His lunge to the side prevented him from being hit. Here was Villus's partner.

The Daimon transformed but he was young, not fully grown. This would be a pathetic fight. Maelcom sighed. He was a warrior at his prime, close to one hundred years old, and here was a green recruit, so weak the Ice Daimons had left him instead of bringing him to battle. It was only fair that Maelcom hadn't unpacked his sword and was in his human form.

He waited till the soldier pulled his sword back to strike. Maelcom raised his fists, pretending to lead with his right, but sucker punched the soldier hard with his left fist. The soldier fell backward and then stumbled upright with blood pouring out of his nose. He shouted a battle cry and raised his sword.

Maelcom pulled his knife out, balanced it then flung it at the Daimon's arm holding the sword. The moment the knife flew from his fingers, he realized the Daimon tripped on a tree root and was in the process of falling. The Ice Daimon gasped and collapsed with Maelcom's knife in his right eye.

Behind him, Nessa's voice gasped. "Oh my god. Oh my god."

Maelcom went forward and knelt by the Ice Daimon. So young, his skin perfect unmarked by the woes of life. He listened for some breath but the young Daimon was dead. At least he'd died in his Daimon form fighting. He would dine in the hall of warriors, or so the poets said.

Maelcom didn't think about his next move because he needed his weapon back. He pulled his knife from the Daimon's eye—it made a pop and a mushy, sucking sound—and wiped it on the sleeve of the fallen Ice Daimon.

Nessa watched him with her mouth open and her eyes dilated. She turned and puked.

Leal held Villus back so he wouldn't lunge forward. His mouth hung open in shock at his fallen comrade's fate. "He was new," Villus said hoarsely. "He was so young."

Leal extended his hand to touch Villus but he screamed something inarticulate and wild. In his pain and madness, he threw himself at Leal with a snarl, lifting his knife to strike. But Leal caught his arm and held the knife away. "No, no, Villus," he begged.

The two of them fell to the ground. Leal struggled to hold the hand with the knife away from his body while trying to pin Villus down. But Villus was a trained soldier and Leal was not. He was a scribe not a soldier. It was not going well as they wrestled on the ground.

Maelcom pulled his gun but there was too much risk of

hitting Leal. He couldn't shoot them as they were rolling around on the ground so he holstered it.

"Do something, Maelcom. Just don't throw a knife or shoot him," Nessa pleaded.

Perhaps some stealth was needed. He went toward them slowly, circling the grunting and thrashing men like one would with dogs fighting. He hovered over them until at the right moment, he grabbed Villus's right hand firmly while quickly twisting in the opposite direction between his hands. The wrist broke with a loud crack.

Villus screamed in pain and Leal shoved Villus off him and scrambled to get away. Maelcom tried to grab Villus but he missed in the confusion. Leal and Villus both jumped to their feet, with Villus cradling his broken hand against his chest.

What a mess. This Ice Daimon needed to calm the fuck down. Maelcom stepped back. "Stop, both of you," he growled harshly.

Nessa froze beside him. He felt her hand on his back, a little tickle of her energy, scared. Villus pulled out another knife with his left hand. He was ambidextrous.

Maelcom snarled, "Villus, concede. Surrender now."

Villus looked lost and looked at Leal sadly. "I loved you," he said. His words rang out in the cool forest.

Birds tweeted and the trees rustled in the wind. He spoke with a sad resignation in his voice, like he was giving up. Like he didn't care anymore. Shit.

Maelcom reached for his gun in his holster but he knew

it was too late. Half a second too late. "No-ooo!" he shouted as he aimed his gun. Villus sliced his own throat open with a flick of his unbroken hand. Maelcom watched the Daimon fall. The idea of another ambidextrous Daimon had never occurred to him. He thought he had disabled Villus.

Maelcom leapt forward and caught Villus. Leal stood, shocked and covered in a spray of blood. Maelcom placed his hand on the wound to see if he could stop the flow but the steady arterial pulse of the blood pushed out between his fingers. *Whoosh. Whoosh.* Villus would bleed out in minutes. Looking up to Leal, he shook his head. The wound was too deep.

Leal fell to his knees beside his ex-lover and pulled his body up on his lap, putting his head on Villus's shoulder, and whispering something in his ear. The two of them on the ground saturated in blood.

Nessa had covered her mouth. Tears poured down her face quietly, her shoulders shaking. Her brown eyes were huge and dilated. She made no noise now.

"Are you okay, Nessa?" Maelcom asked softly. Her gaze darted all over his body with disgust and horror. Glancing down, he realized he was covered in blood from the young Ice Daimon and from Villus.

The brutal breaking of Villus's hand had likely horrified her. He thought a decisive action would stop the violence. He hadn't considered that he wasn't the only ambidextrous Daimon in existence, and assumed he had control of the situation. He had nothing under control. Everything had spiraled into shit. Two dead Daimons and it was his fault.

She stepped away from him and stared at the Ice Daimons lying on the ground, her hand over her mouth as if she could stop her whimpers. The pool of blood was spreading wide. Villus's eyes closed softly. He was gone.

All was quiet. He and Nessa stood next to each other. His knuckles brushed the back of her hand briefly. She jerked back. Her energy had gone dark so he simply held his hand up to tell her to stay. Maelcom went up to the men on the ground in the blood. "Leal. He is dead."

Maelcom stood and transformed in his Daimon form, the world fuzzed as the heat spiraled out from his core, changing everything from human to Daimon. For one second during his change, he was nothing until something snapped inside his energy and then in a breath, his horns were there. He threw his shoulders back, stretched his large hands then cast his gaze down on the dead and pounded his chest three times. He recited the words of a soldier fallen. "Daimon Warriors. Drink with the gods. Rise now."

It was simply tradition. An old prayer. The unlikely hope of drinking with the gods who had left or never existed. So many had died under his sword and fist. No way were they anywhere but dead and rotted in the ground. He didn't believe he was going drinking with those bloodthirsty bastards when he died but he owed it to their memory to pretend he did.

The blood on his face and hands cooled, the wet of it covered him. *So red.* He looked at his huge Daimon hands.

Maelcom could feel himself go into a gray nothing. Barely seeing, he could not move. He was slipping into one of his spaced-out reveries. *Shit.* It was sucking him into the grey. He had a dim awareness of Nessa but he couldn't focus on her. He could see her in his peripheral vision, a pink blob with yellow hair.

He heard her say. "Leal, Leal. You must get up. We'll take them back. Back to his family. Come. Maelcom, Maelcom, I need you to help me."

She put her hand on Leal as if she knew her energy would stabilize him. He wanted to taste it again.

"Maelcom, come on. Now. I need you." Her hand reached out to touch him and her voice floated through his fog, straight to his heart. He concentrated and in a snap, she came into focus. Her little sharp face and the beautiful blonde tendrils that loosened from her braid. A ferocious fairy. The hem of her pretty dress dipped in pools of blood. Her eyes were huge circles of dark and he wanted to kiss her. She needed his help. He had to help her. He snapped awake with a huge inhale of breath and a hum in the air told him the gate would open soon.

"Leal, pick him up. The gate opens soon," Maelcom ordered as he could feel the energy build in the gate. Soon. And the roundish shape on the ground glowed and with a soft sucking of sound and a tiny sonic boom, the gate was open. It was a very small gate.

"Leal, you first," he said.

Leal bent and picked Villus up. He staggered slightly

with the Daimon in his arms but managed to walk forward into the shimmering pool of light.

"We're only allowed to enter the fort and then we must return. The Realm is closed to humans. Soldiers will be waiting for us. Do not be afraid." Maelcom wiped his hand on his pants and held it out to Nessa. Trembling, she took it and walked onto the circle of shimmering light.

Everything went white until they emerged through something bright into the courtyard of the gate fort. A voice called out, "Wait in the gauntlet." He walked forward, tugging Nessa behind him into a narrow hallway without a ceiling. A door closed behind them. Archers peered over the edge. A shield maiden's hair blew in the wind while she looked over the edge, too.

He wrapped an arm around Nessa's shoulders and looked her in the eyes. "You're okay?" She swallowed hard and gave him a barely perceptible nod.

A rumble of voices started above them with everyone talking at once. *It's the Fist. Maelcom. It's Maelcom. Lord Maelcom. He's here.*

All the bows were lowered and a hundred fists pounded on their chests. "Maelcom!" they all roared.

Nessa whispered, "Are you famous?"

"Among Daimon soldiers," he said under his breath while he stood straight to receive his tribute.

Her pupils enlarged and she gave a tiny nod. No smart comeback. No torrent of chatter. He gritted his teeth together. *Shit.*

The gate at the other end of the narrow space opened and they walked into a courtyard with green grass. Two shield maidens bowed to them and then stood guard on Leal. A Daimon medic verified Villus was dead and placed the red cloth over his face. Leal cried, loudly, noisily. Nessa ran to him and comforted him, rubbing his shoulder and making little noises.

"I never loved him. I don't know why I am crying," Leal said in a tight voice between sobs.

"But he was once your friend. I'm sorry, Leal," she said softly.

Leal shuddered and sucked in a tight breath. "I need to sit with him for a while."

Maelcom stepped forward. "Take Leal and the body of Villus to a room where he can sit and grieve." Several Daimon soldiers sprang forward to carry the body away and gestured for Leal to follow. Nessa's face was pale and her mouth tight.

He could feel himself slip back but she held his hand tightly, her nerves apparent, so he settled himself and pulled her close to him.

Someone coughed and they looked up. Maelcom gave a haughty, annoyed stare to the Daimon with the golden eyes and a cool smile—Ephraim Vasteras, Naberius's twin brother and the head of Daimon Intelligence.

"Welcome, Maelcom. You have been successful in locating the last of the Ice Daimons. Thank you."

"This one Leal turned himself in to me. The other two

were hunting him. I wanted to bring them back alive but one was killed when he attacked me and the second took his own life," he said.

Nessa's husky voice piped up beside him. "Hello, I'm Nessa Gustafson. It's a pleasure to meet you."

Maelcom and Ephraim turned to look at her. She stood with her white hair loose around her face, a determined expression and her hand stuck out. Nothing in his life had prepared him for Nessa. He experienced a twinge of anguish that he might be unworthy. That he was this beast, a killer, and the Bloody Fist of the Daimon Armies could have such a woman. He would hold on to her like he was drowning, like she was the only thing that could save him.

CHAPTER 24

Nessa

SHE STUCK HER HAND OUT, even though it was slightly dirty and her fingernails were painted bright blue. The Daimon, Ephraim, stood tall and haughty with sharp gold eyes. He took her hand and shook it firmly. "I am Ephraim Vasteras. Welcome, Nessa Gustafson."

Manners were important when meeting beings from hidden realms. "Thank you so much, Ephraim. I'm sure you can imagine how strange this is for me. I might stare a lot because I'm just learning about Daimons. Forgive me if I am rude." It was all she could do to appear simply amazed because it was like she had slipped through the looking glass.

Ephraim's mouth curled into a small grin. "We understand, my lady. There will be many Daimons staring at you."

"That makes sense. I guess you don't get a lot of tourists or visitors or whatever. We can do a stare-off. Can I ask why are you all in Daimon form and not in your human form?"

"This is a guard post and Daimon soldiers customarily stay in that form. It is good for fighting. Think of it as a uniform for the army, but there are exceptions like medics and support staff who prefer human form. In civilian life, Daimons don't follow many rules but there are norms of behavior which you can learn about."

She frowned. There were subtleties in the Daimon world which were difficult to understand. It was like any culture with different traditions and habits, like when she visited Japan as an exchange student. All the little things were so strange at first and she kept asking why on certain customs. She realized that Maelcom was still in his Daimon form perhaps because it was important business or because they were all soldiers here. *Just go with the flow and make sense of it later.*

All the soldiers were staring at her like she was the one with horns. It was a little uncomfortable with everyone—Daimons—staring at her. Throwing her shoulders back, she stared right back with one eyebrow lifted. She noticed they all had subtly unique horn formations. Different colors and curves. Like shells on a beach.

Maelcom grunted and took her hand. He stroked the inside of her wrist with his thumb, restless, and his distress was almost palpable. He was a walking contradiction, declaring his love with a smile and not trusting that she loved him. She knew it like she was a tuning fork for his emotions, capable of picking up on his discordant unhappiness.

He seemed to have snapped out of the crazy space-out thing the moment she touched him. "Nessa needs to clean up," he said but he didn't move.

"We'll talk more later, Maelcom," Ephraim said and waved his hand.

One of the Daimon Guard stepped forward and gestured for them to follow. "This way."

Maelcom didn't move and appeared frozen. "I need to wash up. Can we go?" she asked him while she tugging at his hand to get him moving. Finally, he started walking, still holding her hand tightly and not meeting her eyes. She frowned because she knew in her gut that this was about her reaction to the deaths of the Ice Daimons. Given everything that had happened, she thought puking and getting a little freaked out was completely reasonable.

The captain of the guard led them to a small house in the back of a large courtyard with tall stone walls.

Once they were alone in the sitting room, Maelcom folded his arms and stared at his boots. "I'm sorry that I killed the Daimon who attacked me. And Villus, I broke his wrist, thinking to incapacitate him. I know violence is abhorrent to you. I know you are disgusted with me," he said softly.

Nessa's mouth dropped open at the ridiculous assumptions. "I don't know what you're talking about. Are you saying that because I freaked during the fighting? I mean, it was horrible, the knife in the eye and Villus slicing his own throat open. But I'm not disgusted with you, I'm disgusted with the events. You think I want to break up with you or something? What is wrong with you? All that blood and gore. Anyone would be a little freaked out."

He ran his hand through his hair. "You're angry and disgusted that I killed the Ice Daimon," he said stubbornly.

Shit. He was in his own little freak-out about what happened and he couldn't be more wrong. "I wish he wasn't dead but you couldn't do anything. I saw what happened." Why was he acting so unreasonably? He should be able to understand her point of view.

"There is lot of violence in the Daimon world. You hate violence. We were a people at war for many years. Terrible wars."

"There's a lot of violence in the Earth Realm. And everyone hates violence. Or, well, everyone sane. Why are you being so weird?" She squinted at him. Perhaps being back in the Daimon Realm triggered something.

"I'm not being weird. You are upset," he said firmly.

Oh, now it was her? They were going to argue this shit out. She marched up to him and stuck her finger in his chest. *Poke. Poke.* "You don't have any trust in me. You think I'm going to freak out and leave or something. You're waiting for the other shoe to drop. Every time you shift or I learn something about you, you give me this worried look. And it's starting to make me angry. Your lack of trust and faith in me is depressing because it means you don't really know my heart. And if you don't know my feelings, maybe I don't know you. It ends up with me being angry at you."

"I knew it," he responded. His mouth had tightened to a flat line like he expected bad news. His reaction hurt her.

She was sure she loved him, because she wanted to strangle him at the same time as she wanted to kiss him. He was annoyingly beautiful with his horns and blue eyes flashing. "You know nothing. Because otherwise you would know that I'm not freaking out and throwing my hands up. I don't like you killing people. Or Daimons, or whatever. Totally normal. Is my staying with you dependent on me never freaking out? Anyway, the point is I saw you aim, I saw that Daimon trip, I knew you wanted to hit his sword arm. I don't even want to discuss that psycho who committed suicide. That was horrible. Yes, I'm freaked out about that. I wanna cry. I need a fucking hug. I don't need you giving me grief about my reaction." The guy with the knife in his eye had been the most horrific thing she had seen since seeing someone whipped on the farm. Her lips started to tremble and her eyes blinked hard.

Maelcom's eyes found hers and she saw the anguish in them. Walking up to her, he wrapped his arms around her and pulled her tight against him. "I'm sorry," he muttered.

She snuggled into his chest and listened to his heart *boom, boom* against her ear. This was better but she was still angry at him. She gave him a squeeze and stepped back. She was concerned about one thing. "Can you tell me if that space-out thing you did happens a lot? Is this what you meant when you said you were damaged? When does it happen? Do your friends know it happens? How can I help you?"

"I don't talk about it with them."

"You should," she said firmly. "You can't just repress that because then you end up—well, like you are now, having space-outs in stressful situations."

"My friends know but we don't discuss as it doesn't happen that much. Anymore."

"Shit, I'm your friend too and I don't know," she said, feeling frustrated. She stepped back out of his arms. Why was he such an ass sometimes? Clearly Daimon men and human men were very similar. An idea grew in her head as she considered his problem and his reactions. "Listen, I think you have some trauma-induced episodes. A form of Post-Traumatic Stress Disorder. You know, your space-outs could simply be a manifestation of that. Take it from a girl who had trauma-induced silence after being abused and starved."

"You said they starved you. Abuse? What abuse? What else did they do you?" he roared. He was impressive when he roared in his Daimon form, but she only saw her gentle, beautiful Maelcom angry at some long-dead ghosts of hers.

She put up her hands to tell him to back down. "First, you will *not* yell at me. Second, sometimes the worst stuff that happens is stuff you see, as opposed to what happens to you. I was beaten but nothing worse. Not everybody was so lucky. I got better because I realized it was fine to feel sad about it. That was how I realized I was still me, because I had all my crazy feelings of despair and sadness. I haven't forgotten anything I experienced, but I learned to live with it. Learned to not let it stop me from living."

He sat silently. All emotion locked up tight. She supposed his warrior culture was not big on dealing with emotions, and although he said Daimons were changing, he was definitely old school. Probably not a lot of mental health support for Daimon soldiers. He was strong and determined. He had radically changed who he was with only the support of his friends, but he still needed to accept the past for what it was—the past.

"Maelcom, I need to shower and I need some time. We can talk more later." She folded her arms across her chest.

He roused himself at her demand. "Why can't we talk now? Also, we need to meet with Ephraim before we return to the Earth Realm." He was pouting which was cute, but she needed some time by herself to process everything that happened.

"You talk to Ephraim. I need to wash all the blood off me. I'm not talking to anyone all bloody. Okay?" She held the front door open.

"But I…"

He looked so lost and confused. Adorable in an annoying way. She kissed him on the cheek. "See you in a bit.

Think about what I said. Trust is really important to me."

"Trust? I trust you completely," he rumbled.

"I just want to wash up and take some time alone." She opened the door and shooed him through it. He stomped unhappily toward the building across the courtyard. Two guards standing nearby jumped to attention for Maelcom.

She shut the door firmly and leaned her head against it.

Yes, he had issues but that didn't get him off the hook. He assumed! Assumed she was freaked out and was backing off from them being together. Really? Did he think her love didn't hold up under pressure? What kind of trust was that? If he didn't trust her, did he trust himself and his love for her? He was the one backtracking. No doubt there were going to be plenty of times when she'd freak out as violence would always be a trigger point for her.

A man or whatever slit his own throat in front of her. She was hurt that Maelcom didn't take what she said and believe it—besides, she was emotionally worked up about everything. She was in the Daimon Realm and she wanted to be experiencing this place, not arguing with her amazing boyfriend-slash-lover. The crazy thing was even though he made her angry, she still loved him.

The horribleness of him pulling the knife out of the eye, the sound wet, and how he'd wiped the blade on the dead guy's shirt—that was going to haunt her for a while. Like it would for anyone.

Not to mention going through the strange portal— they'd stepped down into it and everything blurred as they moved forward. She had held his hand going through, and she could sense his energy, black and low. Totally weird because energy didn't have a color, or did it? Maybe the energy sip was a two-way street and she could sense his energy when he was taking a sip of hers.

She worked herself up into a crazy mood and she stomped around the house. "Nessa, you need to calm down. Think it through, Nessa," she said to herself. The cottage was small so she stomped from the bedroom to the main room and back again. She peered at her reflection in a mirror. *Oh.* She had blood on her dress and hair. She needed to clean up.

There was a room off the kitchen area with a bath and sink. Round windows set high up in the wall provided light through colored glass. The faucets were strange but she turned the water on, put her hands underneath to wash them, and was delighted to find the water warm. Thank god for warm-water technology. She stepped into the bath and rinsed the worst of the dirt and blood off. A brass stopper fit in the drain and she sat down, shivering in the two inches of water until it got high enough to cover her legs. The bar of soap by the tub smelled like flowers, and she leaned back in the warm bath to think.

As she relaxed, she decided that she had overreacted about Maelcom. The shock of seeing Villus kill himself twisted her up inside. Could the PTSD causing the problems between them be hers and not Maelcom's? She was consumed with guilt for not letting Maelcom shoot him, which might have prevented Villus from killing himself.

The steam of her bath made the room misty. She stood up to look around for a towel. Instead, she found a folded length of soft linen, softer and cozier than a regular towel. Wrapping it around her, she stepped out of the bath and went to look in her bag for clean clothes.

She grabbed the most colorful thing in her bag because she needed it, a bright clothing would be bold and it would help her be brave. Her silk shirt made in India had a thousand little shimmery mirrors and lots of embroidery and a pair of slim blue pants. It was one of her favorite concert outfits, great when the laser lights played across the audience.

Looking out the window, she wondered what was outside the walls. This world smelled the same, the sky appeared the same and the plants looked familiar but more lush than at home. A perfect spring day with the air full of green-growth smell. She thought it would be more different. But it was late September at home. The seasons were different here and the climate warmer and more humid.

A little bead of sweat dripped down her neck so she leaned her forehead against the cool glass of the window. She felt terrible about arguing with Maelcom and she wanted to see him. Even if he reacted badly, she should have tried to understand. She could have given him a pass, considering that he'd just accidently killed someone. She hadn't been his friend because she had been freaked out. He was right—she was mad at him and she hadn't realized it.

First, she needed coffee. Then she needed to find Mael-com to apologize. She was the one with great social and communication skills; she could handle this. Or not, clearly, since she'd argued with her boyfriend because he was being him, and she knew who he was even if he didn't think she knew. *Sigh.* She looked around an area which looked like a kitchen, but she couldn't figure out how to light the wood-fired stove and she couldn't find any coffee.

She opened the front door to find two Daimon soldiers standing outside. They bowed slightly to her. They had copper-colored skin, blue eyes and long blond hair. They wore light leather armor with woven pants and no shirts. They had ripped, hard-muscled chests and the younger one had a piercing in his nipple. She had friends, both men and women, who would love to meet these handsome young soldiers. Maybe cross-realm dating could be thing? Someone would need to write an app.

"Hello. Do you know where I could get a cup of coffee? Do you have coffee here?" she asked.

"Yes, we do. In the kitchen hall," the younger one said, smiling happily back and pointing to a building across the courtyard. The older one punched him and he stopped smiling.

They spoke in Swedish but they had a funny accent. It sounded like a north country dialect.

"Thank you." She turned and started walking but she heard footsteps behind her. "Is this your job, to keep an eye on me?"

They both nodded. They were younger-looking than Maelcom, and both had the same skin color as Naberius but their horns were a lighter color, a more golden-brown.

She sighed. "It's strange for me to have two guys I don't know following me around. What would make me a lot more comfortable is if I knew your names. Do you know mine? I'm Nessa Gustafson." She stuck her hand out.

The younger one grabbed it and shook it. "I'm Kian."

She felt a tingle of Daimon energy. "I can't give energy back but you seem like a very polite Daimon."

"You know about the energy? You can feel it? I didn't think—"

The older one shoved Kian aside before he could finish talking and put out his hand. "I'm Ivar."

She shook his hand and received a little tingle of energy from Ivar. "Oh, are you flirting with me?" She lifted an eyebrow and smiled.

Ivar's stern face broke into a shy grin as he stepped back and bowed. "It is my honor to guard you while you are here in the Daimon Realm."

"So where did you get the coffee? I assume the realms share a lot of the same plants and trees but coffee is native to a very small area on Earth. I thought the Realm has been closed for a thousand years."

"Mostly closed. Coffee was not unfamiliar to Daimons before we left the earth realm. I believe some Daimons brought coffee plants with them and we have many coffee farms in the south."

"That's good because if I had to drink mead or whatever old-school stuff Vikings drank, I don't think I could handle it. I tried some once and it was disgusting."

Kian nodded vigorously. "It must have been a sad time before coffee. And we don't drink mead much anymore. Someone obtained the modern recipe for beer. Thank the gods."

"I like mead," Ivar complained and frowned at Kian.

Nessa thought they were both rather sweet young men. Or Daimons. Whatever.

At a large building, Kian held open a thick wood door for her and Ivar gestured to a kitchen area across the room full of Daimons. She scanned them until she found those brilliant blue eyes staring intently back. Maelcom, still in his Daimon form, was taller than other Daimons around him and somehow more graceful, more potent than any of the other horned, fierce soldiers in the room. He glanced at her smiling guards, curling his lip as he growled at them.

Nessa shook her head at his stormy expression and walked up to him. "Hi," she said softly.

"Hello, Nessa."

"I cleaned up and feel much better. Less bloody. Can we talk more now? Because I need to talk. You know I love you, but all the fighting, knives in eyes, blood and death made me angry and scared. So you were right about that, I was angry but not at you, just angry in general, at how horrible it all was. I don't know why I shouted at you about trust. I think it was about me not trusting you. I have a lot to say, but basically, I just wanted to say I'm sorry." As she talked, his face relaxed, and she could see that the corners of his mouth turn up, that little smile appeared which seemed to exist solely for her.

He opened his mouth to say something but she threw her arms around him and hugged him hard. He lightly put his hands around her shoulders, stroking her back gently as if to comfort her but she could feel the slight tremble in him. He was the one who needed comfort.

"You don't have to apologize. I was scared about you, about us," he whispered in her ear. "And I am never scared."

She grinned at him and then realized the entire room had stopped talking and was openly watching them. She cleared her throat and they turned away, everyone talking at the same time. A roomful of horned Daimon soldiers didn't impress her. Well, they did but they shouldn't stare so much.

"Come, Nessa. You wanted coffee?"

He brought her up to the counter where a Daimon stood passing out food and drink. "Hello, I'm Nessa Gustafson. Can I get a cup of coffee? I don't have any Daimon money. Is that okay? Do you have any food? Like that?" She pointed at the Daimon next to her who had a bowl of savory stew and a huge slice of dark bread. Her stomach rumbled.

Maelcom stood beside her. "Nessa—" he started.

She interrupted him. "How about I grab my food and we go back to the guest house? Okay? These guys here look very gossipy," she said softly. She peered over the counter, held up her finger to get the attention of the Daimon who was dishing out the food, "Can I get it to go?" The Daimon behind the counter raised his eyebrows like he didn't understand her.

Maelcom sighed. "Put it on a tray for her. I'll carry it." Instantly, a tray with two bowls and two mugs of steaming coffee were placed on the counter. Maelcom picked it up and nodded at her.

"Thanks. Have a good day!" she called out to the somewhat dumfounded Daimons. They walked back to the guesthouse without the guards, who had been relieved from their duty by Maelcom. "You know, Ivar and Kian are both nice guys. You didn't have to growl at them."

"You know their names? Did you touch them? I smelled you on them."

"That's a very weird observation. And not cool to ask me that. But since you did, I will confess to shaking their hands, being the slutty hussy I am," she said sarcastically. She tried to imagine her reaction if he talked to two hot girls she didn't know, she probably would be a little jealous.

"This Venskat has made me stupid," he said morosely as he balanced the tray in one hand.

She shook her head. "You're not stupid. Maybe we are just adjusting to each other and it's a change so it makes us feel stupid."

He tilted his head to the side with a thoughtful expression. "I think you may be correct."

They sat outside on a bench in front of the little house, and he placed the tray beside them. She picked up the bowl of stew and dug in. "Mm-m, I need this recipe."

Maelcom watched her inhale her stew and bread. "It is a traditional recipe in this part of the Realm."

She mumbled with her mouth full and continued to eat until she finished the bowl. "I feel much better." She cleaned the bowl with the piece of bread. "Super high metabolism. My doctor thinks the long-term malnutrition had a weird effect on my body."

"Did they ever arrest the people who were in charge of the farm?"

"Yes." She closed her eyes for a second at the onslaught of memories. "The children were taken away from the adults at the farm and either put with suitable family members or fostered. My dad was the one who saved everyone. Did I ever tell you that? He searched for me for years. Finally, he called in favors from all the government people who were big fans of his art. 'Sweden's greatest painter' is what they call him. Someone turned up a complaint from a rural town about some religious people who weren't following local regulations about farming. Stupid, eh? You don't think of artists as warriors but my dad accompanied the police to investigate and accompanied them on the raid. He broke the door down on the room they had locked all the children in. I was so tired, I just lay there with all the little babies around me. I couldn't sit up. And he picked me up and carried me out in his arms. He was crying and his hands were bleeding. My dad is my own personal superhero." It always made her weepy to remember the face of her father dripping tears onto her face and whispering that everything was going to be okay.

Maelcom looked furious and she saw another spark fly off his fingertip. Interesting. Like an energy discharge. "I will kill anyone who is still alive. To harm children is an abomination," he said in a hard voice.

She sighed. "Stop, Maelcom. That's all done. They prosecuted the people. Even if they are now out, I don't want to inflict pain on them. That's what they did to me. Their deaths would mean nothing to me. It wouldn't help me and would actually hurt me. In my years of therapy, I learned that spending time focusing on the horrors of the farm did nothing. I had to sort of accept it, grieve and move on. I can't ever undo what has been done. The only way I could do this was to live, do something I loved, which was make art, and try not to engage in dark thoughts. I'm mostly successful, but you know, some days I'm not and that's okay. Isn't that how you are living your life? Isn't that how everybody lives?"

He turned his head and stared off into nothing. "Can you tell me why you were angry with me?"

"It's complicated. I didn't think I had any doubts until you accused me of having doubts. That made me angry, but then I thought if I did have doubts, what would they be? Then, of course, doubts appeared. I guess I wanted to think I was brave but I wasn't. I wish I were braver. And then I hated that you didn't have faith in me that I loved you, even when things became horrible. You understand?"

"I have faith in you. And you are brave. Look what you have done with your life. All your friends, your beautiful art. Yes, I have doubts about me. I'm nervous about my weakness, about what I am and how I appear to you."

"That is the most honest and wordy thing you have said to me about your life. I don't know anything about your war except it was long and brutal."

He rubbed his jaw. "Sometimes I get lost. I space out. I—Well, I become almost unreachable. Blood or death will set me off. I don't remember much. I freeze up. Maelcom, the raging Fist of Naberius, hero of the Daimon wars. I freeze. It's like I am asleep but awake."

She ached at the sharp and pained voice he used. She hadn't realized she would take on his pain because she loved him and it would be her pain. She scooted up next to him and leaned her head against his shoulder. "That is shit."

He laced his fingers through hers. "Yes, it is."

"Maelcom, you seemed to be able to snap out of it when it happened at the gate. So you can control it some."

He made a funny sound. Was that a Maelcom chuckle?

"It was you, Nessa. I touched you, I felt your energy and I came back."

Her throat went tight. She couldn't talk.

She put her hand on his. "I don't know how we are going to do this but I think we can." They sat silently together for a minute before she continued. "I know I'm all wound up, meeting you, learning about Daimons, visiting another dimension, and seeing people kill themselves. It's been a lot. But falling in love with you? That's been the easy part."

"You will stay with me?"

"Is that an invitation? Maelcom, yes, I'm staying. I love you. Just believe in me and I think everything will work out."

"You're my light," he said softly. He bent his head and captured her lips in a deep, open kiss.

She leaned into him and pulled his head down to kiss him back, hot and hard. Slanting his mouth over hers, he kissed like he was talking to her. He bit her lip gently.

He pulled her into a strong hug, leaned his cheek against her head and just held her as if he could get everything he needed from that embrace. "I'll be better. You'll see."

It was a promise that made her heart ache. Even though they clicked and fit together, he didn't think he was worthy. She took his face between her hands. "No, Maelcom, you're not a broken thing. Everyone has scars and a weight of memories, I know this. I love everything about you even your scars. There is no better you that I want to be with. This is the man I want, right here, right now."

She laid her hand flat over his chest. She could feel him in her veins.

"Be my mate, bind with me," he said softly.

"Here, now?" She knew she would without a second

thought. She would follow her reckless heart because she loved him.

"Under the sky, here in this realm." He took her hand and they stood together.

CHAPTER 25

Maelcom

"ARE WE INTERRUPTING?"

Maelcom looked up to see Ephraim and a large group of Daimon Soldiers watching them. "We have come to escort you to the gate. I asked for two men but they all wanted to come," Ephraim said with a shrug.

Maelcom drew himself up. "Before we leave, I need a witness to my binding with Nessa Gustafson."

There was a brief moment of silence then all the Daimons started talking at once. Their names were repeated by all the men.

Ephraim looked at him with a big smile. "You do not wish to wait for Naberius and your comrades in the Earth Realm?"

"No, Nessa and I are going to say the binding words here in the Daimon Realm, here in my Daimon form."

Ephraim put his hand to his chest. "It is my honor to be present, Maelcom Skov-Baern."

Maelcom dropped to his knees before her. "Agnes Gustafson. I'm yours and I bind myself to you for now and ever," he said in a firm voice. His voice echoed in the courtyard.

She was a miracle to him. Reaching out, he took her hand and sighed. It was going to be all right; he was going to be all right. Her delicate, long fingers were pale in his huge, copper-colored hand. A tremble went through her body.

She lifted her hand and stroked his ebony horns, then lightly laid her hands on his head. "Maelcom Skov-Baern. I bind myself to you for now and ever. I am yours. Your mate and your friend."

Maelcom picked her up and kissed her hard. Her energy was sweet and full of love. Stunned, he watched as her appearance shimmered for a second and threw off a strange light. She staggered slightly back, then shook her head as if to clear it, and smiled. The entire courtyard fell silent. He pulled her close to him, ran his fingertips down the side of her face and took a taste of her energy. It was unbelievable. Her energy had changed. She was a hybrid Daimon. A miracle.

Nessa put her hand to her head. "Wow. I feel drunk. It must be the excitement." She punched him in the arm. "We did the runaway and get married thing. We're crazy but good crazy."

His arm hurt. His thoughts were spinning—his mate had simply transformed into a hybrid on a kiss. No stories or documents implied this could happen so fast. Or they'd just read them wrong or hadn't found books with this information. Maelcom was stunned and did not know what to say.

The entire crowd cheered again. Ephraim, with his sharp eyes, came out and held out his hand to Nessa. "I offer my congratulations."

She turned and took Ephraim's hand but stayed in the circle of Maelcom's arms. "This is amazing. I feel amazing."

Ephraim held her hand then let it go abruptly. "Maelcom, she's a hybrid. She just changed. Right there. You know it, you feel it."

Maelcom snapped out of his shock. "Nessa, you are a hybrid Daimon now. Are you okay? Dizzy? Feverish? Weak?"

Nessa looked up at him with her mouth open and her eyes wide. "That was it? I'm a hybrid Daimon? Felt like taking a shot of tequila. It started all hot in my belly and radiated out. I was dizzy for a little bit, but that was it? *I'm a hybrid Daimon.* Wow. Thought it would be a bigger deal. Are you sure? You said I was going to get sick or something before I changed."

"We don't know. It's rare that a Daimon takes a Earth Realm mate."

Ephraim nodded. "It's unbelievable but I can sense your

energy. You are a Daimon. Welcome, Agnes Gustafson. We are honored." He bowed deeply.

Maelcom shifted to his human form. He was worried. This aspect of the binding had concerned him as Naberius's mate, Jessalyn, had become very sick during her transition. But his mate changed in a single ripple. Like nothing. Perhaps she was about to get horribly sick in some delayed fashion. He frowned. "I assumed it would take time. Like with Jessalyn. Are you sure you feel fine?" He watched her suspiciously.

She bounced up and down on the balls of her feet. "I feel awesome!"

"Nessa, please, stop bouncing around. Let me feel your head for fever. We know nothing of the change. Jessalyn was the first hybrid in a thousand years and she became very ill, almost close to death."

She stopped bouncing and he put his hand on her forehead while she grinned up at him. Her temperature seemed normal.

"See, I'm fine. Don't worry. I feel like I had an energy drink but nothing weird. I thought the whole process would be a lot more dramatic but it was nothing." She snapped her fingers with a grin.

Leal fought his way to the front of the crowd. "Nessa, Nessa," he called out.

Maelcom turned and stood in front of Nessa. She tapped him. "Hey, step aside."

Leal's mouth opened in a big circle as she hugged him.

"Oh my god, Nessa. You're Daimon. It's amazing. This shouldn't have happened. It must your Små folk heritage."

Ephraim started in surprise. "What do you mean?"

"We are not sure if she really has Små folk ancestry," Maelcom muttered to Ephraim. "That is Leal's theory."

"We will see if improved genetic testing can figure it out. Leal mentioned it. I don't know if it's important but we can learn something," Nessa said.

"Why do you think she has Små folk ancestry?" Ephraim demanded of Leal.

"I don't, but I guessed from her energy and her appearance. Researching what happened to the Små folk is sort of a personal obsession of mine and I have conducted my own research efforts into what happened to them. They married into human families like Daimons before the withdrawal. It's thought they all died but some may have survived, intermarried and survived on Earth in quiet places. I have just learnt about genetics but from what I've read it could be that the Små folk DNA is recessive but occasionally manifests itself strongly, just randomly like in Nessa."

Maelcom twisted his mouth. "Ephraim, what should we do? Is she okay?" He could feel himself shaking and his field of vision narrowing.

"Maelcom, I'm fine. Really." She wrapped her arm around his waist and sent some energy into him. Like a tickle. Small kisses landed on his chest.

He snapped out of it fast. "I think we should take you back to the Earth Realm immediately. Medical care is better there. Just in case."

Ephraim said, "Captain, retrieve her belongings. Nessa, I think Maelcom is correct and you should return to the Earth Realm. The gate will open soon. Come."

Nessa wrinkled her nose. "You don't need to talk to me more?"

"I have all the information already. I was simply being careful."

Before Nessa could respond, Maelcom spoke in a language that was vaguely Nordic, fast and angry. Ephraim bowed slightly and made some soothing comment back.

Ephraim turned to her. "Apologies. Maelcom didn't like that I implied I didn't trust you. Also, that I don't trust him. I apologize. Maelcom is an important asset to Daimon Intelligence and we trust him absolutely."

She simply raised an eyebrow and twisted her mouth. "Apology accepted. I agree that you need to trust us both," she said. Maelcom liked that she didn't let Ephraim off the hook that easily. Not a lot of people stood up to Ephraim. He was a fearsome personality as a Daimon, the most brilliant mind in all the Realm and a political genius who was the force behind the peace and the move to a parliamentary system.

Ephraim shrugged. "We are in a period of change in many ways. I'm often overly zealous in ensuring the security of the Realm."

"We just had an Ice Daimon slit his own throat rather than surrender. Not everyone is over the hatred from the

Wars. I think they believe they need to still fight and you need to try harder to convince them otherwise," Nessa said bluntly.

Ephraim grimaced. "There are some residual issues with a small group of Ice Daimons who refuse to acknowledge the peace treaty. We are trying to integrate our societies but change is slow."

"I understand. I know you work with Maelcom a lot but we are going on a long honeymoon. He has to meet my father and all my friends. My father will want to throw a party," Nessa said. "I would invite you but you say the Realm still has its borders closed?"

"For now. Safety concerns."

"I told her about the great Daimon killings," Maelcom said.

Ephraim's expression became serious. "They are here in our hearts."

The men around them muttered, "Our hearts remember." This was the traditional remembrance for the many who'd died, a terror that had changed their society and world completely.

Nessa closed her eyes for a second. "I will remember them too," she whispered. Maelcom looked at her, stunned at her declaration. The absolute perfect and right thing to say.

Ephraim cast a sharp look at her. "Lady Skov-Baern, thank you for your remembrance."

"Just Nessa, please. I'm not comfortable with titles even

though I want to be considerate to your traditions. But it feels too weird to use the title 'Lady.' Skov-Baern is a name that holds importance because Maelcom is a hero so I am going to take his name to honor him. And frankly, not being a Gustavfson will be a relief as my father is famous. I am going to call myself Agnes Skov-Baern but all my friends can still call me Nessa."

"You can use whatever name you want," Maelcom said. Like he cared. She was his—that was all that mattered. But he liked that she had considered deeply about her name. How it spoke of her pride in him even though she knew what he was and what he had done. Something shifted inside him. He hadn't considered his love for her could grow.

"You understand what it means to be a hybrid? Extended longevity. Altered DNA. Your children will be Daimons. You must abide by the rule of the leaders of the Daimon Realm and all of it must remain secret," Ephraim said.

"Yes. Yes, I know. You have a weird idea of two people being together if you think they don't talk," Nessa observed. "Maelcom has told me everything, or mostly, and I have sworn to keep the Daimons secret."

"Agnes, I thank you for your oath. Maelcom, you have a fierce and courageous mate. You've saved my brother a million times, and I owe you everything. The Daimon Realm owes you all its gratitude and thanks," Ephraim said and bowed.

Maelcom was stunned. Ephraim was not publicly effusive. He had never seen this side of him—almost emotional in public.

"It was Naberius saved his men, who saved me even when he was lost and troubled. He brought us to the Earth Realm and letting us heal each in our own way."

Nessa leaned against Maelcom. "I want to meet him and Jessalyn."

"You will," Maelcom said.

"Ephraim, thank you." She stepped forward and gave him a kiss on each cheek, smiled and then patted Ephraim's cloak. "That cloak looks beautiful. What kind of sheep do you have here?"

Ephraim blinked his eyes as he was not used to the rapidity of how Nessa's mind worked. "The cape?" Ephraim said, confused. Maelcom enjoyed seeing Ephraim slightly off-balance.

"Yes, I know a lot of fiber artists and craftspeople so I know some about wool. I even knit but not very well."

Ephraim smiled and whipped the cape off his shoulders and wrapped it around her. "You like it? Then it's yours. It will keep you warm."

What was a short cloak for Ephraim was a full-out to-the-floor cape for her. "You don't have to give me your cape. I just said I liked it. I could buy one?" she said to Maelcom.

Maelcom shook his head. "I think that was made just for Ephraim. Special sheep for the Vasteras family." Later, he would tell her that it was a mark of Ephraim's office and his rank, that giving it bestowed on her the visible approval of one of the most powerful men in the Daimon world. For now, he simply said, "It makes you look like a snow princess."

Ephraim held up his hand. "Nessa, it is yours. A small wedding gift that you can take back to the Earth Realm and remember this day."

Maelcom noticed Leal watching them, pale and biting his fingernails. He had promised to help Leal stay in the Earth Realm, and he needed to honor his word. Plus, he liked Leal even if he was an Ice Daimon. Perhaps it was because he'd never been a soldier. It would be good for his men to learn to interact with their old enemy on a professional and friendly basis without the worry of having fought him in battle. In the new Daimon Realm, Ice Daimons and Jotun Daimons needed to work together.

Turning back to Ephraim, he said, "Leal should come with us. His knowledge about Ice Daimon rebels and their history is important. Secondly, if Nessa is descended from Små folk, he is the only Daimon with extensive knowledge about them. I want him working for me in the Earth Realm if that is acceptable to you, Ephraim."

Ephraim pursed his lips and nodded. "Fine. He swears an oath to you and you are responsible for him. By allowing an Ice Daimon in the Earth Realm and having them work with the Jotun Daimons, it will show to all Ice Daimons that we are interested in working together for the future of all Daimons."

"I'll gladly work for Maelcom," Leal said. He straightened up and gave Ephraim a brilliant smile. Everyone stopped and stared as if they hadn't realized that Leal was beautiful and stunning when he smiled. Maelcom wondered if he could use Leal as a honeypot in intelligence work. He wouldn't really have to do anything but smile.

Maelcom picked up Nessa's hand and brought it to his lips. He could feel her take some energy like a little tickle in his core. "Are you ready?" She nodded.

As they walked slowly to the gate, she whispered, "Tell me how much you love me."

The gate hummed and it would open soon.

"You are my heart, my breath, my life," Maelcom said softly.

Her huge brown eyes glistened but she smiled. A muted boom from the gate. They turned together and walked onto the portal holding hands.

CHAPTER 26

Maelcom

MAELCOM STOOD IN THE MIDDLE of the garden, shaking hands with what seemed like an endless stream of people. Nessa was beside him in a beautiful white lace and silk dress with a short skirt, which made her look like an old-fashioned fairy. As each person stopped to congratulate them, she talked extensively with them, and he nodded to whatever was said without saying much. Everyone appeared to be slightly nervous around him and he was able to avoid long conversations.

When he first met Nessa's father on their return to the Earth Realm and told him they had married, her father looked at Maelcom with suspicion and distrust, like he could sense something was off.

Eric Gustafson was intelligent, fierce and a big, shambling bear of a man who looked like he had been a boxer when he was young, broken nose and all. Almost as tall as Maelcom, he had familiar chocolate-brown eyes. When they shook hands, Maelcom remembered that this was a man who had never given up on his daughter and who accepted nothing but the truth. This was a man who broke down doors to save his daughter.

Eric suggested Maelcom and he take a walk to get to know each other. Alone. Nessa smiled and kissed them both. Off they went on a long hike during which time Maelcom told her father everything about who he was and the Daimon Realm. Deep in the woods, far from everything, he'd shifted and bowed his head to her father and asked for his blessing because Nessa would be unhappy otherwise.

Eric was unimpressed. He folded his arms across his chest and grumbled. "Well, the myths are true. You know, I had you investigated. I talked to your commander in Denmark who said you were the best soldier he has ever known. He is obviously in the dark about this." He gestured to Maelcom's horns.

"Yes. I'm telling you because you are family now and it would physically pain Nessa to keep a secret from you."

Eric stared at him in silence before nodding. "You and Nessa have my blessing and you have my oath to keep your secret. I agree it would be unwise to make this knowledge public." Eric laid his hand on Maelcom's shoulder and whispered, "You know she talks nonstop."

"I enjoy it. It's like music, her talking. It's Nessa," Maelcom said firmly.

Eric nodded and clapped him on his shoulder with his broad and meaty hand. "She is her own woman. Do not try to change her and you will be happy. But I swear, you hurt her or make her unhappy, I will make you pay in whatever form you choose to take." He said this so mildly and lightly that it sent a chill through Maelcom. This was a man who did not make vows lightly.

"Agreed. I swear to make her very happy."

"Good. We will have a party to celebrate your marriage. In a week. Invite your friends," Eric informed him.

Gusion, Oona, Bobby, Naberius and Jessalyn had flown to Sweden to attend the wedding party. Bobby stood beside him as he spoke the wedding vows of their Earth wedding. Jessalyn was thrilled to meet Nessa and pulled her aside for private discussion. They talked rapidly and with great animation, interspersed with shrieks and giggles.

Naberius, Bobby and Maelcom stood watching them. Gusion downed a beer and burped. They both turned to frown at him.

"You guys are lovesick Daimons. Who'll party with me or come to strip clubs with me now that you are settled with your mates?"

"Marcus and Barth?" Maelcom suggested.

"I never went to a strip club with you, Gusion," Naberius said. "You kept asking me, but I said no. And the night you had all the ladies come to the bar doesn't count. That was someone's birthday."

Gusion grinned. "Marcus and Barth are good kids." Marcus and Barth were the youngest of the Daimon soldiers here in the Earth Realm, not children but fierce warriors, and certainly far younger than Gusion.

Naberius chuckled and turned to Maelcom. "I think he's jealous of you. His last lady friend dumped him because she went to school to be a nurse."

Maelcom tilted his head to look at Gusion. "Cherry Blossom? Good for her. She was a very sweet lady." Gusion glumly nodded.

Oona walked up. "Checked the perimeter and got some champagne." She lifted a bottle to show them.

Oona was a Pale Daimon. Tall with long black hair, white skin and big black eyes. She was dressed in black leather but wore crystal necklaces. A fierce warrior, she Jessalyn's bodyguard.

All of them caught the scent at the same time and they stiffened. An Ice Daimon was here and it wasn't Leal. They all watched intently as a tall and beautiful woman who smelled like an Ice Daimon walked across the garden to Nessa.

Oona held up her hand. "Careful, she is a friend of your wife, Maelcom. Interesting."

Nessa shrieked when she saw her friend, "Tatianna!"

Shit. Another Ice Daimon.

Much hugging, kissing and talking. Nessa held on to Tatianna's hand, giggled and waggled her finger at her.

Tatianna lifted an eyebrow with a resigned smile and then whispered into Nessa's ear. Nessa nodded shyly.

Bobby shook his head. "Wow." Oona gave him a cold stare. Maelcom shook his head at his friend who was engaged in a relationship with the fearsome Oona. Bobby walked over to Oona and threw his arms around her. "But not as beautiful or as deadly as you." Oona smiled happily at Bobby who always seemed to know what to say to his Pale Daimon girlfriend.

"Come," Nessa said and brought Tatianna, the Ice Daimon, over to say hello to everyone. "Say hello. I will be back. I need to finishing talking to Jessalyn." She hurried back to where Jessalyn waited for her.

Tatianna stood proudly before them as if she expected them all to bow. Maelcom realized this Tatianna was astonishingly beautiful in an old-fashioned way, with long, chestnut hair, creamy gold skin, perfect rosebud lips and large dark eyes. She was the oldest daughter of Rayme and had disappeared several years ago from the Daimon Realm. Apparently, she had always hated her father who had been cruel to her mother.

"Lady Tatianna, I'm Maelcom Skov-Baern. My wife considers you a good friend and speaks of you as a sister. Any friend of Nessa's is a friend of mine." He held out his hand.

She hesitated a second before taking it firmly. "The same for me. We are on the verge of many changes in the Realm. It is amazing." She gave a little energy to him—polite to offer first—and then he returned the gesture.

"Allow me to introduce you to Lord Naberius Vasteras," Maelcom said softly and very politely. He was improving his diplomatic skills.

Tatianna bowed her head with a polite but cautious smile. "Lord Vasteras."

Naberius bowed slightly, "Lady Tatianna."

"I have been in contact with Ephraim and explained my presence here. I am not and never have been involved in my father's political actions. We agreed that I would keep in touch with you if I wished to stay here in this realm."

"Agreed. I have your contact information," Naberius said.

Gusion stepped forward. "I will keep an eye on this one."

Tatianna lifted an eyebrow with disdain. "The dog speaks?"

Gusion growled. "Tread carefully. I will not hold back in fighting a shield maiden."

"I'm not frightened of you." Tatianna said disdainfully. They glared at each other.

Maelcom shifted his stance to step hard on Gusion's foot while frowning at Gusion. Gusion looked sheepish and grunted an apology. "Lady Tatianna, my apologies for being rude."

Tatianna rolled her eyes and darted a look at Nessa who was still talking to Jessalyn. "Apology accepted. For Nessa's sake. Maelcom, best wishes to you and Nessa."

"Thank you, Tatianna. I'm honored to have you as a family friend."

She gave a regal nod and Maelcom was relieved. Tatianna was his wife's best friend and he planned to recruit her into his intelligence organization here on earth. But he needed her to relax. And he didn't need Gusion riling her up.

Oona stepped up to her. "Greetings. I am the personal guard of Lord Naberius and Lady Jessalyn." He could see how Oona kept her hand on her hips, no doubt with her finger tips on knives hidden carefully in her clothes.

Bobby waved his hand. "Nice to meet you. I'm her boyfriend," he said with his big friendly smile.

Tatianna hid her shock well. A Pale Daimon Assassin as a personal bodyguard was an intimidating fact and meeting her surfer boyfriend was probably strange.

Naberius gestured to Jessalyn. "Walk with me, Lady Tatianna. I would like to introduce you to my mate, Jessalyn. She is also a hybrid. She is working on improving relations with your people. You and she will have much to discuss, although perhaps at another time. There are many friends of Nessa's here."

Tatianna looked surprised. "Another human hybrid mate as well? This is amazing," she whispered.

Naberius nodded. "It is. Many things are changing. I would like to hear more about your people."

Maelcom and Gusion watched them walk away together with Tatianna talking rapidly to Naberius. Oona whispered into Bobby's ear about who Tatianna was and he frowned unhappy the daughter of the man who had tried to kill his sister was here.

Gusion growled under his breath. "You cannot trust an Ice Daimon."

Oona shrugged. "People used to think you could not trust a Pale Daimon."

"And I still don't," Gusion grumbled.

"Do not be rude to Oona. And, Dude? You have some unresolved anger issues," Bobby said firmly.

Gusion grimaced and looked sorry. "I apologize, Oona. I am honored to fight alongside you. It's just strange, Rayme's daughter."

Oona rolled her eyes. "She is the daughter of his first wife who left him. She hated him. I got the intel on her yesterday."

"And you didn't tell me?" Gusion complained.

"I told Maelcom," Oona said. "You were busy."

Maelcom held up his hand to stop the chitchat. "She'll be working with me for my Earth Realm division of Daimon Intelligence. Gusion, you might work together."

"First, Leal. Now her. I like Leal but I will see about her."

Maelcom nodded. Everyone like Leal, thankfully. He had charmed his way into the good graces of all the Daimons on Earth. "We can lead the way for everyone in the Daimon Realm, demonstrate cooperation and under-standing. We will need to make reparations and formal apologies to each other. I plan to be first. But we must move forward together," Maelcom said with determination.

"Shit. Okay. I'm with you." Gusion ran his hands through his red hair. "This will be interesting."

They all watched Naberius talking to Tatianna. A new future for Daimons was being created.

Nessa

MAELCOM CAME UP BESIDE HER as she was hugging some old cousin. "Excuse me, you're needed in the house."

As they walked away, she said, "Thanks for rescuing me. Helena talks nonstop. She heard we'll be living in California and demanded to hear everything. I told her about our plans to live part of the time there and part of the year here. Hopefully she won't visit."

He wasn't really listening to her as they walked into the house. She hummed the wedding march song while he led her to their bedroom upstairs. He slid her a glittering blue look of desire, pulled her in and locked the door.

She pretended to be shocked. "Maelcom, there're people out there who have come to see us, give us their best wishes. We have social obligations." She giggled as he ran his finger down her cheek, giving her a little energy.

"They'll still be there in fifteen minutes."

"Fifteen minutes. That's pretty fast," she said with a grin.

Her beautiful husband tucked his hair behind his ears and flicked another hungry glance at her. "If we have people waiting, we should be quick." He took off his silk tie and his jacket then unbuttoned his shirt.

She licked her lips and grinned. "I guess we should try to be fast." She pulled the lacy white dress off over her head and put it carefully over a chair. She was wearing a lacy white bra and a garter belt with white stockings, very high white shoes and no underwear. "Come here." She crooked her finger at her handsome mate.

He sucked in his breath and stepped forward to obey her commands.

She shook her head. "Transform, Maelcom. I desire you as a Daimon on our wedding day."

Clear bright eyes stared at her. That rare, wide smile appeared on his face and she knew he was saying he loved her. Then he transformed in a spiral of color light.

THE END

AUTHOR'S NOTE

Please review my book. *You are an influencer.* Just a couple of sentences – nothing big. Thank you.

This is a stand-alone book in the Daimon Soldier Series.

The moment Maelcom walked onto the scene in <u>Naberius: Daimon Soldier</u>, I knew the next book would be about him. His gentleness, his sorrow and his sweetness made me fall in love with him even if he didn't think he could ever be worthy of love. Maelcom suffers from a Daimon form of post-traumatic-stress-disorder but this is a fantasy book, and he is a Daimon so please forgive me if my depiction of PTSD is inaccurate in how it affects human beings. Maelcom is a Jotun Daimon, and readers should take the depiction of his issues and his recovery with a bucket of salt.

Follow me on Facebook and Twitter. Sign up for my newsletter on my website.

Website: www.katebigel.com
Twitter: @katebig
Facebook: @Kate.Bigel.author
Instagram: katebigel_author

DAIMON SOLDIER SERIES

Naberius Daimon Soldier
Maelcom Daimon Desire
Gusion Daimon Craving (5/18)

ABOUT THE AUTHOR

Kate Bigel grew up a bookworm in a family of book-worms—the kind of little girl who walked down hallways at school reading and bumping into people. Kate went to art school and painted narrative works from her imagination. She received a BFA and MFA but, tired of waiting tables, she started working in the digital world as a visual artist doing UI design in the software industry. She soon found her way into the computer game business and worked as an Art Director at Microsoft Games in Seattle and as a Development Director at Electronic Arts in Los Angeles.

Kate and her husband decided they needed an adventure, so they spent five years sailing around the Pacific Ocean with their young son visiting many beautiful tropical nations. Currently, they live in sunny southern California, still on their sailboat because it's home. Kate has over five thousand books on various devices and is grateful for e-books because otherwise, the boat would have sunk by now.

Made in the USA
Columbia, SC
11 April 2018